The Fe

Shade Owens

THE FERAL SENTENCE
THE FERAL SENTENCE, BOOK 1
© Copyright 2019 Shade Owens
www.shadeowens.com

SERIES INFORMATION

The Feral Sentence – Book 1
Beasts of Prey – Book 2
Primal Instincts – Book 3
Reign of Blood – Book 4
Game of Death – Book 5

Edited by Nikki Busch
www.nikkibuschediting.com

Published by

RED RAVEN PUBLISHING

ISBN: 978-0-9813530-2-9

Content Advisory: Although this book falls within the young adult genre, it does contain some violence and foul language and is intended for readers 16+.

PART one

PROLOGUE

Were the handcuffs really necessary? I rubbed the inflamed skin on my wrist, trying to understand how an eighteen-year-old girl such as myself could possibly pose a threat to two soldiers in a combat helicopter, four thousand feet above sea level.

They wore black masks to match their thick uniforms and SWAT-like goggles over their eyes. I could tell they were both men by their height and build, but I hadn't seen their faces. I eyed their machine guns, but not for long, because I felt them watching me from behind their dark shades.

I peered through the helicopter's fogged window, and the shape of an island surrounded by nothing but open blue came into view. I had so many questions—so many fears—but the overpowering sound of the rotating helicopter blades, coupled with the menacing looks I was receiving, encouraged me to keep my mouth shut.

The larger of the two soldiers stood up and reached for a lever. A burst of sunlight came into the helicopter, along with the loudening of the helicopter blades, and I inhaled fresh ocean air. I could see the entire island through the open helicopter door. From this distance, it appeared to be nothing more than a house floating on the ocean's horizon. I hadn't noticed how far we'd descended until I saw water splashing in all directions beneath us due to the helicopter's force.

So this is my prison sentence, I thought, gazing across the open water at what I'd only read about in news articles—Kormace Island: the Island of Killers. How had I managed to get myself into so much trouble? I wanted to wake up. It wasn't real. It couldn't be.

The smaller of the two soldiers uncuffed me and led me to the edge of the helicopter. I didn't bother struggling. I was too frail, and his thick hand around my wrist was so tight, I was losing blood circulation. Was he going to throw me out? They couldn't do that! And why weren't they flying any closer to the island? The water underneath us was dark blue...black, almost. It was too deep. I'd never make it to the island alive.

I could have sworn I saw shark fins circling below as if hungrily anticipating my fall. But I knew these were imagined—I was panicking. I didn't have the time to visualize my death any further, because I was instantly pushed out of the helicopter, with only two words echoing behind me, "Swim fast."

It didn't feel like water at all. It felt like I'd broken through a thick sheet of glass. My body temperature dropped instantly, and my fingers quickly numbed.

"Swim fast," I remembered. I moved forward, motivated by the thought of a shark ripping off my leg with its razor-sharp teeth.

Almost there, I lied to myself. Who was I kidding? I could see the island, but only barely. It looked like it was made of Legos from this distance—like it wasn't even real. Was the plan to have me die before successfully reaching Kormace Island? It was a good plan.

The helicopter regained its altitude before flying off in the opposite direction. Couldn't they have dropped me off any closer? Bastards.

The taste of salt coated my tongue, and I coughed up several mouthfuls of ocean water. It was satisfying in a sense. It was the closest thing I'd tasted to food in the last few days. How would I feed myself, anyways? Did the government drop supplies every week? I hadn't been informed of anything.

I was out of breath by the time the island doubled in size. I was getting closer, but it wasn't fast enough. I kicked harder and threw my arms forward, wanting nothing more than to feel the warmth of the sun on my body as I lay in a soft bed of golden sand.

But as the island continued to expand in my line-of-sight, it became clear to me that this fantasy of a remote, paradise-like island was precisely that—a fantasy. The sand, from what I could see, was dark brown with large rocks positioned sporadically across the shore alongside skeletal remains. I finally felt the ocean bed beneath the pads of my feet. Gooey seaweed slid in between my toes as I walked across a hard, uneven path. I couldn't believe I'd actually made it. I felt something slimy wrap itself around my thigh, and I almost screamed before I realized it was just another ocean plant.

I crawled through the filthy sand, feeling both deathly and relieved. Water dripped from my hair and onto my hands, causing goose bumps to spread out evenly across my skin. I just wanted warmth. I hadn't realized I was trembling until I heard my own teeth chatter. I hurried out of the ocean, kicking ocean junk away from my calves, and collapsed onto my stomach.

Although the sand was rough and dirty, it felt warm and dry. I caressed my face into it and closed my eyes. I couldn't remember the last time I'd slept. I remembered the prison cells; I remembered the cold cement walls; I remembered feeling starved; and I remembered the shouts and wails emitted from the surrounding cells. The noise kept me up for days.

Surely, being a prisoner on an island would be much more comfortable than in a prison cell, I thought. I breathed in the scent of saltwater fish, feeling suddenly hungry. I mustered the bit of strength I had and crawled up onto my hands and knees. I tried to wipe sticky sand off my face, even though this only spread it more.

Branches broke in the distance, and my eyes

followed the noise. My heart began to race. There must have been four or five of them just standing there, blending effortlessly with the trees. Their eyes were outlined in black and dark markings spread across their faces.

One of them stepped forward, and the others followed. I considered running, or at least trying to, but I was beyond exhausted—I wouldn't make it.

The fiercest-looking one walked forward, as would the alpha of a wolf pack, and I knew this was their leader. Her dark skin glistened in the sunlight and her muscles bulged as she gripped and regripped what appeared to be a spear carved from wood and stone. She had rope, or vines, wrapped around the muscles of her arms, and I could only assume these were holsters of some type. There was a bow strapped to her back with feathered arrows protruding from a leather quiver. She made a hand gesture and cocked her chin up in my direction.

The other women moved in closer toward me.

"Grab her," the leader ordered.

There was a heavy blow to the side of my head, and everything faded away.

CHAPTER 1

"She ain't no huntin' material."

"She isn't *island* material."

"And you are?"

"Shut up."

"No one is until they're forced to be."

I cracked my eyes open. The skin on my face was warm, and a fire danced from side to side in the near distance. From what I could see, there were five of them sitting around the flames. They bickered back and forth, and I knew they were arguing about me. I closed my eyes when the one nearest to me swung back to look at me. She scoffed and said, "Murk can decide."

Who, or what, was Murk?

I peered through the narrow crack of my eyelid when they began to argue again. They all looked the same at quick glance—dark skin, painted markings, and clothing made of skins and vegetation.

There were spears, ropes, and other sharp objects around their feet. And then I smelled it—

the warm, mouth-watering smell of roasted meat. Atop the fire was a small animal dangling upside down. It looked like a bunny, but I couldn't be sure. Its skin had darkened and crisped, and there was no fur left.

Had I been offered roasted rabbit a week prior, my stomach would have churned at the thought of munching down on a family pet. But I hadn't eaten in days, and at this point, I was willing to eat just about anything.

Suddenly, cold, moist fingers gripped the skin of my upper arm, and I was forced to sit upright.

"She's been awake for a while," came a woman's voice.

She was standing directly beside me, but I was afraid to look up. Where had she come from? The rest remained seated, just staring at me from behind partially shadowed faces.

"Who are you?" asked the woman sitting behind the fire. I remembered that face. She was their leader.

I couldn't speak. I took several deep breaths, ordering my mind to wake from its heinous nightmare. But nothing happened. The more I hoped, the more I realized just how frightening my reality had become.

"Trim asked you a question." I felt something cold and razor-sharp dig into the skin of my neck.

I swallowed hard. They were so barbaric—so wild looking, with their unevenly cut hair and dirty faces.

"Lydia," I said.

"Last name?" the leader asked.

"Brone."

The leader—Trim—tilted her head back and smiled. She was ugly in every sense imaginable with disproportionate features: a long pointed nose, small black eyes, blemished skin, and thick, untrimmed eyebrows that matched her frizzy black hair. Her name now made sense to me.

"Brone," Trim repeated.

I stared at her. Had this been a question? I wasn't sure what to answer.

"Do you like your name?" she asked.

What kind of a question was that? It was my name. I didn't like it or dislike it.

"I'm Rocket," said one of the women seated by the fire. She pressed her hand against her chest as a way of introducing herself. She was very petite and sweet looking despite her savage exterior, which was rough and filthy. She had a cute button nose and bright forest green eyes, but her beauty was masked by a thick crooked scar that ran across her left eyebrow and cheek. Her caramel-brown dreadlocks were pulled back into a knot at the base of her skull.

"'Cause I'm fast," she added. "You pick your own identity here on the island. In prison, you'll always be called by your last name. You can change that here. You know—if you want to be someone else."

Did I want to be someone else? Yes. I wanted to be someone who hadn't been convicted of first-degree murder and dropped on an island to rot.

But my name wouldn't change that.

"Brone's fine," I said.

"This here's Flander," Rocket said, pointing to the woman beside her. Flander cocked an eyebrow but didn't smile. She looked much older than the rest of them, with her wrinkled skin and dull, colorless eyes. She had short grey hair and hundreds of freckles across her nose, cheeks, and shoulders. "That's Biggie, that's Eagle, and that right there," she said, pointing at the woman standing at my side, "is Fisher."

Biggie, as her name insinuated, was the biggest of them all. She had squared off shoulders, a rounded belly, and legs the size of my torso. Her hair was short and woolly, and she had small silver loop earrings running down both ears. She had glossy brown eyes, and wide nostrils the width of her lips. She tried to smile, but it had looked more like a twitch.

I quickly glanced at Eagle, who was eyeing me carefully from behind eyes that were neither green nor blue, but rather, dark turquoise. She nodded as way of acknowledging my presence, but she didn't smile or speak. She had short greasy blonde hair that stood up in all directions. Her lips were thin and flat, and she had an unusual moon shaped birthmark on her forehead.

I finally looked up at Fisher. She grimaced, baring a set of crooked teeth, and said, "I don't like fishing."

I wasn't sure whether or not this had been a joke. Her dark eyebrows were nearly touching at the center of her forehead, and her colorless lips were curved downward. I could tell she'd once been very pretty with her high cheek bones, her dark brown eyes, and her defined jawline, but the island had damaged her. I smiled awkwardly and returned my attention to Trim.

"You hungry?" Trim asked.

She must have caught me eyeing the piece of dangling meat, because she stood up, pulled a dagger from her side, and moved in. She cut the animal loose and propped it up onto a flat rock beside Flander. She tore into it without a second thought and ripped off one of its legs. Although disgusted by the sound of bones cracking and muscle tendons tearing, I'd never been more excited to eat meat.

"Welcome to Kormace," Trim said, tossing me a crispy leg.

CHAPTER 2

I heard a throat-like growl and flinched at the thought of a wild beast lingering nearby. But the sound hadn't come from an animal—at least not a four-legged one. Trim hovered above me with her arms crossed tightly over her chest.

I rubbed my crusted eyes and sat upright. The sun was still up, although for a moment I'd thought it to be night time because of Trim's overly frizzy hair casting a shadow around me. I must have fallen asleep after eating. I was exhausted. I hadn't slept in days due to the reality of my new life.

"On your feet, Brone," she ordered.

I crawled onto my knees and then onto my feet. I didn't have the time to appreciate the melodic chirping that came from the trees or the warmth of the sun penetrating the thousands of leaves overhead.

"Change," Trim said.

Warm suede hit me in the face before landing on my lap. It appeared to be a shirt and a pair of poorly sewn pants.

"What's wrong with what I'm wearing?" I asked.

This had obviously been a stupid question. Trim leaned in and cocked an eyebrow.

"You look new. You smell new. You'll be treated like new."

"Since when is new bad?" I asked.

Rocket was suddenly standing beside Trim. "Since now," she said. "Being new makes you more vulnerable to attacks."

"Attacks?"

Rocket smiled, seemingly amused. "Yeah, that's what I said."

I stared at her, but she offered no consolation.

"Welcome to the wild, Brone." She pointed at my new attire, raised both eyebrows, then walked away.

Trim simply waited, arms still crossed over her chest. So I slowly slid off my chalk-blue T-shirt, something I'd bought at a thrift shop a few months ago, and replaced it with the leather. It hung loosely over one shoulder, leaving the other shoulder completely bare. I couldn't quite tell whether this was the actual design or poor craftsmanship.

"Appreciate that while you have it," I heard.

I followed the voice. It had come from Eagle. She was slouched against a slanted birch tree, sharpening a blade.

"Sorry?" I said.

She smirked, her turquoise eyes gazing into me to the point of discomfort. "Your bra."

I then realized that everyone was looking at

me. Had they all been watching me change? I became fully aware of my red bra straps, which were clearly visible at both my shoulders. Had they expected me to remove it? I noticed most of them weren't even wearing bras; those who were had made them using tight leather, which offered no support, but rather, a flattening functionality.

"Just sayin'," Eagle said, now striking harder with her rock, "that's a luxury most of us islanders don't have."

I couldn't tell whether she'd simply stated a fact or had blatantly threatened me. Her eyes remained glued to me for a moment, and I wondered what she was thinking. She struck harder, and a few sparks spat in all directions.

"Ignore the bird," Rocket said, flicking her wrist out at Eagle. "Come on, put the pants on."

So I slid off my jeans and replaced them with the rugged, uneven pants Trim had so graciously given me. I wiped a line of sweat off my forehead. It was so humid. Hadn't they thought of sewing shorts instead?

Rocket must've read my mind, because she laughed and said, "Yeah, it's hot. Can't be wearin' skanky shorts with all them poisonous snakes around here."

My eyes widened. Snakes? Poisonous?

The others laughed. I didn't understand how any of this was funny. Had I seriously been dropped on an island, surrounded by dangerous creatures and poorly civilized women? When would the government come back for me? How would I know when my three-year sentence was up? I didn't have a calendar. I didn't have my iPhone to keep track. I just wanted to go home. I wanted to slip into my favorite satin pajamas and spend the night lazing on my leather sofa watching reality television.

"Let's have a look," Rocket said, standing me up straight. She eyed me from top to bottom. "Ain't Prada, but it'll do."

"All right, enough already. This ain't no fashion show. Murk isn't gonna wait around. You know the rules," Biggie said. Her muscular dark brown arms were crossed over her chest and her lips formed a flat line. She was the darkest skinned of all the women, and she was built like an ox—her shoulders wide and her chest robust.

"What rules?" I asked.

I knew I was pushing my luck asking so many questions, but I wanted answers. How was I supposed to be calm in such a situation? I'd just been dropped on an island to rot for three years.

"You ever read Harry Potter?" Eagle asked.

I nodded, not quite understanding the relevancy.

"Think of Murk as the island's sorting h—"

"Shut up!" Fisher hissed. "We were all forced to face the island blindly. Brone isn't any different."

Eagle looked away, not daring to challenge Fisher. I didn't blame her. Fisher was the toughest-looking woman I'd ever seen, aside from Trim. She was definitely a mixed race, with dark hair pulled back and round black eyes. She was short, with

10

broad shoulders that gave her the appearance of a professional wrestler. I knew she was Trim's right hand by the way she hovered nearby, constantly glancing her way like a pit bull on guard, as if ready to pounce on anyone who posed a threat.

Trim glanced back at us, at Fisher, and then said, "Fisher's right. Let's go."

She turned toward the sun and led us through an array of trees, plants, and flowers. I could hear birds chirping from above, followed by other sounds I was unfamiliar with. I flinched when a monkey—or a chimp—screamed ahead of us. The women didn't seem bothered by this at all.

I watched my every step, careful not to step on any hard-shelled critters or giant spiders. I'd seen jungles in movies before, so I knew what I was up against—sort of.

Trim led us farther and farther away from shore, and I couldn't help but feel that the deeper we ventured, the more we became vulnerable to Mother Nature.

It was just like I'd seen in the movies. Everything was green or brown, with the exclusion of colorful flowers routed at the base of overly large trees. Even the water flowing through a narrow stream nearby had a greenish tint, most likely due to reflection.

I breathed in the scent of wild flowers, which masked the subtle scent of moist dirt and widespread mildew. I wouldn't get used to this. I'd always been disgusted by the smell of my cat's litter box; I used to remedy the problem by spraying excessive amounts of air freshener throughout my apartment. And I wasn't the outdoorsy type. I'd never survive.

Trim quickly crouched, and the others followed. Rocket tugged on the back of my shirt to bring me down. What was going on? I parted my lips to speak, but Rocket nudged me in the ribs. Fisher's nostrils flared and her muscles bulged. She wanted to fight. But who? Or what?

I heard the cracking of forest vegetation in the distance, and my heart began to race. I realized that aside from these women surrounding me, I was entirely unprotected. The others had blades and spears and even arrows, yet I had nothing. How was I supposed to defend myself in the event of an attack?

Eagle slowly slid a wooden arrow from its quiver on her back. She placed it against the bowstring and drew it back, her gaze fixed intently on her target up ahead. I held my breath, fearful to lure in the unseen predator.

Eagle's eyes narrowed, and she released the arrow. Her bowstring made a snap-like sound, and her arrow whistled through dangling vines and past several tree trunks. There was a squeal in the distance followed by rapid footsteps and the stirring of leaves. Eagle bolted forward, and the others followed, leaving me at the back. I hurried to keep up, but the moment I arrived at the site of her wounded target, I cringed.

Across the root of a tree lay a dying boar, its eyes wide and its head swaying desperately from side to side. Eagle pulled a grimy hatchet from her holster, grabbed the pig by one of its tusks, and raised the weapon over her head.

Rocket barely had time to warn me to look away when Eagle swung downward at the boar's neck. The sound of impact nauseated me. There was a violent squeal, followed by another blow and another and another until the boar stopped moving entirely. Eagle stepped onto the boar's body, and with a hand on each one of its tusks, pulled upward. I nearly threw up at the sound of flesh and soft tissue tearing.

"Nice shot," Trim said, staring down at the arrow protruding from the animal's chest.

"Thanks." Eagle raised the boar's head to eye level, analyzing its face, tusks, and teeth. "Better than my last," she said.

I threw my hand over my mouth at the sight of blood dripping from the wild pig's severed head. Rocket laughed and squeezed my shoulder.

"You get used to it," she said.

Eagle wiped her bloody blade against several vines to clean it, then quickly sliced through one of them before placing her blade back into its holster. The thick, green rope-like plant fell to the ground with a thump. Eagle wrapped the vine around the boar and secured it by tugging hard. She then bent over and tore her arrow out of the boar's chest. She inspected it quickly, then wiped it and tossed it back into her quiver.

"Need help?" Fisher asked.

Eagle shook her head and began dragging her

kill through the forest's bed.

"That looks really heavy," I whispered.

"That's nothing," Rocket said. "Maybe two hundred pounds, at most. A while back, Eagle killed one that was at least five hundred pounds. Had to cut it up to bring it back to the Village."

I grimaced.

"The Village?" I asked, enthused by the prospect of a civilized society.

"What were you expecting?" Flander said, her wrinkled face suddenly near mine. "You were dropped off on an island with over a thousand square miles of land, along with hundreds o' criminals. You really think it's a free-for-all? Humans are social creatures. We wouldn't survive without each other."

Rocket rolled her eyes as if to say, 'Old woman. Here she goes again...'

"How do you know all of this?" I asked.

"I do my research," Flander said.

"Let's keep moving," Trim interrupted.

She continued her lead through the jungle, hacking away at the overpopulation of tree branches and vines.

"Hundreds of criminals?" I whispered, leaning in toward Flander.

She nodded all knowingly.

"Are they all in the Village?" I asked.

She smiled, as if this had been the dumbest question she'd ever heard.

"Like any society, Kormace has its outlaws and its rebels. And like any prison, women fight to hold

14

a position of power," Flander said. She wiped several beads of sweat away from her shiny forehead and gazed around, as if paranoid of being heard. "A few years ago, someone challenged Murk. Didn't agree with the way she was runnin' things. Long story short, she and her loyal followers were removed from the Village. Rumors say they moved to the north the island and created their own society. They're dangerous— merciless. They attacked a while back, killin' a dozen women in their sleep."

I swallowed hard. Flander paused, and I knew she was vividly reliving that terrible night. I couldn't help but wonder if she'd lost anyone she truly cared about.

She cleared her throat. "The Northers all deserve to be killed."

"Fucking right," Rocket interjected.

Fisher joined in on the conversation, shaking a clenched fist in the air. "I'll be the first to rip off Rainer's fucking head!" Her muscles bulged out from underneath her tanned skin, and I could tell she'd been born to fight.

"Rainer?" I asked.

Trim stopped walking. She slowly turned around, as if insulted by the very name.

"Their leader," she said scornfully.

"Whatever you do," Rocket warned, "don't mention that name in front of Murk."

"And Murk is your leader?" I asked.

In an instant, Trim was standing in front of me, her cold blade pressed against the base of my throat.

"Yours too," she said, glaring. "Or would you rather go find the Northers?"

I swallowed hard.

"That's not what Brone meant—" Rocket said.

"Shut up," Trim ordered. I felt the sharp edge of her knife press harder into my skin. "Well?" she asked.

"No," I said. "No. I just meant... I was just trying to understand the hierarchy. I don't know how things are run here... I'm sorry if I..."

She quickly pulled away and stored her weapon.

"Good," she said. "Just making sure."

I noticed a satisfied smile curve at the corners of her lips, but I failed to see the humor in her reaction. My heart was racing, and my mouth was completely dry. Why was I being treated like the enemy? I wasn't here to harm anyone.

"Don't take it personally," Flander said, tapping me hard on the back. "She wouldn't be a good leader if she didn't instill fear every once in a while."

I resentfully accepted this advice and decided it was best to continue following, despite my anger toward Trim. We continued through the jungle for a while, Fisher and Eagle alternating turns pulling the boar.

My legs were about to give out when I finally noticed light being cast through the trees. As we moved closer, the light expanded, and I realized we were exiting the forest—or at least, nearing an opening. Had we crossed the island? My feet were throbbing and my muscles burned. I wanted to collapse. As we moved closer to the light, I realized that the brightness was not being cast by the sun, but rather, by its reflection over a beautiful bed of green water. The water was surrounded by some of the tallest trees I'd ever seen—walls built of greenery that formed a natural enclosure.

A cool mist floated in the air. I parted my lips, allowing several droplets to land on the tip of my tongue. I swallowed hard, my throat sticking, and I wanted nothing more than to dive into the water and drink until my stomach blew. I'd never felt so thirsty in my life.

A consistent static echoed in the distance—the sound of water crashing against water. I knew we'd reached a waterfall. We stepped out into the opening; it was encircled by tall trees and a rocky surface, and I immediately realized we weren't alone.

Surrounding the large circular shaped body of emerald green water were women with similar attributes to those who'd found me. They were wild looking with their tangled hair, their tattooed arms, and their suntanned skin. The ages varied— from adolescents to elderly who required assistance with their bodily movements.

There were women skinning animals and removing their bloody body parts for meat and other materials; women working with some type of contraption in the sand, which appeared to be a handmade water filtration system; women sewing animal hide to construct clothing and shelter; women chopping away at logs of wood; and women working the earth, cultivating and planting a multitude of fruits and vegetables—a society working together to ensure all basic needs were being met.

We moved in closer, and I felt several eyes turn my way. These women stood tall, their chests heaved and their shoulders drawn back as if preparing to face a potential threat. I didn't blame them—they didn't know me, after all. I could have easily been a Norther or even one of the outlaws, as Flander had explained.

A young girl, maybe in her early twenties, was the first to approach me. She had frizzy, dirty blonde hair that was tied back and a fresh cut across her lower lip. She smiled, and I knew it was genuine. She reached out her hand, as did I, but there was no time for introductions.

She was instantly propelled into the air by a woman twice her size, who I could tell ate enough food to feed an army. She had rolls on her arms, her belly, and her legs. How was she so obese while everyone else was so muscular and lean?

"You don't talk to da newcomers, stupid girl," she said, her ugly face contorted as she eyed me with disgust from head to toe. She waddled away with such confidence that it made me wonder if she was Murk.

Rocket chuckled. "Welcome to paradise."

CHAPTER 3

There was no Hogwarts sorting hat.

In fact, there was nothing magical about it at all. She just sat there against the leather of her ruling chair, gazing into me so intently I felt as though I'd be billed for the psychiatric evaluation upon exit.

She smiled, and there was something genuine about it. She didn't look menacing or mistrustful, yet there was something intimidating about her. She had crystal blue eyes and short silver hair that looked white in comparison to her suntanned face. There was red paint, or blood, smeared across her cheeks, and she wore a necklace made of sharp canine teeth. She leaned back in her chair, then crossed her legs and interlocked her fingers over her knees.

I had been led underneath the large waterfall, through a damp cave that smelled of mould, and into a room illuminated by wall-mounted torches. I'd been told to get on my knees and bow the moment I saw her, and I realized then that the bully I'd run into earlier had not been Murk. This woman was Murk.

"Welcome," she said.

I was told to stand, and I did so—for what felt like hours—being scrutinized by the leader of the island. I realized the power she had over me. With a click of her fingers, she could have me dragged away from their society and fed to the sharks. It was best to remain silent until asked to speak.

"What's your name?" she asked.

"L—Lydia. Lydia Brone."

"Why are you here?"

I swallowed hard. I wanted Trim, Rocket, Fisher, Eagle, Biggie, or Flander to speak on my behalf, but the only other person here was Trim who was standing silently at the cavern's entry point, arms crossed over her chest and eyes focused away from us.

"Well, the government—" I started.

She waved a hand and shook her head.

"I know all about the government. What did you do? What crime?"

"M—murder," I said.

"Cold-blooded?"

I shook my head. "It was an accident."

"I don't need the details," she said.

"What did you do?" she asked.

I wasn't sure what she was referring to. I'd just explained to her what I'd been convicted of.

"Well... I... Um. It was a complicated situation. It all happened really fast."

She cut me short again with a wave of her hand.

"What was your profession?"

"Oh. Cashier. Local flea market."

She smirked. I immediately knew that I wouldn't be of much use to her.

"Are you strong?" she asked.

I knew I wasn't the toughest of girls, but I needed to sell myself.

"I'm not weak," I said.

"Ever been in a fight?"

"Does fourth grade count?" I asked.

"No."

"Then no," I said.

I wondered if I should have lied, but there was something about the way her eyes gazed into me that made me want to reveal only truths. If I lied, she would somehow know.

"What about your parents? What do they do?"

I hesitated.

"Well, my mom doesn't work, and my dad... Well, I'm not sure... I haven't spoken to him in years."

She nodded slowly.

"My dad worked in a warehouse—when he was around, that is," I continued.

She shook her head. "That's fine. What do you like to do for fun?" she asked. "Any hobbies?"

I felt like I was being interviewed for a salary-less job. How many more questions did she have up her sleeve? And how did my hobbies have anything to do with my life as a prisoner on Kormace Island? It wasn't like I'd be given a flat-screen TV with a cable box that fed off some magical source of electricity. My hobbies really didn't matter.

I shrugged. "I like to cook."

"Anything else?"

"I like to read."

She was still staring at me, and I knew she was unimpressed.

"I like beading and bracelet-making. I don't earn money doing it, but they make nice gifts."

No response.

"Look, I'm just the average person. I spend most of my time watching TV, which is obviously something I won't be doing anytime soon. I have a cat at home, but you know how cats are... pretty independent. I don't take him to the park. I don't have many friends or a social life. I'm nothing special—I'm sorry. I know you'd rather have a doctor land on the island, but that's not me. I don't have any special talents, but I'm a quick learner, and I'll try anything."

I hadn't meant to ramble for so long, but I couldn't bear another minute of her analytical gaze. It made me feel not only judged but completely unworthy of living among the other women on this island. She had a way of making me feel comfortable while also completely helpless and in need of her guidance.

"Trim," she said.

Trim turned her way.

"Have her join the Needlewomen."

Needlewomen? Who were they? I wanted more information, but I knew I wouldn't receive it. Murk simply smiled and nodded at me as a way of saying good-bye. I met Trim at the entryway, and she led me out through the cavern.

"What're Needlewomen?" I finally asked her, but she ignored me.

The sound of the waterfall crashing into water grew louder as we approached the exit. I would have had to yell to communicate, so I remained quiet and allowed Trim to lead the way. We slid out through the side of the waterfall, and to my surprise, the women working in the open space and around the water stood still, their eyes fixed toward the waterfall. What were they looking at?

Trim led me up a crooked path, away from the fall. I realized then that my paranoia was warranted. They were all staring at me—watching me. We finally reached the path's peak—an elevated surface that sat on a rocky wall. A cliff, almost.

There was an unlit torch jabbed into the earth of the platform. Trim wrapped her fingers around it, almost ceremonially, and threw her fist into the air before shouting over the people, "Brone! Needlewoman!"

There were shouts of anger and resentment and then shouts of joy, but I couldn't tell which were coming from where. I scanned the crowd in hopes of spotting one of the women I knew, but I couldn't see them.

I was led back down the cliff, alongside the waterfall and through the crowd of wild women. I received several glares, most of which I could tell were attempts at intimidation.

"This way," Trim said.

We approached a group of women sitting in the forest's cool shade, away from the body of water.

"Savia, this is Brone, your new girl."

There was a woman—Savia, I presumed—sitting against the root of a tree with her head tilted back against its coarse bark. Around her were several women who'd been sewing a variety of items, most of which I could tell were garments, but they all stopped to look at me.

Savia smiled at me. I wasn't quite sure what to make of it. She seemed good-hearted, yet I knew no one on this island could be trusted. She had frizzy silver hair tied in a braid at the side of her head and emerald colored eyes. There was a pink, unsightly scar above her right eyebrow that took attention away from her crooked teeth.

"Grab a needle, m'girl," she said.

I glanced at the woman nearest me. She must have sensed my discomfort, because she threw her head sideways, signaling me to sit beside her. Trim walked away, and I wondered how long it would be until I saw her again. Although Trim and her group of women had basically kidnapped me, I felt as though I'd made new friends only to have them immediately taken away.

"You ever sew before?" Savia asked.

I shook my head.

"Jeena 'ere will show you," she said, pointing a loose finger at the woman next to me.

"Hi, Jeena," I said.

She tried to smile, the corner of her lip twitching, but she didn't respond or look at me.

"You can talk to her all y'like, but she won't talk back," Savia said.

I glanced at Jeena, whose eyes were fixed on the ground. She seemed like a sweet girl—like someone who wouldn't hurt a fly. She was very petite, light skinned, and frail looking, and all I wanted to do was protect her.

"Got a bad infection in her mouth 'while back," Savia said. "Had to take out most of 'er teeth and part of 'er tongue."

Jeena cringed at the sound of her own story.

"I—I'm sorry," I said.

"That's what happens when y'only got two medics for several hundred women and when the Northers kill one of 'em off."

"You only have one doctor?" I asked.

Savia laughed.

"Medic," she corrected. "Ain't no prisoner here a doctor. But we're lucky enough to have one woman who knows anything and everything about the plants on this island. Knows how to heal the injured and the sick. 'Er sister was our other medic, but she was killed not long ago."

I couldn't believe what I was hearing. It had never occurred to me that medical care among felons would be completely stripped. We were on our own with nothing more than bare necessities. What would happen if food were to run out? If the last medic were to be killed?

I watched the other women as they punctured

holes through thick sheets of suede, cut numerous shapes out of the skin, and stitched pieces together by sewing through the holes they'd made. I'd get the hang of it.

There were several sheets of skin stretched out across what appeared to be giant slingshots. Pieces of wood held the skins at an angle, which I assumed was to allow the sun to dry them out.

"What do you guys make with all this leather?" I asked.

Savia smiled, and I noticed a few of the other women smirk as if I'd just asked the most idiotic of questions.

"Anythin' and everythin'," she said. "Women on the island need to survive. We've gone back to the native times. We need clothing, water satchels, weapons, footwear, tents..."

Jeena handed me several long pieces of leather. She pointed at it and made a fist-like gesture, but I couldn't make out what she was trying to tell me.

"Arrows," Savia intervened.

I stared at her. Was I supposed to make arrows out of flimsy leather?

I felt a tap on my thigh, and I glanced back. The woman sitting beside me pointed at a pile of finely carved arrowheads, and then at a pile of smooth pieces of wood with beautiful multicolored feathers attached at the tips. I watched Jeena as she tied the pieces together, her fingernails whitening as she repeatedly wrapped the leather band around both the arrowhead and the stem of wood. When she was finished, there was no telling these two pieces had ever been apart—what she held in her fist was a genuine hunting arrow.

I knew it would take practice. I felt humiliated by my twelfth attempt, still unable to solidly conjoin the two pieces.

"Why'd they give 'er Needlewoman?" I heard one of the women whisper to another.

I glanced up, but what I met was a pair of fearless black eyes beneath uncombed eyebrows. I could tell that confrontation was no alien matter among these savages.

"Got a problem?" she asked.

I shook my head and looked away. I wasn't the type to talk back to anyone. I'd been raised to respect those around me, to avoid conflict at all costs, and to mind my own business. The woman scoffed, as did the other, and then she said, "Probably here for some stupid shit like drinkin' and drivin' and killin' a family."

"That's enough," Savia intervened.

I didn't bother to look up. I felt my throat swell at the memory of it. He hadn't deserved death. Prison—maybe, but not death. I cringed at the image of his lifeless body lying on my mother's kitchen floor surrounded by a pool of thick blood, his empty eyes staring past me into nothingness. I'd only meant to knock him out. He'd had my mother pinned against the wall, his thick hands around her collapsing throat, and I'd swung the iron pan at the back of his head.

I hadn't meant to kill him.

"Brone?"

I was shaken from my past by a beautiful young woman standing by Savia's side. She had thick, wavy brown hair tied to the side of her head and dark chocolate eyes shaped like almonds. Her build was strong, but her features were soft. She had a small butterfly tattoo on her right shoulder, and a necklace made of seaweed and seashells. I felt at ease.

"I'm Ellie," she said, extending a hand. "I'll be your new peer support worker."

I rose to my feet and shook her hand.

She smiled.

"We try to maintain a prison's standard societal structure, even though we're in the wild."

A peer worker? I had no objections. I was very welcoming to the idea of having someone show me the ropes.

"Come with me," she said.

I felt several eyes on me as I walked away from my new post, but I didn't mind—I was happy to get away from the hostility.

She led me through a narrow path in the trees, away from all of the commotion around the waterfall.

"That," she said, eyeing the loud voices and noise behind us, "is the Working Grounds. You'll be spending most of your time there, working with the leather. Murk sometimes gives us the opportunity to change posts, but don't count on that. It's happened twice since I've been here, and she only allowed a handful of people to change jobs. Disrupts the expertise otherwise, you know?"

I nodded, even though she was ahead of me and couldn't see me.

"Hey, Tal," Ellie said.

I glanced up just in time to step to the side and allow the woman to pass. Her head was shaved on both sides, and she had skull tattoos covering both arms. She eyed me from top to bottom and released a growl-like sound.

"That's Tal," Ellie said, smiling back at me.

Was I really supposed to remember all these names? I didn't bother to look back at the woman. I feared she might attack me if I so much as looked at her.

"She can be a bit scary at first, but she means well," Ellie said. "Come on."

The sound of the waterfall faded behind us, and the jungle's orchestra returned. Birds chirped in the distance, rustling leaves shook above us, and vegetation crackled underneath us.

"Through here," Ellie said, sliding her way through a thick curtain of vines.

When I entered the opening, I couldn't believe what I was seeing. An entire village. What caught my attention first and foremost was the seclusion of the Village. Trees and branches had been bent, vines intertwined, and stones compiled around the area to form an enclosure—a barrier around the Village, which appeared to be the size of an average football field.

There were several dozens of tents constructed of wood and leather positioned in an uncalculated fashion across the land. The color of the tents varied due to sun damage—some were beige, others light brown, and the tents closest to the trees were dark mocha. Many women roamed the area freely, some socializing, others keeping to themselves. There was a fire pit at the center, around which a group of women gnawed on cooked meat and pieces of bone.

"Welcome to the Village," Ellie said, wrapping a warm arm around my shoulder.

I tried to smile to acknowledge her presence, but I was too intrigued by what I was seeing.

At the far back were three huts positioned side by side. These were constructed mostly of wood, with what appeared to be seaweed atop tree branches to form a roof. The one at the center was the largest and most beautiful of the three.

"That's Murk's," Ellie said, watching me eye the hut at the back.

"Who is Murk, anyways?" I finally asked.

Ellie smiled at me, and I could tell she'd been in my shoes before.

"Murk's what you call the top dog," she said. "Like wolves in the wild, there's always an alpha. Murk's the alpha—the pack leader. And we're the pack."

"So she's the boss," I said.

Ellie smirked. "I'll show you your tent."

She led me to the farthest corner of the Village, past the largest of tents, and we headed for the smallest and shabbiest of them all. Mine was slanted toward the right, and several dozen cobwebs were gathered around the base and underneath the leather flaps.

"Think of this as initiation," Ellie said. She punched me in the shoulder, but only hard enough to capture my attention. "I know it looks like shit," she admitted, "but you're the new kid on the block. Can't expect luxury."

I scoffed. "I'm assuming Murk's hut is considered luxury?"

Ellie smiled, but her eyebrows quickly came together. "I get it, trust me, but no talking about Murk. Got it? She's a good leader, and if you walk around here disrespecting her, you'll disappear in no time."

"I wasn't disrespecting her—" I tried.

"Check it out," Ellie said, extending an arm toward the tent.

"Can I clean it off first?"

Ellie tilted her head and cocked an eyebrow.

"You're living in the jungle now. You'd better get used to bugs and creepy critters."

"Creepy cr—" I started.

"I'll lead the way, princess." She winked back at me.

The moment she pulled on the large hanging front door, something hairy and black fell from above. She didn't flinch or make a sound. Instead, she reached up and pulled the oversized spider out of her hair. I cringed. It had long stick legs and a round body, and I couldn't tell whether it was a spider or a tarantula. She held it gently in the palm of her hand.

"Aw, it's just a baby," she said.

Just a baby? The thing was the size of a golf ball! I swallowed hard. I wanted to tap the heels of my muddy sneakers together and say aloud, "There's no place like home," over and over again.

The thought of cleaning my cat's litter box somehow became less repulsive to me, as did the idea of crushing little white spiders in between thick sheets of napkin to remove them from my apartment.

Ellie knelt on one knee and freed the baby monster. I could only pray it wouldn't find its way back to me.

"It's a good idea to keep your tent closed when you aren't around," she said. She pulled the door to the side and wrapped a piece of rope around it. She did the same thing to the other side, allowing sunlight to enter my new home.

The interior was bare and somewhat cool in comparison to the island's sticky heat. I stared at the dirt beneath my feet. Where was I supposed to sleep?

"You'll have to find your own bed and blanket," Ellie said, eyeing the ground.

"Where am I supposed to find that in a jungle?" I asked.

Ellie ignored me, and I knew I'd just posed a silly question. I would have to make my own comfort with the items I could find. I cringed at the thought of gathering leaves or seaweed—I'd be left vulnerable to oversized bugs.

But the thought didn't linger. My shoulders jerked forward at the sound of a deep, hollow horn that resonated across the Village. I glanced at Ellie, hoping to be eased and reassured that the sound was no more than an invitation of sorts, but I knew it wasn't the case because Ellie's eyes seemed to double in size, and she crouched like frightened prey.

Something was wrong.

She muttered something, but I didn't understand her. She glanced back at me briefly and placed a finger over her lips, then quickly reached outside of the tent and loosened the door's straps.

The curtains fell forward with a heavy swing, and we were left in the dark.

CHAPTER 4

The sound of footsteps and voices drifted in from outside. The only thing I saw was Ellie's silhouette as sunlight broke through several cracks in the tent. I could hear her breathing heavily, and all I wanted to do was ask her what was going on.

I'd been tempted to crawl to the front of the tent—just one glance, that was all I wanted. But that's when I heard it—a scream like none I'd ever heard before. It was the most horrific sound I could have imagined: the sound of excruciating torment...the sound of torture.

Ellie raised a hand over her mouth, almost as if to keep sound from involuntarily spilling out. There were more screams—some were pained, others vengeful. These sounds were the cries of battle.

I couldn't think. I could only feel adrenaline flooding my body. Everything felt surreal, as if at any moment, I'd awaken from this gruesome nightmare to the sound of my cat purring beside my pillow. This couldn't be happening.

There was a loud rip-like sound from above, and I immediately felt heat spread across my face and atop my shoulders. My sense of smell was quicker than my eyes, though. I smelled the smoke before I knew it was fire. Up above, through a hole in the leather, was an arrow lit on fire, sticking out from one of the tent's wooden support beams.

"Shit," Ellie muttered.

She reached for my hand and pulled me toward the front of the tent. She peered through the cracks, and then back at the dancing flames above us that had begun to spread. The heat became unbearable, and the smoke thickened to a dark gray. I couldn't believe how quickly it was catching.

"We have to run," she said.

My heart was pounding, and my ears were ringing. I wanted to object, but I couldn't speak. Nothing came out. She pulled on my hand, tore through the front of the tent, and ran out toward the Village's outer wall.

I heard an arrow whistle right by me and more voices shouted from afar. I glanced back—something I shouldn't have done—only to witness a woman running in all directions, lit on fire with several arrows protruding from her body. Women ran to her aid, attempting to fight the flames with torn pieces of clothing.

Many tents were engulfed with flames; others were punctured by arrows. I heard a few more arrows whistle through the air, followed by shouts of rage. Ellie pulled us against the Village's barrier, through which I knew we couldn't pass. It had been woven together so tightly, with little to no space in between the materials. I suddenly realized that the attack was coming from above...from the trees.

She brought us to a corner, where we knelt in an attempt to camouflage ourselves with the surrounding greens and browns. She was still holding onto my hand, squeezing so hard I wondered if my fingers were breaking, but I couldn't feel anything.

What felt like hours may have lasted mere minutes. I watched as wounded women were dragged away from the center of the Village and into one of the larger wooden cabins at the south end. I could only presume that this was where the medic resided. The shouting had faded, only to be replaced by moans and cries of sorrow and agony. The fires had subsided, and now thick gray smoke hovered above us all. I felt sick to my stomach.

I turned away from Ellie just in time for acid to come pouring out of my mouth—burning my throat raw in the process—before I collapsed.

* * *

For a moment, I thought I was being attacked.

"Told you she wasn't jungle material," I heard.

I wiped the lukewarm water off my face and away from my eyes, then glanced up. Trim was standing in front of me with a shell-shaped piece of bone I assumed was meant to be used as a bowl. Behind her were Rocket and Fisher, whose arms were crossed over their chests.

"Well, she's still alive, isn't she?" Rocket said, eyeing Fisher.

"Luck," Fisher said.

I could tell she wasn't impressed by the way she gazed down at me as if I were nothing more than a rock in her way.

Trim raised a hand, silencing them both instantly, before kneeling down onto one knee in front of me. I then realized that Ellie wasn't anywhere near me. Trim must have sensed my panic, because she smiled, and said, "She's at the cabin, helping the injured women."

I sighed.

"You okay?" she asked.

I wasn't sure whether to nod or cry. I wasn't sure what to feel.

"The Northers attacked us," she said, matter-of-factly.

"W—why?" I asked.

Trim looked away, then shook her head. "That's just how things are here. We're at war."

"Yeah, but they've never attacked us in broad daylight!" Rocket shouted.

Trim grimaced and waved a hand behind her head.

"Is anyone hurt?" I asked.

Fisher's and Rocket's eyes wandered away from mine.

"Do you wear glasses?" Trim asked me, cutting right through the silence.

I shook my head, not quite understanding the relevancy of her question.

"Many women on this island do—did," she said, "when they were living in the real world."

"Like me," Rocket said, attempting to smile. "Your face is a bit blurry from here."

I didn't understand why they were talking about glasses when we'd just been brutally attacked by wild women from the north. Why wasn't anyone devising a battle plan? What if this attack had been a warning of sorts—a precursor of something much worse to come. I wanted to ask, "What's your point?" but I'd always been taught that if I had nothing nice to say, it was best I keep my damn mouth shut. So, I did.

The stupefied look on my face may have given away my thoughts.

"Look," Trim said, "Eagle's been hit, and Murk's already trying to gather potential archers. She's the best we had—the best we *have*," she corrected.

Rocket refused to make eye contact. I could tell she was hurting, which made me wonder how long she'd known Eagle.

"What are you asking me?" I asked.

"What's your vision?" Fisher asked, stepping in closer.

"What?"

"You got twenty-twenty?" Fisher asked.

I hadn't been to an optometrist in several years. I'd never bothered to go because my vision had never posed any real problems. I'd always been one of the lucky kids in class who was able to sit at the back corner and still make out the many mathematical equations written on the chalkboard by Mr. Adams.

I nodded.

Rocket scoffed. "Lucky... Wish I hadn't played so many video games growing up."

Fisher elbowed her. "That ain't what caused your shit vision," she said.

"Yeah, it is!"

"Guys, shut up!" Trim hissed. She gazed at me from head to toe, cocked an eyebrow, and extended an open palm. "Come on, Murk wants you assessed."

* * *

Some women were crying; others excitedly mimicked archers shooting at invisible targets across the Village. It was clear that being the object of analysis for the purpose of creating soldiers hadn't been voluntary.

"There hasn't been an Assessment like this in years," I heard.

I glanced behind me to where the voice had come from. There were two women facing each other within the lineup, gabbing away about the history of Kormace Island and the changes brought forth by Murk over the last ten years.

I stood near the back of the line, behind dozens of other women, waiting to enter Murk's cabin. The Assessment was being performed on an individual basis, which was not only intimidating but also terrifying. I wasn't ready to be a fighter. I didn't want to be a fighter. I was perfectly content sewing leather together for the next three years. The only fight I'd ever been in was in fourth grade, and it had been over a boy stealing my peanut butter and jelly sandwich.

I was so involved in my memory of young Steven Poulis, I failed to hear how silent the Village had grown. I peered over one of the women's shoulders and toward Murk's cabin which appeared to be attracting many eyes.

Murk had stepped outside, surrounded by Trim, Fisher, Flander, Biggie, and Rocket. There were two other women standing tall on either side of her, who I assumed were her personal guards. She walked forward, and the women around me began to kneel. I followed suit and placed the weight of my body onto one knee.

"Women of Kormace," Murk shouted. Her chest heaved and her fingers wrapped around a spear. "Today came to us all as a surprise." She paused for a moment, eyeing each person with such care and empathy that I realized she thought of her people as family. I understood how she'd earned everyone's respect.

"A beautiful life was taken," she said, raising her voice as she spoke, "but this was not in vain. Today has shown us how uncivilized and cruel the Northers have become." She took another step forward and raised her spear. "We will not allow this to happen again!"

There were shouts of angst among the women, but all I felt was fear. Several other spears and weapons were thrown up toward the sky, and I felt surrounded by animals. Everyone wanted blood.

"We've spent years surviving with our divisions of Farmers, Needlewomen, Builders, Medics, and Hunters who have also been our Battlewomen. But today, this changes."

Another uproar shook throughout the Village.

"We need more Battlewomen to protect our people—to fight for what's ours and to defend what we've worked so hard for."

I was knocked in the back by one of the islanders who was throwing her fists into the air, shouting nonsense with determination. I wanted to push her back but knew she'd tear me to shreds. All she wanted to do was fight.

"Let the Assessment begin!" Murk said.

I covered my ears to block out the surrounding screams and cries of motivation to murder. How had I managed to be dropped onto a remote island that was in the midst of war? Trim's crew had been right when they first found me—I wasn't island material.

I was shoved from side to side a few more times by overbearingly loud women practicing their fighting skills. They were tackling each other to the ground and pulling at limbs and joints, acting like young boys.

"Hey, stranger," I heard.

It was Ellie. She stood directly behind me with her arms crossed over her chest, a grin stretching her face. Although still upset by the fact that she'd completely abandoned me the moment I lost consciousness, I was happy to see her.

"Sorry about earlier," she said.

I frowned, but all it did was make her smile grow wider.

"For the record, I slapped you at least a dozen

times before I left," she said.

I rubbed my cheek; it was tender to the touch.

"Thanks for trying," I said.

"You're welcome." She patted me on the arm. "Couldn't sit by your side all day. I knew you'd wake up eventually."

"Yeah, well—" I started, even though I had no clue what to say.

"So what's the deal?" she interrupted. "You're taking part in the Assessment?"

I cleared my throat. "Guess so."

"Voluntold, not volunteered?" she asked.

"Pretty much."

She nodded, eyeing the competition around me.

"It's a noble status to have, I guess," she said, "being a Battlewoman and all."

I shrugged. I didn't care about statuses. All I wanted was to live a quiet life for the remainder of my sentence, and if that meant being the Omega of the pack, so be it.

"Is it hard?" I asked.

"Is what hard?" She tilted her head to the side, scrutinizing every inch of me.

"Being a Hunter—a Battlewoman," I said.

"For you, probably," she admitted. "No offense."

"What's that supposed to mean?" I asked.

She laughed, even though I'd shown no sign of amusement.

"You aren't exactly built for battle," she said.

I couldn't argue. I'd never been one for sports, let alone any type of physical activity. The only exercise I ever performed on a daily basis was bending over to scoop my cat's litter box. I'd always been the scrawny kid in class, and in high school gym class, I'd once been used as a bench press weight by one of the guys.

I sighed.

"Don't be so hard on yourself." Ellie threw an arm around my shoulders and pulled me in. "Everyone has a purpose."

I scoffed. I wasn't buying it.

"Murk's desperate for Battlewomen," she said, leaning in closer. "Her standards aren't what they usually are."

Was this supposed to make me feel better? It definitely didn't. This was equivalent to offering someone a job not because of their qualifications, but due to an unexpected layoff and an immediate requirement to replace the former employee.

It sounded so official—the Assessment—like something so monumental it could only be experienced through a form of ceremony. But there was no ceremony. In fact, there was nothing special about it at all. I watched as women were brought into Murk's cabin one at a time, led by two Amazonian-built women on either side. Some women were escorted from Murk's cabin within mere minutes; others did not return.

Everyone stared as one woman came storming out, cursing and swinging her fists into the air. You could tell she was a fighter by nature. Why hadn't Murk selected her? What was she really looking for?

"Brone," I heard.

I swallowed hard. It was finally my turn. I glanced at Ellie, who was now leaning against a tree not far from the cabin. The sun had begun to set, casting an orange hue across the Village, and I couldn't tell whether she was smiling or grimacing at me.

"Your turn," Trim said. She didn't smile or make eye contact.

I walked into Murk's cabin, holding onto the comforting image of my immediate release. I wasn't cut out for this. Surely, Murk would come to realize this and demand to have me removed from her presence. But what I saw carried no comfort at all. Murk was sitting on a wooden bench of sorts, sucking on a stick, and exhaling a cloud of gray from the corner of her mouth.

"What's your vision?" she asked, staring into me as a mother would a disobedient child. She leaned in, placing both elbows onto her parted knees.

I glanced at Trim, but she offered no guidance.

"I'm sorry?" I asked.

"Your sight. What is it?"

For a moment, I was tempted to lie—to say that I was nearsighted and required glasses for clear vision. No one would have known. No one but Trim, that is. I couldn't trust her to protect me.

"Good," I admitted.

"Perfect?" Murk asked.

I nodded, even though all I wanted to do was shake my head. I visualized the woman on fire and the way she'd danced from side to side in an

45

attempt to outrun the flames melting her skin.

She laid her cigar onto the floor, sat up straight, and stared into nothingness. I shot another glance toward Trim, but again, received no indication as to what I was supposed to do.

I watched as Murk's eyes followed the smoke from her cigar, which curled several times, before drifting to the left. She nodded slowly, then reached down and pulled the cigar back into her mouth.

"Archer," she suddenly said, and I thought I might faint.

CHAPTER 5

I felt as though I'd been involuntarily recruited into police foundations. The islanders around me spoke of training and of enhancing one's survival skills. All I heard was *death*. We were just a bunch of women who'd been chosen to defend the Village without adequate time to develop the necessary combat skills to fight—we'd been assigned a suicide mission.

Trim led the twelve of us who'd been chosen to the Working Grounds to commence training. I was already so exhausted from the long day I'd had—from being assigned the task of Needlewoman, to the Village falling under attack—that I wasn't prepared for any of this. My legs burned, and my head throbbed. I couldn't remember the last time I'd eaten, let alone had anything to drink.

"Archer?"

I side-glanced at the woman standing beside me, not wanting to make full eye contact.

"I don't bite."

I turned to face her. Her smile revealed a set of

brown, rotting teeth and large nostrils which were flared beyond normality. She had the strangest eyes I'd ever seen: dandelion yellow and charcoal gray. They stood out even more in contrast to her dark brown skin. Her hair was cut close to the skin of her head, not quite shaved but not quite long enough to be considered a haircut. She was built thin, with protruding muscles that I knew were not the result of strength, but rather, lack of fat.

"Yeah, I got Archer," I said.

"Me too." She smirked as if this title was something to be proud of. "Sunny."

I glanced up at the sky, which was covered in a thin layer of gray, but when she extended a calloused hand, I realized she hadn't been talking about the sky.

"I'm Ly—Brone," I said.

"Pleasure to meet you, Librone," she said, shaking my hand vigorously.

"Just Brone," I said.

"You're new," she said. It was a statement more than a question. "You'll get used to it around here."

I nearly said, 'I doubt that,' but she patted me on the arm as a father would his son, then added, "Took me about six months to adjust."

Six months? It had only been two days, and I was already craving the feeling of warm soap being lathered against my skin; the taste of cold Pepsi against the tip of my tongue on a hot summer day; the sound of club music blasting through my car speakers while I sped on the highway with my windows rolled down. I'd taken so much for granted, not ever realizing how luxurious a life I'd truly had.

"How long have you been here?" I asked.

She shrugged. "Can't say for sure. Stopped counting after two years."

"Why two?" I asked.

She shook her head and laughed, but I knew she wasn't amused.

"I didn't believe them," she said. She bit her lip, then scratched her cracked fingernails against the skin of her head. "Thought they were lying."

"Who? What're you talking about?" I asked.

Her eyes narrowed on me and then shot from side to side at the other women nearby.

"My sentence," she whispered, "was s'pposed to be two years."

I turned away at the smell of her rancid breath.

"What happened?" I asked.

She curled her lips upward, resembling a Rottweiler guarding a junkyard. I could tell the island had made this woman feral. There was an emptiness in her eyes—a lack of morality, of self-awareness, and of empathy. This island had taken from her what had once made her human, and I feared it would do the same to me.

"I'm still here, ain't I?" she said.

I wasn't entirely sure what she'd meant by this. Had she committed a second crime? Had she been reconvicted to serve a life sentence? I'd been given three years of isolation on Kormace Island as punishment for my crime, which was rather short in comparison to standard sentences imposed on criminals convicted of murder. My lawyer had fought for *manslaughter*, but he hadn't won.

* * *

"Fuck sakes, Janet, how many times I gotta tell you to wash my clothes at the end of the week?" Gary said.

He'd found his work clothes sitting at the bottom of a hamper, only to realize it reeked of sweat and old water. Gary, my mother's boyfriend, was always verbally abusing her. He was a big guy, weighing at least two hundred pounds, with large hands and a thick neck the size of one of my legs. My mother had always told me he'd had a hard life—that he had demons but that deep down, he only meant well. I didn't believe her. I just wanted her to leave him.

I watched as my mother hurriedly gathered his dirty socks and stained shirt, nearly falling over in the process.

"This too," he said, throwing a pair of booze-stained boxers at her feet.

He walked right past me into the kitchen and opened the fridge door. He reached inside and pulled out a cheap brand of beer. Piece of shit, I thought.

"You know how Gary is," my mom said, flicking her wrist as if to insinuate that his ways were no worse than those of a child throwing a tantrum. She sipped her red wine, then gazed out through the trees and toward a row of parked cars down below our balcony.

"Mom," I said, "he's too much." But I knew she

wouldn't listen. She was too soft—too capable of looking past one's worst qualities, only to see the good in them.

She went on and on about how most days, he treated her like a queen. I had a hard time believing this. If only I'd known how terrible things were about to become, I would have tried harder to convince her of the danger he posed.

By the time we went back inside, he'd gotten piss drunk, and he began accusing my mother of all sorts of nonsense. It was difficult to make out what he was saying. She tried to calm him, but it only angered him further.

Everything then happened so fast... He'd swung an open hand at the side of her face, and I remember thinking she hadn't survived the blow. She fell to the carpet by the living room's coffee table, and a thin line of red slid around the curves of her lips.

He grabbed her again and I came at him with a cast iron frying pan. I'd only intended to knock him out long enough for the police to show. I raised the pan above my head with both hands, and with all my might, swung directly at the back of his head. I hit him so hard, he collapsed instantly.

I hadn't meant to kill him.

* * *

"Archers, let's go."

I glanced up. It was Trim. She stood directly in front of me with three wooden bows in one hand and a fistful of arrows in the other. The carving work on the bows and arrows was meticulously done—smooth, with barely any unevenness. The bows were shaped like half-moons, and the wood was fresh white.

She led us away from the water and toward the trees, where handmade wooden targets stained in blood hung unevenly. I wasn't ready for this.

"Is Eagle gonna be okay?" I asked, wanting nothing more than to be dismissed.

She glanced sideways at me, but she didn't respond. I couldn't help but wonder how long she'd been on the island. She was so cold—so emotionally impenetrable. I supposed this made her a strong leader.

By my fourth arrow—which flopped down into the sand—it became clear to me that Murk's expectations were to have women trained into Battlewomen overnight.

"Keep your elbow up," Trim ordered.

Sunny caught on. Her form was good, as was her aim, but she lacked patience and obedience. She'd release the arrow before being ordered to do so, which only enraged Trim.

"Fuck you!"

I turned around to spot two women battling with wooden sticks across the shore of the Working Grounds. One was black and the other white. The black woman had managed to climb atop the other, and she was pressing a wooden spear against her victim's throat. Her muscles were hard and her back was round. She'd lost control.

"Enough!" Fisher shouted, moving in closer.

The black woman didn't listen. She pushed down harder, causing the other woman's face to turn a deep shade of purple.

"I said enough!" Fisher grabbed the black woman by the back of her hair and pulled up hard, but the woman swung backward and punched Fisher in the face, rendering her dazed.

I hadn't realized how tightly I was holding my bow until Trim pulled it out of my hands. She took one step forward, slid an arrow into the bow, and then raised it to eye level. Her movements had been so quick—so swift.

There was a scream.

Suddenly, the black woman was lying in the sand, crawling backward like a crab on her heels and elbows in an attempt to get away from Trim who was now marching her way. I noticed a trail of red sand grains underneath her as she moved.

Trim stepped on her chest, causing the woman to collapse instantly. She reached down and tore the protruding arrow out of the woman's shoulder. I turned away at the sound of her tormented bellowing.

"You know the rules," Trim said, hunched over the woman who appeared to be begging for her life.

"Trim, please, I didn't mean it," the woman pleaded.

Trim pressed her foot down harder, and the woman gasped for air.

"You turn on your own, and you're no longer one of us."

"Trim, I won't survive. I'm begging you!"

Trim turned around to meet the eyes of her audience. There were other women surrounding us; many of them had not been part of the combat training, but their curiosity had lured them to the scene.

Trim stepped toward the observing women with my bow in one hand, her features hardened.

"Let it be known, from this day forward, that this woman has committed treason and is no longer one of us."

Conversation erupted all around us, and large eyes were glued to the injured woman in the sand. Trim turned her face toward the black woman, and without making direct eye contact, said, "Leave."

"Trim, please!"

Fisher moved in with several other Battlewomen who were prepared to drag her out of the Working Grounds by any means necessary. I caught sight of Flander among these women, her silver hair bright in comparison to the skin tones around her. Although older than most islanders, I could tell she possessed the strength of a dozen women.

I heard the name "Marlin" several times and realized this name belonged to the woman who'd just been banished. I watched as Marlin ran past us toward the jungle's verdure. She disappeared within moments, leaving nothing but a trail of messy footprints and a pool of dark blood in the sand.

"Let me remind all of you," Trim said, "of the

rules you must obey if you wish to remain one of us."

Everyone went silent. I stared at the water behind Trim, wondering how such a paradise came to be so intoxicated by the women's egotistical desires to prove themselves within the island's hierarchy system.

"This isn't a prison," she said. "You aren't prisoners. There are no walls around you—no cells. The women around you aren't your cellmates."

The women exchanged discerning glances.

"If you want to leave—leave. No one's stopping you. Whether you'll survive out there is beyond me, but at least the option is yours. Murk has worked for years building our colony to create a civilized space for us to live among each other. If you're going to act like a prisoner—like an animal—who attempts to prove herself better than others by use of force, then you have no place among our people."

She tossed the bow into the sand.

"We need each other to survive. If you turn on your own, you're turning on all of us. Anyone who kills or attempts to kill another fellow convict will be banished to the outside."

I felt a nudge, followed by, "What'd I miss?"

It was Rocket. She was standing beside me with her hands on her waist and her eyebrows drawn close together, trying to make sense of what she'd just heard.

"Marlin," I said, glancing sideways at her. "Trim banished her."

"Shit," Rocket said, her piercing green eyes fixed on Trim. "She must've done something pretty bad to be sentenced to death."

CHAPTER 6

The Village was quiet and gloomy. The sky had turned a translucent gray, and a cool breeze ruffled the tree leaves overhead. The name Marlin was brought up again and again throughout the Village, mostly in a sympathetic tone, but also in a fearful one. I watched as people visited the medic's cabin, entering solemnly and exiting just the same.

I could sense everyone was on edge—terrified that the next attack might be the one to kill them. We were weak and vulnerable, but I'd overheard Trim say that Eagle had injured the attacking archers before being shot, so maybe time was on our side.

I wondered if Marlin stood a better chance than us in the Village. I couldn't get her face out of my mind. Within days, she'd probably be dead.

And although I didn't agree with banishing a woman to the outside world—away from civilization and closer to the Northers and wild animals—I understood why Trim had done it. She was a leader among wild women: felons. These women were dangerous, and they possessed the capability to kill one another if order was not established. They needed to fear Murk—to fear the head of their hierarchy system. I'd come to realize that Trim was Murk's right hand and she enforced Murk's beliefs and laws.

I was brought to my tent by Rocket after Trim's speech and told to rest as much as possible. She explained to me that supper was served when the sun descended to the level of the trees or when I heard a brief drumming sound, which was the method used for announcing mealtime on cloudy days.

"We're lucky," she said. "Battlewomen and Hunters don't have a portion limit."

I could only assume this was to allow adequate caloric intake to promote strength and endurance for the purpose of battle and hunting.

"Hey, Rocket?" I asked as she was leaving through the tent's front curtain.

"Yeah?"

"What's the difference between a Battlewoman and a Hunter? Which one am I?"

She smiled.

"A Battlewoman is a soldier, and a Hunter is just that, a hunter—someone who gets food for the Village. Don't worry about your title—just do what Trim tells you. I've always been a Hunter alongside Trim. But things are getting pretty bad now..." she sighed. "So I get to do both."

"So you'll fight?" I asked.

"To the death."

She stared into nothingness, and I could tell part of her was afraid.

"Let me put it this way," she added, "all Hunters are Battlewomen, but not all Battlewomen are Hunters."

"So, what am I?"

"A Hunter."

"Why's that?" I asked.

"Because you're being trained as an Archer. Most women are being trained as Battlewomen, which doesn't make them useful during a hunt."

I nodded. I didn't want her to leave. I didn't want to be alone.

"Hey, Brone," she said, before sliding out of the tent, "if you decide to build yourself a bed, just remember to always have the Village or the Working Grounds in sight. Any further, and you're no longer on our territory. I'll see you at mealtime."

And I was left alone in the dark, the skin of my feet illuminated by a ray of light coming from the hole in the roof of the tent that had been punctured and burned during the attack.

Although I wanted to construct a comfortable sleeping area for myself, I was unable to muster the strength. I slowly leaned to my side, until finally, I lay flat in the damp soil beneath me. I closed my eyes, wanting nothing more than a few minutes of rest after such an oppressively long day. My muscles ached, and my back felt as though I'd spent all day building an ancient pyramid among thousands of slaves.

I breathed in the scent of earth, the freshness

of the island beneath me. I could hear women talking and moving about around my tent and throughout the Village, but their voices became faded and indistinct.

* * *

"Lydia Brone, I hereby sentence you to three years on Kormace Island," the judge said. He smacked his gavel hard and made a gesture at the guards.

"Korma—what?" I tried, but the guards moved in quickly.

They looked more like military staff than correctional officers with their padded black uniforms, their oversized bulletproof vests, and their shaved heads.

"But I didn't...it was an acc—"

I heard my lawyer shout out the term *manslaughter* in an attempt to argue with the judge, but it accomplished nothing. Two guards moved in on me, and the most menacing-looking of them snatched me up underneath my arms. I didn't stand a chance. How was this even happening? I'd heard of the government's implementation of new criminal punishment, but I'd never actually given it much thought because I never imagined I'd be convicted as a felon. Me? Lydia Brone? Sentenced to three years on a remote island for murder?

* * *

For a moment, I thought I'd fallen asleep on my mother's living room sofa. Everything was dark, and I wondered if perhaps my mother had forgotten to lower the air conditioner as she often did on the nights of hot summer days.

But the smell of earthworms and sea water brought forth the reality that I was nowhere near home—nowhere near my mother. I hadn't spent much time thinking about her, having been too distracted by my need to survive among wild women and my unwavering belief that my circumstance was nothing more than a dream.

As I remembered the many nights spent by my mother's side, watching reality TV and ordering takeout, I began to feel grief. I felt as though I'd lost her forever—the only person who meant anything in my life. Sure, I had some acquaintances, but none of them would have ever taken the time of day to visit me had I been incarcerated behind bars. My mother had attended every court date and meeting with my lawyer.

I remembered the sound of her sobbing at the sight of her only child being dragged away by heavily armed men after my sentence. She'd sat in the back, tugging at her white pearl necklace as she always did when she was anxious. Not only had I abandoned her, but I'd taken Gary from her, who I knew would be mourned regardless of his abusive tendencies.

What had I done?

I shivered and wrapped my arms around myself. I could hear faint sounds in the distance—waves crashing against the shore and animals lurking nearby, but overall, the entire Village was silent. My stomach growled, and I feared I might wake someone up. Although I was tempted to peek out through the curtain of my tent, I was still too exhausted.

So I closed my eyes and allowed my mind to venture into the depths of my imagination—to a place where I'd never been convicted of murder and where I was free to do as I pleased. I woke up with drool on my face and a stiff body. I wasn't sure whether my aches were the consequence of an uncomfortable sleeping area or of the stressful events I'd endured the day prior.

I jumped when my tent curtains flew open and Ellie popped inside, seemingly frantic.

"Where've you been?" she asked.

I wiped the gooeyness off my face. I must have looked like a complete dirtbag—literally.

"Here," I said, matter-of-factly.

"What'd you mean, here? I didn't see you anywhere last night. Didn't you hear the supper drums? The breakfast drums?"

I shook my head.

"Well you'd better get up," she urged. "Eat something, because after breakfast, everyone gets to work."

"Work?"

She cocked an eyebrow at me.

"You didn't think your sentence would be a getaway, did you?"

"No, not at—" I tried.

"Just get up. I'll lend you some pearls."

"Pearls?"

But she was gone. I looked around my new home, not quite certain what to make of it. It was basically a house made of suede leather walls and dirt flooring, without any furniture or decorations. At least I had some sunlight, I thought, gazing up at the tear in the tent. The arrow was lying on the ground, its sharp point dug into the dirt.

Welcome to *paradise*, I thought.

I sighed.

I threw my greasy hair up into a messy bun, suddenly realizing how valuable my hair elastic had become. I'd only had the one tied around my wrist. What would I do if it broke? If it was stolen? Perhaps I'd do as most women did and cut off all my hair.

Another thought crept into my mind. How would I wash my hair? My body? I smelled of sour sweat and rotting water. I slid my tongue across the front of my teeth. My toothbrush, I thought dreamily. God, I missed my life.

I stepped out into the Village, completely devastated by my inability to maintain proper hygiene. Ellie was standing there, waiting for me, with both arms crossed over her chest. Her dark hair was braided to one side, and at the end of the braid was a thin rope tying it all together. That works too, I thought.

"Here," she said, handing me six small pearls.

I could tell these were natural and not the type you'd find attached to an expensive necklace. They were all mismatched—one was small and metallic blue in color, two were purple and unevenly shaped, and the other three were a gold-like color, all perfectly round, but different sizes.

"What're these for?" I asked.

She smirked as if she'd just handed me a Christmas gift.

"Consider these Kormace currency."

"Sorry?"

Her eyebrows fell flat.

"Moola, Benjamins, cheddar."

"I get it," I said, "but what do I need this for?"

She sighed, then turned toward the Village and glared through the morning sun.

"We have a pretty good thing going on," she said. "You work and you get paid, just like in the real world. You can use your pearls for just about anything—rope, clothing, hygiene products, food."

"Hygiene products?"

Ellie laughed.

"That would be tent number four," she said, pointing several tents down.

I noticed there were five of them, lined up evenly in front of the Village wall. There were planks of wood jabbed into the earth, with numbers carved into them.

"One is food, two is clothing, three is tools, four is health and hygiene, and five is miscellaneous."

I knew I wouldn't remember this, but I'd be able to walk by to peek inside later.

"Everyone here does something," she said. "What's the point if you can't contribute to the community? You'll meet Tegan in tent number four. She's what you call our pharmacist. She can make anything and everything with natural ingredients."

"Like soap?" I asked.

"Like soap," she said, amused.

I stepped forward, prepared to purchase any type of soap available. I'd lather myself in squid guts if it guaranteed my cleanliness.

"You might want to eat first," Ellie said.

I glanced back.

"Meals are free, but once it's over, it's over, so you have to be punctual. Breakfast is at sunrise, and supper's at sunset."

"What about lunch?"

She scoffed. "This isn't the Marriott hotel."

I shifted my attention to the center of the Village, where women were gathered by the dozens, some sitting, others standing while enjoying what appeared to be meat and eggs.

"By the way," she added, "you'll get over it."

"Get over what?"

"That need to be clean all the time."

I smiled. I'd always been a priss when it came to cleanliness—borderline OCD, even. If my fruit wasn't washed with soap, I wouldn't eat it. But I was starving, and at that point, I was prepared to eat an apple covered in a layer of filthy wax. I would have to be less picky when it came to food.

I approached the many women who were gathered around a small fire that danced in a shallow pit. There were large spotted eggshells piled beside it and cookware that appeared to have been constructed from bone.

"What is that?" I asked, eyeing the oversized bowl of cooked eggs and pieces of meat.

I received several glares, but no one responded. My stomach growled. Several women were hunched over their own bowls, scooping gooey pieces of egg into their mouths with their hands. I analyzed the area. There were no bowls or plates for me to use: no utensils...nothing. How was I supposed to eat?

"Brone!" I heard.

It was Sunny. Although I'd hoped I wouldn't run into her again, I was happy to see her.

"Sunny," I said.

"Guys, this is Brone. She's cool shit."

Several dark eyes glanced my way. There were a few nods, some hand gestures, but overall, there was still hostility and mistrust.

"You gotta bowl?" she asked.

"Sorry?"

"Girl, if you wanna eat, you gotta have your own bowl. You can buy one in the Tools tent. You can use mine for now, though." She handed me what appeared to be a broken piece of skull.

It was of average size with a slight curve all around to form a bowl. It had egg and meat residue inside, and although disgusted by the thought of using someone else's dirty dish, I was too hungry to refuse. I grabbed it with both hands.

I could feel the hatred around me as Sunny scooped an oversized spoonful of cold eggs and meat bits into my bowl.

"S'all you get," I heard.

There was a young Asian girl sitting on the ground with her legs crossed in front of her. She raised an eyebrow when I glanced at her, so I quickly looked away. The other women around her laughed.

"Brone, meet Sumi. Sumi, meet Brone," Sunny said nonchalantly.

"Pleasure," Sumi said, although she sounded more disgusted than anything.

"Sumi's the cook," Sunny said. "And the portion size she tells us is the portion size we eat."

"I thought Hunters and Battlewomen—" I tried.

"Trim's rules," Sumi said. "You gonna snitch on me?"

I looked at Sumi once more, and she smirked up at me. I could tell that integration into the Village wouldn't come easily.

I ate my food, forgetting entirely that I was shoveling bacteria from Sunny's mouth into mine.

"Thank you," I said, handing the piece of skull back to Sunny. I turned my attention to Sumi, and although I disliked her already, I thanked her for the food. She simply scoffed, and the others followed suit.

I couldn't believe I'd be spending the next three years of my life with ignorant women like this. I made my way to the tents Ellie had told me about, fuming.

"Brone!"

My name had been followed by rapid footsteps behind me.

"Sorry 'bout that," Sunny said.

"It's okay."

"Here," she said, placing three pearls into the

palm of my hand. I was already holding onto six of them which had been given to me by Ellie.

"Start by getting yourself a pouch—you know, for your pearls." She tapped the side of her belt, from which hung a leather pouch filled to the point of hardness. "And a belt," she quickly added, eyeing my waist.

I stared at the fist-sized pouch dangling at her side. "Aren't you scared of theft?"

She shrugged.

"It's always a possibility. That's why you don't carry it all with you. I bury mine." She grinned and showed me her fingernails, which were filthy brown in every crevice. I couldn't believe we'd shared a dish.

I nodded slowly.

She pinched one of the pearls in my hand and stared down at me from behind her bright yellow eyes.

"Pouch."

She then pinched the other pearl she'd given me and said, "Bowl."

She finally grabbed the last pearl, but this time, she smiled.

"Anything you'd like."

I smiled back, feeling completely awkward and wanting nothing more than for her to remove her germ-encrusted hand from mine.

I thanked her again and continued my path inside the Tools tent. It wasn't like any store you'd find in the real world—everything was dim, and there was no welcome bell, no "Hello, how are you?" from a tired cashier, no bright florescent lights shining down from above; I was still in the wild.

I received a glance from a butchy woman with thick arms and a protruding belly who sat at the back of the tent atop a wooden box. She was carving something—a knife, maybe. She didn't speak; she just watched me. A table at the center of the store displayed various handmade items: carved tools, bones, bowls, arrowheads, rope, blocks of wood, elastic-like bands, and boxes constructed of solid wood.

I noticed several small leather pouches in a pile with strings long enough to tie them closed and around one's waist or belt. I picked one up and rubbed my thumbs against the grainy leather.

"Lookin' for something?" the woman asked.

"Um, yeah," I said. "Just a pouch. Oh—and maybe a belt." I raised the leather to eye level. "How much?"

"How much you got?" she asked.

I hesitated. Did the price really depend on how many pearls I was carrying? What kind of a store was this?

"Well?"

I opened my palm.

"Nine."

"That pouch is six pearls," she said nonchalantly before turning to her chiseling.

I couldn't help but feel like I was being conned, but who was I to argue? I needed the pouch.

I held on to the item and approached the

merchant. I'd been about to hand over my pearls when I heard someone walk in.

"Hey, sup, Hammer?" Ellie asked.

The woman grunted.

"You buying something, Brone?"

I nodded.

"Whatcha got there?" she asked me.

I extended the leather pouch, and she pulled it out of my hand.

"Nice," she said. "How much you charging this time, Ham?"

"Four," the woman growled.

"You said six," I said.

Ellie laughed, although I knew she hadn't found this funny.

"Six pearls? For a flimsy little sack of leather?" she wiggled the pouch in front of Hammer's face who immediately lost her nonchalant attitude.

"I said four," she said.

"But you originally asked for six. Is this how you treat newcomers? By ripping them off?"

Hammer didn't speak, and I immediately became uneasy. I didn't want to be hated by someone else.

"It's okay," I said, "I'll pay the four."

"No, you won't," Ellie said. "Hammer knows better."

I could see the fury building behind Hammer's eyes, but it was evident that Ellie had some kind of leverage over her.

"You need anything else?" Ellie asked me.

I shook my head, even though I'd hoped to get

myself a belt. I couldn't risk being completely despised.

"In that case, you get one pearl," Ellie said, "and even that's generous."

She pulled a pearl out of my palm, dropped it onto Hammer's lap, then poured my remaining pearls into my new pouch before leading me out of the tent. I hoped I wouldn't have to return to the Tools tent anytime soon, but that was wishful thinking.

"That was close," Ellie said as we walked out into the open.

I wasn't sure whether to thank her or scold her. I could have handled myself.

"Oh don't look at me like that," she said. "You almost got gypped."

"And now Hammer hates me," I said.

"What do you care? You'll always have enemies here on the island, Brone. But if you let them push you around, you'll become a victim."

I parted my lips to thank her, realizing that she was right, but the sound of rapid footsteps caught my attention. They were walking right toward me—Trim and her usual crew. There were about six other women behind them, and the only face I recognized was Sunny's.

"There's a drop coming," Trim said.

She threw a bow into my hands, and I nearly dropped it. Was this a joke? I hadn't received proper training. I didn't know how to hit a target. What good would I be with a bow?

And what was a drop, anyways?

CHAPTER 7

If I hadn't known any better, I'd have assumed we were running from a wild panther. I'd fallen to the back of the line, with Trim and her crew at the front and Sunny and the other women following closely behind.

They hopped and lunged forward over fallen trees, masses of muddy water, and even animal carcasses. It was already hard enough keeping pace; it was even harder with an oversized wooden bow in one hand and a loose pouch filled with pearls. Trim had tied a quiver around my shoulders, and I could feel the arrows bouncing up and down as I ran forward. I feared they might go flying out, but they did no such thing.

I glanced back several times as we ran, praying no one, or nothing, was following us. I could see an opening up ahead, and I realized we'd reached the end of the jungle. Trim stood still, hiding behind several overlapping branches and rotting greenery.

She signaled us to remain quiet, which was

hard to do being that I was entirely out of breath. What were we looking for, anyways? I stretched my neck in an attempt to peer over the many shoulders in front of me, but it was useless. The only thing I saw was the ocean: sand, water, and sky.

Trim raised a finger, signaling us once more to remain as still as possible. That's when I heard it—the blades of a helicopter. But they weren't getting louder. Rather, the sound was becoming fainter, until finally, I could no longer hear it.

"They're gone," Fisher said.

"Where's the drop, then?" Biggie asked, towering above all of us.

Trim muttered something in anger, but I couldn't make it out. Were they receiving supplies?

"She must have found her own way," Flander said.

"Yeah, right," Rocket said. "Northers probably got to her before us."

It all made sense to me now. A new felon had been dropped onto Kormace Island, and their hope was to recruit her, as they'd done with me. I couldn't believe anyone would have found their own way through a wild jungle after such a long swim. I remembered dragging myself onto shore and how utterly exhausted I'd become, almost to the point of absolute incapacity.

"Why don't we just track her footsteps?" asked one of the other women. She stepped forward, but Trim threw her arm against her chest.

"I give orders, and you obey," she growled.

"This could be a trap."

The woman stepped back indignantly.

"Let's go," Trim ordered.

She walked past us and moved into position to lead. Fisher was by her side as always, with Rocket, Biggie, and Flander close behind. How was Eagle doing, anyways? No one had spoken her name since she'd been injured. I couldn't imagine anyone surviving grave injuries on this island. There was no proper medical care.

"Well, that was pointless," Sunny said.

She smirked at me, clearly attempting to force a smile on my face. But I was too exhausted to feign interest in her comedic ways. How was anyone built for this type of physical exertion? We'd spent the last hour running east to the shoreline of Kormace Island, and now we were expected to simply return to the Village?

Just then, I remembered gym class in ninth grade. Our teacher, who'd also been nicknamed *Little John* for his unusually large size and his borderline obsessive fascination with Robin Hood, had always been keen on making us do *beep* tests— a test consisting of continuous running from one point to another, quickening in pace by the sound of a *beep* being emitted from an old cassette player. I'd hated him for this. I'd never reached past the fourth beep, being the only person left sitting out of the race, alongside Gail, the fattest kid in class.

Trim was basically my gym teacher, only much harsher and more barbaric. If I'd disobeyed Little

John, he'd have sent me to the principal's office. Trim, however, might have my head, or worse, ban me from ever returning to the Village. The latter of the two possibilities was bound to lead to a painful, tortuous death caused by starvation, or more likely, an attack.

I'd simply have to obey.

I hopped over sharp-edged rocks being cleaned by a narrow stream of water. My sneakers had turned a shade of brown, but I was grateful to have them nonetheless. The last thing I wanted to run in were shoes constructed of wood and leather, which appeared to be what everyone else was wearing. Rocket had advised me to remove any *real-world* pieces of clothing and accessories, explaining to me that the newer I looked, the harder time I'd have integrating within the Village's society. I'd tossed everything but my sneakers, my bra, and my hair elastic, even though I knew their lifespan was limited.

I heard a soft whistle followed by a gentle pat on my back. It was Sunny. She'd slowed her pace, and she was moving away from the group and toward a slanted tree in the distance. She held her bow in one hand, and from her quiver, slowly drew an arrow. I knew she'd spotted an animal.

But what was she doing? She'd never hunted before. Trim hadn't given the order to hunt, either. I couldn't determine what she was aiming for. All I saw was darkness, surrounded by drooping greenery and shattered rocks.

The string of her bow made a squeaky sound as

she pulled hard, preparing to kill her target. But I didn't see the arrow leave her bow or hear a cry in the distance...

I was suddenly lying flat on my back, my head aching and my vision blurred. I was alone.

I blinked several times to gain clarity, but all I could see was a shape being dragged into the thick of the jungle. I blinked several times again. It was Sunny. I could tell by the frizz atop her head and by the way her scrawny arms dangled on either side of her body. She was being taken away by someone or something. The creature stood as a human but had the face of a black panther with skin hanging all around its edges. A mask?

I tried to cry for help, but nothing came out. I couldn't move. For a moment, I wondered if perhaps I'd been killed by this half-beast.

"Brone," I heard, over and over again.

Warmth slowly returned to my extremities, and my sight began to clear.

"Brone, what happened?"

"She's in shock."

"Don't touch her."

"There's blood," I heard. I wasn't sure whether they were talking about mine or Sunny's. I had droplets sprinkled across my chest, and the mud around us was stained a deep red.

"What happened?" Trim asked.

She knelt in front of me, her eyes fierce and her breath heavy.

I shook my head. I wanted to vomit.

"Brone, what did you see?" she pressed.

"Someone—something..." I tried.

She rested a hand on my shoulder.

"I think it was a Norther... I think. They took Sunny. I don't know," I said, causing an eruption of fear among the new Battlewomen.

Her brows came together, and she quickly stood up.

"Did anyone else see anything?" she asked, pacing around everyone.

"I did," Rocket said, her face hardening, and her eyes meeting mine.

Everyone fell silent.

"That wasn't a Norther."

PART TWO

PROLOGUE

Its thick black head blocked out all surrounding light. It stared down at me as would a cat at a quivering mouse, tilting its head from side to side, analyzing me entirely. I wanted to scream, but nothing came out.

The skin around its jaw hung loose, dangling as the creature moved in closer. I couldn't see its eyes—I saw only a shadowed face; curved horns atop its head pointed toward the sky.

I moved back, but no distance came between us. I wanted to disappear, to die, but not at the hands of this beast.

There were voices throughout the trees, and suddenly, the creature was gone. There was blood smeared everywhere: on my skin, across the jungle's soil, and on my clothes, yet I couldn't remember what had happened. All I saw was this beast's face, and all I felt was its thirst for blood.

The voices drew closer, and distorted figures began to surround me. I couldn't make sense of anything. But these figures soon became hazy, and their voices were replaced by a rhythmic drumming in the distance.

CHAPTER 1

I cracked open my tired eyes, and reality set in.

I lay on a bed of dirt with cruddy hair stuck to the side of my neck and my skin covered in uneven goose bumps. I heard women gathering in the Village, surely making their way to the feeding area.

The breakfast drums sounded in the distance. I was back on Kormace Island—the island of killers.

I couldn't get her out of my head—Sunny. I remembered seeing her blurred silhouette being dragged into the trees.

"That wasn't a Norther," I heard beside me.

But no one was there. I saw Rocket's face as clear as it had been the day before, her brows close together and her nostrils flared. She'd been the only one to see the beast—the only one who knew what had taken Sunny.

* * *

Savages, uncivilized, violent... *Ogres*, as Rocket has called them. They were known for surviving the island without the comfort of civilization or sympathy for human life.

"We've always been told that Ogres were nothing more than a myth, a fictitious tale to keep women from straying too far from the Village," Trim said. I could tell that she too had blindly believed this.

And who could blame her? Ogres? It sounded like something you'd hear in a children's story—a one-eyed monster vengefully seeking out human flesh.

"They're the most ruthless and barbaric women you could ever imagine," Rocket said, brushing her dreadlocked hair against her head. I'd once thought her to be barbaric; I couldn't even begin to imagine how terrible Ogres were.

"What makes you think they're women?" Fisher asked.

Rocket smirked knowingly. "It's an island for female felons only. They've never dropped a man."

Fisher snorted. "Yet."

Trim eyed everyone curiously. "What makes you so sure they're even felons?"

And everyone fell silent.

* * *

"Brone?"

It was Ellie.

She stood in the entryway of my tent, her wavy brown hair over one shoulder, a patient smile on her lips.

"Didn't you hear the drums?"

Exhausted, I rubbed my eyes and nodded. I wondered if I'd even slept.

"Well?" she said. "What're you waiting for?"

I eyed my pouch of pearls lying in the dirt, and I hesitated, feeling guilt ridden because of Sunny's abduction. Only yesterday, she'd given me three pearls—the island's currency—to buy myself something from the market tents. And today, she was gone—dead, most likely.

I reached for the pouch, knowing all too well that I'd have to spend its contents eventually. I still needed an eating dish, utensils, bathing products, and possibly materials to build myself a bed.

A bed... God, I missed my bed. I missed sliding on a fresh pair of pajamas after a hot bath. A bath... I sighed. I didn't even want to imagine how much filth covered my body; every inch of skin, every crevasse, every fingernail...

But I didn't linger on this thought, because I knew that my old life was nothing more than a distant fantasy, and the more I reminisced, the shittier I felt about myself and my present life. I'd just witnessed more horror in a few days than anyone should be forced to see in a lifetime. I didn't have the energy to dwell on materialistic desires or on the luxury of cleanliness and comfort.

For all I knew, I could be dead tomorrow.

I followed Ellie toward the center of the Village, where women had begun gathering around a large fire. I could see Sumi, the Village's cook, moving around so quickly I wondered how she kept track of what she was cooking.

I heard the name Sunny several times, and I

knew that word had made its way to all the women of the Village. Information on the island was like malaria—it spread quickly, leaving nothing but pain and misery in its wake.

"Here," Ellie said, handing me a dish made of bone. "Got you one."

"Thanks," I said.

I grabbed the bowl and waited in line to be served by one of Sumi's helpers. When it was my turn to receive a hot spoonful of wild turkey eggs, Sumi appeared, eyeing me from head to toe.

"She gets half," she said.

I fumed inside. I was starving. What did Sumi have against me? What had I ever done to her? Ever since landing on Kormace, she'd given me a hard time.

"Brone's a Hunter," Ellie intervened. "She gets whatever she wants."

She tore the spoon right out of Sumi's hands and filled my bowl to the brim. I glanced at Sumi, who stared right at me, but what I received was not a hateful glare. Instead, she smiled, as if she knew something I didn't or as if she were contemplating a gruesome revenge.

"You didn't have to do that," I said quickly.

Ellie glanced sideways at me. "Why can't you just be thankful you have someone looking out for you?"

"Because you're making me enemies!"

She led us to a thick tree log away from the center fire. She sat down and began shoveling egg into her mouth.

"Br... Brone," she said, still chewing on gooey yellow bits and pieces, "you're too soft."

I stared at her.

"You're a Hunter now." She swallowed the last piece. "People should respect you and fear you."

"I'm not a Hunter. I'm nothing like Eagle."

I hadn't meant to sound mopey, but the title I'd been given was beyond my physical capabilities. I felt hopeless. I stared at the grass beneath my feet, where a blue-shelled beetle hopped from blade to blade. Even he had more stealth than I did.

I wondered how Eagle—our finest Archer—was doing ever since she had been wounded when the Northers attacked the Village. No one had mentioned her name since. Had she died? Why hadn't we heard about it? Would I be quickly forgotten if injured? Was I just a number?

"Eagle was—is," Ellie corrected, "a great Hunter. But that doesn't mean you can't be. It takes time to shoot an arrow the way she does."

I stood silent. Was she trying to make me feel better? It wasn't working. I was useless to the women of the Village. I couldn't protect them... or feed them for that matter. Holding a bow and arrow felt so unnatural to me; so foreign.

Ellie sighed. "This isn't about being good at what you do. It's about knowing your worth on this island." She leaned forward, her shoulders rounded and her fists clenched. "Or at least... pretending to know it. You have to be assertive, Brone. Weakness won't get you anywhere."

"You calling me weak?"

Her lips curved upward. "Well, yes," she said, matter-of-factly.

"You're not a citizen anymore, Brone. You're in the wild. Learn to act like it. If someone gives you a hard time, challenge her. You're a Hunter now, for God's sake." She threw her arms up and laughed. "That's one of the most respected positions on this island. You could cut everyone's food supply. You have leverage."

I scoffed. "No, I couldn't. I'm not the leader of the Hunters. I just do what I'm told."

"You don't have to be the one who runs shit," she said. "You just have to make people believe that with a few spoken words, you could turn Trim against them."

I was finally beginning to understand what she was getting at. Everything was a game. Although we functioned well together as a society, we were still human beings. We were still women who felt the need to prove our worth to be greater than another's.

"It's all about survival," Ellie added, "and I won't always be around to defend you." I finally sat down beside her and scooped a spoonful of cold egg into my mouth.

"So what leverage do you have?" I glanced sideways at her. "No offense, but you don't seem like the fighting type. I can't picture you beating your way up to the top."

She raised her chin proudly toward the sky. "Pearls."

"Pearls?" I repeated.

But she didn't answer me. Instead, she eyed the pouch of pearls on my waist and raised both eyebrows.

The island's currency? Did she own it?

"You could call me the bank," she finally said.

My jaw dropped.

"You're the one who pays all of us for doing our jobs?" I asked.

She placed her empty bowl into the grass by her feet and nodded proudly. I couldn't help but laugh.

"That explains a lot," I said, remembering the defeated look on Hammer's face in the Tools tent when Ellie had caught her in a scam and the way Sumi had remained silent when Ellie filled my bowl with food.

"Which means you have even more leverage," she said.

"What do you mean?" I asked.

"Not only are you a Hunter, but you're also friends with the Village's bank."

I smiled—not because of the power I suddenly realized I had over other women but because she'd called me a friend. All I wanted on this island was a friend. She placed a hand over mine and squeezed it, and I felt comforted for the first time in a very long time.

CHAPTER 2

"This is soap?" I asked, rubbing the edge of my fingernail against the waxy surface.

"The finest in all of Kormace," she said slowly. She walked around the wooden table, her slender figure swaying from side to side as she moved. She picked up the unevenly chopped brick of soap and smirked all-knowingly.

"Coconut oil, seaweed... and a few other ingredients." She rubbed the soap's surface with the side of her thumb. "The rest is a secret. Keeps me valuable."

There was a certain elusive quality about her. Her pale, crooked smile made her appear all knowing, almost to the point of arrogant, yet her plant-constructed jewelry and messily braided hair gave her the appearance of simplicity and authenticity.

She dropped the soap into my hands and I pressed it underneath my nose. It smelled fresh but also earthy and somewhat salty—if salt had a smell. I'd take anything at this point. I just wanted to rid my body of its filth. I couldn't remember the last time I'd showered.

"How much?" I asked.

"Three," she said quickly.

I knew she was referring to pearls, the Village's currency. I couldn't understand how she was charging three pearls for this little bar of soap. I remembered Hammer, the butch woman from the Tools tent, and how she'd tried to scam me into spending all my pearls on a flimsy little leather pouch.

"Weakness won't get you anywhere," I remembered Ellie telling me.

Although it wasn't in my nature to be assertive or confrontational, I reached into my pouch and extracted one shiny pearl.

"One," I said, holding the single pearl out in front of me.

She eyed me carefully from top to bottom, and I became uncomfortable. I stood there, with my arm stiff out in front of me, refusing to back down.

"You're the new girl, aren't you? The one Murk's assigned as an Archer among the Hunters?" She rubbed her chin with her thumb and index finger.

I nodded.

She stared at the bar of soap for a moment.

"Consider it a welcome gift," she said.

I hesitated. Was this a game? A test? Why would someone hand over free merchandise? This had never happened to me before. I'd never had anything handed to me for free.

"Don't overthink it, sweetheart," she said. "I happen to have a working relationship with you Hunters... I'd like to keep it that way."

And there it was—leverage.

She smiled. "Maybe one of these days, I'll be in need of ingredients farther out on the island, and you'll be the one to help me."

"Sounds fair," I said, realizing that our exchange was mutually beneficial.

"I'm Tegan," she said.

"Brone."

"You need anything else, you know where to find me." She walked to the back of the tent and sat on a thick piece of log. Beside her were coconut shells, plants of different lengths and colors, powders, feathers, skins, and many other ingredients thrown into a pile for future creations.

I was about to leave Tegan's tent when I realized something.

"Tegan?" I asked.

"Yes, doll?"

"Where do I clean myself?"

She smiled at me the way a teacher would her student—with patience and kindness.

"Anything on this island look like a shower to you?"

Had this been a joke? Of course not. Had I seen some magical shower, I'd have... "The waterfall?" I realized.

She nodded. "Word of advice, though... Don't stand directly underneath it. It'll knock you right off your feet. Most women stand at the edges or use the pool of water underneath it to bathe in."

I thanked her and left.

When I stepped out into the Village, the first thing I noticed was the silence. There were no women arguing about fighting the Northers; there were no footsteps nearby; there was no fire at the center of the Village.

Had we been attacked? There was no sign of struggle or damage.

I rushed out through the Village's entrance, where trees were slanted to form an arch. How could so many women disappear so quickly? I could feel my legs trembling, but I had to keep moving. Although I'd never gone to the Working Grounds alone, I knew which direction to go.

I ran over the path that had been gradually constructed through usage over the last few decades: broken branches, flattened leaves, and hardened mud. I knew this path quite well now, having travelled it several times to train as an Archer near the Working Grounds' waterfall.

I'd been running so fast—so blindly, being led by fear and adrenaline—that I'd failed to see her running in my direction. I felt the impact of our bodies before I heard my name, "Brone!"

It was Rocket. She had both hands gripped around my arms, and she was breathing heavily, although not quite as heavily as I was. She was a runner—a true hunter. I had a lot of catching up to do, physically speaking.

"Where were you?" she asked.

My heart regained its natural pace, and I

slowed my breathing.

"I... I was just buying something." I raised the seaweed and coconut soap for her to see, only to realize my fingers' tight grip had melted holes into it. I sighed.

"Nice." She laughed at me, and I smiled.

"You're supposed to keep products like that in your tent and on the ground, where it's coolest," she said.

I stared at her as if to say, 'How was I supposed to know that?'

"Anyways," she said, "you can't clean yourself now. You're a Hunter, Brone, which means you report to Trim every day after breakfast. We train or work until suppertime. Then you get clean if you want."

She reached for my deformed soap and placed it at the base of the nearest tree. She then covered it with several leaves and branches.

"There," she said.

"And how am I supposed to remember where that is?" I asked.

"Monkey Brush," she said.

"Monkey what?" I asked, shifting my attention to the trees overhead.

"Right there." She pointed at a strangely shaped plant that resembled a snow brush, only it was vibrant red and orange.

"Did you just make up that name?" I asked.

Rocket chuckled. "No, it's the actual name. I did a project on it in high school before I dropped out.

Always stuck with me."

I'd been about to ask her how she'd landed herself on Kormace Island, but even I knew that interrogating a felon about their life in the real world was a faux pas. It didn't matter what she'd done— who she'd killed—because life on Kormace wasn't the same as life in the real world.

"Come on." She turned around. "Trim's waiting on you. No one makes Trim wait."

I followed her into the Working Grounds, where I received several impatient glares from the new Battlewomen who'd been forced to wait for me before beginning their training.

"You're late," Trim said. She threw me my bow, but I wasn't ready for the catch and it landed in the sand.

Laughter erupted around me, and I felt like a complete klutz. How would I ever hunt an animal if I couldn't even catch my own bow? I'd never hit my target. I suddenly remembered the blurry sight of Sunny being dragged away by the dark figure in the mask, and I couldn't help but feel responsible. If only I'd known how to shoot... if only I'd been as good as Eagle, I might have been able to save her.

I picked up my bow, its smooth wood feeling even softer than usual against my now calloused palm. I was turning into a true Islander, with my rough skin and dirty fingernails. It disgusted me.

Women fought around me with sticks, rope, and their bare hands while Trim led me closer to the waterfall to continue practicing target shooting with two other Archers, Pin and Hamu—

two Asian twin sisters who'd been selected for their perfect vision and small builds, which, as Trim had mentioned, was advantageous for the purpose of stealth.

For the last few days, Pin and Hamu had managed to shoot their arrows several feet away from the target, which was far better than anything I'd managed to do. If the arrow didn't fall out of my hands, it landed mere feet away from me; it was both embarrassing and frustrating. I began to wonder if Murk had made a mistake in assigning me the task of Archer.

But today was different. Their movements were sloppy and their aim was terrible. It made me feel better.

"You're supposed to get better, not worse." Trim moved in, eyeing them both curiously.

"Sorry, Trim," Pin said. She was the more vocal of the two, and unlike Hamu who hid her face behind her hair, Pin appeared to be quite confident. Hamu barely spoke, and she followed her sister like a puppy on a leash. "We're just really tired."

"I don't care if you're tired," Trim said. "We're all tired. We're all tossing and turning in our sleep, afraid that there might be an attack in the middle of the night."

She tore the bow out of Pin's hand and picked up an arrow from the pile beside us. Without hesitating, she raised the bow, positioned her arrow, and pulled the bowstring. There was a snap, and her arrow penetrated the middle of the blood-drawn target.

"Tired or not, we still have enemies," she said, before turning away and toward the Battlewomen.

"You young people are too impulsive..." I recognized Flander's old voice. She was leaning up against a large flat rock at the base of the waterfall's cliff, observing the new Battlewomen spar.

"You old people are too slow," Rocket said. She swung her fighting stick at the shins of the woman she was battling before tackling her to the ground.

Flander smirked, unoffended by Rocket's words. It was as if she were proud of her overly freckled, leather-like skin and colorless hair—as if it represented wisdom.

"Always keep your guard up," Rocket said, extending an open palm to the young Battlewoman lying in the sand.

The girl smiled and grabbed Rocket's hand. I could tell she was soaking all of this in. She was eager to fight, and she was willing to take a few punches to become as good as Trim's crew.

The clicking of sticks and fighting cries continued, and I was instantly thankful to have been given the title of Archer. I wouldn't have lasted two minutes in a fight with a wooden stick. At least, as an Archer, I could shoot from a distance. The only thing I had to worry about was not getting shot by one of the enemy's Archers.

"Always stay hidden," Trim had told us Archers on our first day when Sunny had been by my side. "The enemy always tries to take out Archers first, so they can attack on foot."

I remembered Sunny's dandelion-yellow eyes and the way she'd nodded at Trim's every word. She too had been eager to fight alongside the Hunters. I wondered why I lacked such eagerness. Maybe I was still too fresh. I still possessed this notion that we, as human beings, should be able to cohabitate without wanting to slit each other's throats. What was the purpose of this war? Why did the Northers want our heads? What had we ever done to them?

I knew there was a lot I didn't know and a lot I had to learn.

I was still shooting arrows into the sand when I noticed Fisher move in slowly. I'd been intimated by her since the first day I'd seen her. She had such a badass look with her long dark hair pulled back into a tight ponytail and protruding cheekbones— the type of girl you didn't want to make eye contact with.

"It took her a while too, you know," she said, a crooked smile on her lips.

I eyed her curiously. I couldn't tell whether she was being nice to me or blatantly degrading me.

"Eagle," she clarified.

I lowered my bow. There were dozens of arrows sticking out of the sand several feet away from the wooden target, which was completely undamaged.

"It takes time, kid," she said. "Here." She moved in closer and signaled me to get into position.

I placed an arrow into the bowstring and pulled

my shoulders back.

"Knees bent a bit," she said.

Pin and Hamu were now standing still, trying to absorb any bit of advice Fisher had to offer.

"Don't hold your elbow straight like that."

I did as I was told and sighed, not quite understanding how my stance would change the direction of my arrow.

"It's an art, really," she said. "There. Now pull back, up to your lips, and keep your eyes on the target."

I followed her instructions and kept my gaze on the target's bloody circle, but it was hard to concentrate with her practically pressed up against me and her breath warming the back of my shoulder.

"Visualize the arrow hitting your target, and when you're ready... let go."

I held onto the idea of a Norther standing in front of me—the very same Norther who'd maimed Eagle. I didn't know what she looked like, but I'd drawn myself an image for the purpose of directing my hatred: torn garments, arms full of faded ink, facial piercings, and yellow plaque-coated teeth.

I released the arrow.

There was a loud crack, and the hanging target swayed gently from side to side upon impact. To my surprise, I'd managed to strike just above the bullseye. I couldn't believe it. I glanced back at Fisher, but she'd already walked away.

Pin and Hamu hopped into position, prepared

to follow Fisher's advice. The practicing continued, and although I didn't hit the bullseye, I managed to hit my target more than once. I'd been so caught up in the moment that for the first time in several days, the cacophonous bickering of female felons became nonexistent to me. I couldn't hear women swearing or yelling at each other, fighting sticks being knocked against one another, the waterfall's static noise, the inconsistent chirping and whistling of insects, or the faraway screams and calls being emitted by the jungle's wildlife.

The only thing I knew in that moment was the feeling of the bow's wood against the skin of my calloused palm. The target ahead seemed to blur out all surrounding objects. It felt instinctual.

I'd been about to grab another arrow when Biggie came by, almost waddling due to her size. A beam of sunlight landed across her face, and she glared at us through the bright light. I wondered why Fisher was Trim's right hand, when Biggie was the size of a full-grown man—six feet tall, at a minimum, and definitely weighing more than two hundred pounds. I could only imagine the kind of damage she was capable of causing.

"We're going on a hunt," she said. "Trim's orders."

CHAPTER 3

To my surprise, Pin and Hamu had been told to stay behind and continue practicing along with several other Battlewomen.

"The fewer women, the better," Biggie said, looking down at me.

She led me to Trim and the usual crew, and I immediately felt nauseous at the realization that I was the only Archer. Were they really going to entrust me with the responsibility of capturing food to feed the entire Village? I'd managed to hit my target today—big whoop. How was I supposed to hit a *moving* target?

The sound of women sparring grew distant as did the waterfall's powerful roar. Trim led us into the jungle, and I felt a lump swell at the base of my throat. The anxiety was not the result of my having to prove my worth as a Hunter, but rather, the result of one horrifying memory: Sunny. I couldn't get the image out of my mind nor the idea of Ogres lurking nearby, women who'd turned away from civilization and succumbed to living like animals.

I couldn't imagine what these women would do—if they hadn't done it already—to Sunny. Rocket had let it slip that cannibalism was one of the many myths associated with the concept of Ogres, along with sacrificial rituals and baiting.

I'd feared the Northers ever since being dropped onto Kormace Island, but if there was one thing far worse than Northers, it was Ogres.

I followed Trim and the others into the jungle, my heart racing every time I heard a noise in the distance. The farther away we were led from the waterfall, the more anxious I felt. I gripped and regripped my bow, afraid that it might slip out of my sweaty palm.

"This way," Trim whispered.

She led us through a narrow path fabricated of moist verdure and along the current of a crystal-clear stream that originated from the Working Grounds. I ducked just in time to avoid an oversized spider web—an intricate pattern fabricated at the tips of two tree branches.

The further we ventured, the more uncomfortable I became.

"Brone," I heard.

My name had come from the front of the line led by Trim.

"At the front," Trim ordered.

I wasn't accustomed to being at the front of the line. The front of the line had always been reserved for Trim and Fisher, and oftentimes Eagle during a hunt. I remembered Eagle's short, messy blonde hair and the way she'd stared down at me the first time we'd met. I didn't know her, but I knew she was still a human being, and for the sake of the Hunters and all other women on the island, I truly hoped she'd be okay.

I walked by Trim's side, shifting my eyes toward every sound I heard to the point of paranoia.

"Relax," Trim said, glancing sideways at me.

I parted my lips to speak, even though I had nothing to say, but Trim raised a hand and everyone stopped moving. How was I supposed to relax when even Trim knew danger lurked nearby?

"Tracks," she said.

Fisher moved in closer. She crouched beside us and analyzed the print that had been left in a patch of mud. The print was sloppy, and a good part of it was missing, but it didn't take a genius to see that this print didn't belong to a human being.

Fisher gently touched the inside of the print with her index and middle finger then glanced up at Trim and said, "Leopard."

A leopard? This was the kind of jungle I'd been dropped on? The kind that had wildcats? I felt lightheaded. How was anyone supposed to survive this island without facing a painful, gruesome death? If it wasn't a Norther, it was an Ogre—and if it wasn't either one of those, it was some predatory animal in search of its next meal.

Trim turned around. "Keep your eyes open for spots or silky black."

"Silky black?" I asked.

"Black panthers. They tend to hide in trees," she said.

"Yeah and drag their carcasses up there," Rocket added.

Fisher suddenly lunged forward and stood face-to-face with Rocket; both her fists were clenched on either side of her body. I could see Fisher's shoulders rising up and down to the rhythm of her rapid breathing.

"Fisher, I... I wasn't trying to bring up Emilia," Rocket said. "I just meant in general."

"I know what you fucking meant, and no one needed to be reminded," Fisher said.

"That's enough," Trim said.

But Fisher didn't move. It was apparent that the thought of tearing Rocket's face off was running through her mind.

"Bring her up one more time," Fisher said.

"I said enough!" Trim grabbed Fisher by the arm and pulled her back.

I could tell the confrontation had shaken Rocket up a bit by the way she nervously tugged on her fingers and bit down on her lip, and I didn't blame her. Fisher was a fighter, a born killer while Rocket was fast but small and frail in comparison. Rocket wouldn't have stood a chance.

"Let's keep moving," Trim ordered. "We go west, away from the prints."

Fisher and Trim moved forward quickly, leaving me behind with the other Hunters.

"Who's Emilia?" I asked.

Flander glanced toward Fisher and Trim, ensuring safe distance, and said, "Fisher's girlfriend. She was killed by a panther."

"And dragged into a tree," Rocket added.

Flander shook her head. "It was awful. She was screamin', but we couldn't stop the attack. When it finally killed her, it dragged her up above us, and we just stood there, listen' to the crunchin' and tearin' sounds of the cat eatin' through her bones and muscles."

"Shut up," Biggie interjected, "all of you. You know better than to talk about Emilia. Ever."

She brushed passed us, nearly knocking Flander over in the process, and followed Trim through an array of multicolored flowers.

"You'd better get up there too, kid," Flander said. "Archers always stay at the front."

I did as instructed and caught up with Trim and Fisher. I only prayed they weren't relying on me to save them from a wild panther with my mediocre archery skills.

The sound of water caught my attention, and I licked my dry, chapped lips. Trim led us to an opening filled with moss-covered trees and smooth stones scattered across a shallow bed of water. There was a small waterfall at the far back, although one could barely call it a waterfall. It was a flow of water that poured down from one rock to another.

"Rest," Trim said.

Rocket was the first to remove a dark brown leather water bladder from her belt. She rushed to the clear water spilling over the sharp-edged rocks and filled it to the brim. The others followed, and I realized I had more purchases to make from the merchant tents.

"It's fresh?" I asked.

Although my mouth was pasty and my lips felt as though they'd shriveled up like raisins, the last thing I wanted to do was drink salt water.

"Sure is," Biggie said. She'd sat down at the edge of the pool, and she began splashing water on her face, her neck, and throughout her short woolly hair.

I wanted to jump into the water, but instead, I placed my bow against the nearest tree and crept up to the waterfall, then formed a cup underneath with the palms of my hands. The water was cool and hard—a texture dissimilar to the large green bed of salt water found on the Working Grounds, which was warm and silky. I pressed my lips against the edge of my palm and slowly tilted back, allowing the fluid to pour past my lips and into my parched mouth.

The taste was beyond satisfaction. I was given filtered water on the Working Grounds in a stone-carved cup during training, but it was always warm. This water was fresh and crisp, and it slid so effortlessly into the bottom of my stomach, cooling my insides in the process.

I drank some more until I felt my stomach might explode. I could feel the water splashing around inside, and it felt as though I'd just eaten an entire meal.

The other women had already filled their water bladders by the time I was finished loading up on a day's worth of water, and they'd all sat down to rest around the small pond, their bare feet dipped into the water. I knew I'd have to stop our hunt on several occasions to pee. I could live with that—I only hoped Trim and the others would be so patient.

I slid off my sneakers—which were now entirely brown and ripping at the soles—and sat down between Flander and Biggie. Flander was playing with her water bladder—rubbing the thick stitching with her index finger and brushing her hand over the smooth exterior.

"Three pearls," she said, glancing sideways at me.

"Oh," I said, "I don't want to take—"

She chortled as if I were dumber than a dead battery. "I ain't selling you mine."

I stared at her.

"When you go see Hammer," she said, "don't let her charge you more than three pearls."

Trim laughed. I'd never heard her laugh before. She was much nicer to look at with a smile on her face. It seemed to take away from the ugliness she'd been cursed with at birth.

"You got gypped," she told Flander.

"Whad'ya mean?" Flander furrowed her eyebrows and grimaced.

"You're a Hunter," Trim said nonchalantly. "All necessities are free."

"And water's a necessity when hunting," Fisher chimed in, raising her water bladder.

Flander grunted. "Well ain't nobody told me."

"We just did," Trim said.

Flander rolled her eyes toward me. "What're you here for? How long's your sentence?"

I shot several glances at the rest of the Hunters, feeling both violated and tricked. I'd been told that our past lives were irrelevant on Kormace Island.

"What's said here, stays here," Biggie said, towering over me. "I killed a boy in high school during a fight. Dey waited for me after school, to prove that I wasn't too big to take down. Two of 'em ran, but when I caught the leader, I couldn't stop myself. Just kept beatin' down on his face over and over 'gain." She sighed. "Got sentenced to three years here."

"How long do you have left?" I asked.

She quickly looked up at Trim. "Don't matter."

I didn't have the time to question her any further.

"I shot someone, got seven years," Fisher said, glaring at the water around her feet.

"That's it?" Biggie said. "I just gave my life story and dat's all you gon' say?"

Fisher grimaced then rolled her eyes. "I was involved in some illegal shit—you know, gangs." She widened her eyes at me as if I was too stupid to understand the concept of street gangs. "Anyways... I had to shoot some guy who'd been selling on our corner. Turns out he was a cop's kid."

I wasn't sure whether to feel sorry for her or frightened by her. Was this sharing of information supposed to make me feel closer to these women?

"Got three years too," Rocket said, throwing

her chin up toward Biggie. "Seems to be the popular sentence." She shook her head, as if this would break apart any emotion she felt toward her past. "His name was Ben..." She clasped her hands together. "We'd been dating for a while, and I was heavy into heroin at the time. I wanted him to try it—just try it, you know?" She glanced up at me, and I could tell the memory still haunted her. "I had some, so I convinced him to try it. He was a good kid... Never skipped class, never talked back to his mom. But he didn't tell me he had a heart condition. I wouldn't have given it to him. I wouldn't have... After my high, he was just lying there, pale as a ghost, and... Well, you know..."

Flander got up and crossed through the shallow water. She sat beside Rocket and wrapped an arm around her shoulders. "It's okay, kid. We know."

Rocket pressed her head against Flander's shoulder. Despite their criminal backgrounds, I could tell these women had grown to be a family. They cared about each other even when their twisted faces or snarky comments suggested otherwise.

"I got three years, too," Flander said. She swirled her hand through the water by her feet and glanced up at me. "I'd been out all night at the bar, drinking my sorrows away, and when I left, I climbed into my car—just like that. I don't remember anything... I just remember waking up in the hospital and being told I'd killed two little girls and their mother."

I swallowed hard. I couldn't even begin to imagine the guilt she felt. I felt sick to my stomach at the thought of killing Gary when he'd attacked my mother, and he'd deserved it. But an innocent family? I was nauseated.

"I'm sorry," I said, not knowing what else to say.

"Don't be," Flander said. "We all make mistakes, and we pay for them. I've spent enough years here to forgive myself. What happened was horrible, but it can't be undone, and hatin' myself for it ain't gonna make it better."

"How long have you been here?" I asked.

"Almost done my three years now," Flander said, forcing a crooked smile.

"Like Fisher here," Trim said, "I got seven years." She leaned forward and placed her elbows on her knees as though she were a summer camp leader about to tell ghost stories around a campfire. "I was a dealer... One night, I got a call from one of my boys asking me to deliver. I trusted the guy, so I showed up at his place. There were other guys there, though, fucked out of their minds. Long story short, they tried to pin me down and have their way with me. I always carried a pocket knife in my boot, and that night, it saved me." She zoned out, most likely reliving that awful night. "They forced my face against the dining room table and ripped my pants down to my knees, and I remember thinking... I'd rather die than get raped. So I pulled out my knife and swung back as hard I could. Next thing I knew, I was covered in red, and there was a guy lying on the floor, gargling his own blood."

I just stared at her.

"System's fucking corrupted," she added. "It was self-defense."

"My lawyer was going for manslaughter," I finally said. Everyone fell silent, waiting to hear my story. "My mom's boyfriend... He was a drunk. He attacked her one night, with both hands around her throat. He would've killed her... So I found a frying pan in the kitchen, and I swung it at the back of his head to knock him out."

"A cast iron pan?" Biggie asked.

I nodded.

She laughed. "Damn, girl. Everyone knows those things are deadly."

"It all happened so fast," I said quickly. "I wasn't trying to... Anyways, I got three years."

"Don't sweat it, kid," Flander said. "We're not judging you."

I forced a smile.

Trim suddenly slapped her knees, breaking the silence. "Enough rest, let's keep moving."

CHAPTER 4

"You got this," Trim whispered.

I wasn't sure what I struggled with most—feeling pressured to feed a village of hungry women or taking the life of an innocent animal. I'd never hunted before, yet there I was, gazing down the length of my arrow, aiming its pointed head at a wild boar. Its tusks were barely visible, and I knew it wasn't very old.

Aside from fish, wild boar was the preferred meat among the women, Trim had explained. It tasted like pork—the best pork I'd ever tasted—and it fed many. The Hunters would walk for miles in search of boar. Male turkey was also hunted on occasion, with females captured for egg production.

"Chin up, now pull back," Trim said.

I kept my eye on the boar's chest to aim for the heart as I'd been taught.

"Release," Trim hissed.

I let go of the bowstring, and with a snap-like sound, fired my arrow directly at the boar. It squealed, before quickly darting in the opposite direction. Trim quickly tore the bow out of my hand, and without warning, jolted forward to catch the wounded boar.

By the time we caught up, Trim had stopped running. She handed me my bow, and said, "Almost."

The boar was lying in the dirt several feet away with an arrow protruding from its hairy neck.

"Biggie," Trim said, and at the sound of her name, Biggie moved in. Just as Eagle had done, Biggie reached down and pulled on the boar's tusk, exposing its neck. She pulled a sharp blade from her belt and began sawing through the animal's thick muscles, tendons, and bones.

I turned away at the sound of its head being torn from its body.

"Why do you do that?" I asked.

"It's respectful," Flander said.

"Cutting off its head is supposed to be respectful?" I asked.

"There's always a chance that the animal might still be alive. We take off the head to make sure it bleeds out—to make sure it's dead and not sufferin'."

I noticed my arrow sticking out of the creature's leg. I'd missed my target.

"Let's head back before sundown," Trim ordered. She led the way, with Biggie dragging the boar by its hind legs across the jungle's uneven soil.

We were almost at the Working Grounds—I knew, because I'd recognized the stream we'd followed at the beginning of our hunt—when I felt a tap on my shoulder. Everyone had stopped moving, and Trim was pointing across the flow of water.

It was just sitting there, at the base of a broken tree log, chewing on plants as if nothing else in the world mattered. It was bigger than any gorilla I'd ever seen at the zoo, with its thick, short-haired chest resembling that of an armored knight. Its black eyes were glued to us, and for a moment, it stopped chewing and just stared.

I swallowed hard. Why were we just standing there? I'd heard of gorillas attacking humans, and who knew where this one had come from? Maybe it was a mother. I noticed that the Hunters were all smiling—something I didn't see very often.

"Beautiful, ain't it?" Flander whispered.

It really was, but the fear I felt toward the animal eliminated any excitement within me.

"Let's keep moving," Trim said quietly, and she turned the other way.

I couldn't believe I'd just seen a wild gorilla dozens of feet away from me.

Flander was still smiling ear to ear by the time we reached the Working Grounds. She must have caught me staring at her because she laughed and said, "In all my years."

I cocked an eyebrow. Had she never seen one before?

"I seen a black panther—just once, mind you—chimpanzees, cougars, wild turkey, and birds of all sorts, but never once have I seen a gorilla," she said.

"Me neither," Rocket said. "What a beauty!"

"Are there many around here?" I asked.

"Probably," Flander said. "Kormace is huge. There's still tons we haven't seen. We like to stay close to the Village."

I was beginning to understand why criminal sentences on Kormace Island were so short in comparison to the duration of actual prison sentences—survival was a daily struggle. In prison, all basic necessities were provided and overall safety was guaranteed—somewhat.

The moment we entered the Working Grounds, everyone fell silent. But this silence was not brought forth by our presence, but rather, by someone else's. She'd just entered the Working Grounds from the Village path with Ellie underneath one arm and a long wooden staff underneath the other.

She struggled to move forward, her face contorting with every step taken.

"Eagle!" Rocket shouted.

Eagle glanced up, her blue eyes resembling glass marbles underneath the sunlight's intrusive rays. Her lips curved upward at the sight of Rocket running her way.

Trim and the others were quick to follow, leaving the dead boar on the ground. Even though I felt out of place, I followed too.

Rocket threw her arms around Eagle, and although Eagle's arms were busy maintaining balance, she reached around Rocket's shoulders with her staff and held her tight.

"You okay?" Trim asked.

Several other women had circled around us, curious to hear about Eagle's recovery since the attack.

"I'm okay," Eagle said, shrugging, but the way she struggled to stand upright proved otherwise.

"Medics never tell us anything," Fisher said. "Everything's always a big secret."

Eagle laughed, her blonde hair dancing atop her head. It had grown a bit over the last few weeks. I couldn't imagine how hard it must have been sitting in a cabin, secluded from everyone.

"Just how Navi is," she said. "She says the more people talk about something, the more power they give it. Guess she didn't want anyone talking about my injuries."

"Who's Navi?" I asked, turning to Flander.

"Our Medic—and before y'ask," Flander said, "she named 'erself after a video-game character—some fairy. 'Course the geek would turn out to be the Medic."

I smiled, even though I didn't really care where her name had come from.

"Did Navi tell you when it's safe to start hunting again?" Trim asked.

Eagle regripped her staff and hopped sideways to straighten her stance. "I won't be hunting anymore."

"What?"

"What?"

"How's..."

"What about…"

Eagle waved a hand to quiet everyone.

"I'm just grateful to be alive… Got hit here," she said, pointing at her inner thigh, "and here." She pulled the leather of her shirt over her right shoulder, revealing a pink circular-shaped scar surrounded by blue and yellow bruising. She made a fist with her hand then stretched all her fingers into an open palm.

"Can't really feel them," she said.

"There was nerve damage," Ellie said, her eyes lowering to the ground. "Doesn't look good."

There was a moment of silence, which was uncomfortable but required for the absorption of Ellie's news.

"Does Murk know about this?" Trim asked.

Eagle nodded, defeated.

"Murk's reassigned her to be a Night Watcher," Ellie said.

"A Night Watcher?" I asked.

Everyone turned to face me. It was as if they'd forgotten I was standing behind them.

"It's basically a glorified Battlewoman," Rocket said, seemingly disgusted. "They stay up during night hours and keep watch over the Village while the other women sleep. There's no fighting involved. If there're any intruders, they sound the alarm—well the horn."

Eagle scoffed. "There's fighting, all right. Fighting to stay awake."

But no one laughed. It was evident that being a Night Watcher was a task assigned to those incapable of working any other job due to physical limitations—like having the fat kid in a group of friends "stand watch" while the other kids sneak into the teacher's desk drawers to steal candy.

Rocket moved in again, leaning her head on Eagle's shoulder.

"I'm so sorry, Eag," she said.

Eagle shrugged. "It is what it is." She shook her head and laughed. "I just feel sorry for you guys. You're gonna starve without me."

"I'll do my best to make sure everyone keeps eating," I said, although I wished I'd kept my mouth shut.

Everyone's eyes turned to me.

Eagle raised an eyebrow and eyed me from head to toe. "She's my replacement?"

"No one could ever replace you, Eagle," Biggie said, casting a shadow over all of us as she moved in closer. "But we did need an Archer, and she was one of the chosen ones, along with Sun—Pin and Hamu."

I knew she'd held back from mentioning Sunny, and I felt a knot form in the pit of my stomach.

"Trim can shoot." Eagle crossed her arms over her chest.

It was apparent that my being an Archer was the last thing Eagle would have agreed to. I wasn't sure whether it was because I was new to Kormace Island or because I somehow rubbed her the wrong way. But I'd never done anything to offend her—at least not intentionally.

She was still staring right at me, her eyes

narrowed and her nostrils flared. I'd always been taught to steer away from confrontation—to make friends rather than enemies. Even though I boiled inside, wanting nothing more than to ask, "What's your problem with me, anyways?" I was unable to. I just didn't have it in me, which I knew would be my downfall on this island.

"Cheer up, Eag. We're having a celebration in your name tonight." Rocket nudged her.

"Tegan always makes the best brew during celebrations." Flander licked her lips and rubbed her palms together.

I remembered Tegan. I'd purchased soap from her in one of the merchant tents. She had a way of mixing ingredients to create new items and potions. I wasn't quite sure, but I could only assume Flander was referring to alcohol when she said *brew*.

"A celebration?" Eagle scoffed. "It may as well be a memorial... or a funeral. I know how these things work. I defended the Village, and now I'm a cripple."

"No one's celebrating your injuries," Trim said sharply. "We're celebrating your bravery. You took out most, if not all of the attackers that day."

Eagle shrugged. "Look, I'll catch you guys later."

Ellie shot a glance at me before ducking underneath Eagle's arm and moving forward with her.

"Don't pay any attention to her," Flander said, leaning in toward me. "She's just hurtin'."

"With good reason." Fisher was quick to come

to Eagle's defense. "It's like being a gold medal Olympian and losing a leg. Eagle's always been our number one Hunter, and now she's nothing."

"She's not nothing!" Rocket said.

Fisher rolled her eyes. "In the eyes of the Village—yeah, she is. If you can't contribute, you're basically a waste of space."

Rocket lunged forward and shoved Fisher back as hard as she could. Fisher tripped backward several steps, but she somehow managed to stay on her feet. She had a cryptic smile on her face as if amused by Rocket's lack of strength.

"Enough!" Trim grabbed Rocket by the leather of her shirt and extended an open palm at Fisher.

"She started it," Fisher said, smirking at Rocket.

Rocket pulled out of Trim's grip and stormed off in the opposite direction toward the Village's path.

"Why do you do that?" Trim asked, turning her attention to Fisher.

Fisher laughed. "Come on, Trim. I was being realistic. You know better than anyone that emotions don't belong on Kormace, and emotions aside, Eagle's useless now."

Trim clenched her jaw, mulling over Fisher's words. It was clear that she found truth in them.

"You're right," Trim said coldly. "But Eagle still deserves recognition for all she's done, so I expect you all to be at the celebration."

Everyone nodded and made their way toward the Village. I was about to follow when I felt someone tap my shoulder.

"You should be proud," Rocket said, her gaze fixed on the waterfall.

I didn't know what she was referring to until I followed her eyes. Several women had dragged the bloody boar across the sand to the side of the waterfall where a bountiful garden filled with fruits and vegetables was located. Beside this garden was a cage constructed of branches filled with wild turkeys.

I remembered Murk mentioning Farmers as one of the divisions of the Village, and I realized that these women were responsible for our food and water consumption. There were two women kneeling in front of the garden, reaching into it and pulling out bits and pieces of either weed or actual fruit—I couldn't quite tell which.

There was a water filtration system located beside the turkey cage—it was a massive hole dug into the ground with some meshing or skin stretched out above it. I had no idea how the contraption worked, but I'd seen Trim approach it to fill her water bladder.

I looked away when one of the women raised a carved blade and began tearing into the boar's flesh.

"You shouldn't watch that," Rocket said. "The last thing you want on this island is to be grossed out by meat. It's all we eat."

"I thought you left," I said.

"I did." She smirked then opened her hand and revealed the piece of seaweed soap I'd purchased from Tegan's tent. "I knew you'd forget where it was, so I grabbed it for you. Come on, I'll show you where to get cleaned up."

I followed her toward the waterfall on the opposite side of the bloody scene. There was a gentle flow of water spilling out over several flat rocks high above. Underneath this natural shower was a young woman lathered in a silky substance, with her eyes closed, her wet hair pulled back, her bare skin and small pointed breasts glistening underneath the water.

"This is it," Rocket said. She leaned in close then whispered, "Some women still try to shave—others don't even bother. Not like there are any men to impress. Mind you, most women on the island learn to play for the other team, if ya catch my drift."

"What?" I asked.

Rocket ignored me, and instead, offered me a flat pointed rock, which had been sharpened along one of its edges. "Nothing like a razor, but it manages to get some of the hair. Just be careful."

She raised an arm above her head and revealed an evenly trimmed, short-haired armpit. "Personally, I don't like the long pit hair." She glanced at the woman who was now rinsing the top of her head, revealing thick black patches underneath the pits of her arms. "Some people don't seem to care."

I grabbed the rock and thanked her.

"When you're done," she said, "just sit in the sun for a while. It'll dry you off."

A little farther away, lying in a bed of grass

alongside the Working Grounds' pool of water were three naked women sunbathing.

"Like that," Rocket said, following my gaze.

How was I supposed to be naked around complete strangers? I'd never been the type to shamelessly remove my top at the gym or change in front of my friends. I'd always been self-conscious of my petite body. I suddenly felt the urge to return to the Village, unclean but with my pride intact.

"I'll catch you later." Rocket winked at me and turned the other way.

I moved farther down the side of the waterfall, away from the naked women, and I slid off my top. I held both breasts in my hands, feeling entirely vulnerable and exposed. With one hand, I awkwardly began pulling at the rope of my pants, when a familiar voice startled me.

"You must be happy," Ellie said.

I turned around so fast that I nearly slipped on the cold stone ground underneath me.

"Got something to hide?" She raised an eyebrow.

I realized I was hunched forward, holding onto myself as if afraid my breasts might fall off.

"I... um," I tried.

"I'm not judging," She slowly slid her leather top above her shoulders and over her head, revealing large round breasts and a softly defined stomach.

I hadn't meant to stare, and I immediately felt my cheeks warm to what must have been an uncomfortable shade of red the moment she caught me looking. But this didn't seem to affect her. She simply smirked then went on to removing her bottoms.

"These are washable too, you know," she said, dangling the sun-dried skin between her fingers.

I nodded quickly, avoiding eye contact.

"I usually go for a soak at the base of the waterfall. It's deep enough to walk all the way into," she said.

"To wash your clothes?" I asked.

"To wash everything."

I peered toward the waterfall—or at least what I could see of it from this angle—and I noticed that the number of women who had been sunbathing naked had doubled in number.

"Murk doesn't want anyone using soaps in the Working Grounds' pool," she said, "but salt water still cleanses, so most women opt for a quick bath. The showers lead out into a stream, so it doesn't affect the pool." With her big toe, she pointed below, where flat rocks made a stair-like descent, with translucent water trickling out into the jungle.

I much preferred the idea of using soap. I hadn't showered in over a week.

"Are you showering, or what?" She turned away from me to rinse her hair, her hourglass figure shifting from side to side as she moved to catch the falling water.

I realized I was still holding my chest. I stepped toward the water with my bottoms still in place. I wasn't ready to expose my nudity like the rest of these women. I flinched at the water's impact—not because it was heavy in any way, but because it was cold in comparison to the jungle's hot sticky air.

"I'd use that up fast, if I were you," Ellie said.

I turned toward her, crossing both arms over my chest.

"The soap," she said. "This isn't some cheap-brand pharmacy soap. It's all natural, and in this heat, it doesn't last."

I opened my right palm, only to find a thick glob remaining; an oily substance leaked through the cracks between my fingers. I understood why most women preferred to use the Working Grounds' bed of water for bathing—it was essentially free, while showering alongside the waterfall was costly in the sense that each shower required one piece of soap. I couldn't believe that I'd be spending three years of my life bathing in salt water and only occasionally treating myself to an actual shower, which I'd come to realize was a privileged luxury among the Islanders.

I rubbed the gooey soap all over my body, feeling as though I were taking a shower for the first time in my life. It wasn't like spreading commercial body wash on your body. The texture was balmy and sleek and smelled of coconut, but it didn't lather. I could tell Tegan's concoction was oil-based.

"See you tonight," I heard Ellie say.

My eyes were sealed tight, with soap layering over my entire face, so I waved awkwardly in her direction. The cool water from above rinsed through my sand-infested hair and across my skin, making me feel whole again. I gently rubbed the water out of my eyes, feeling the smooth skin of my face underneath my fingertips, when out of nowhere, an overwhelming sadness came over me. The celebration had made me realize that caring for one's physical appearance was no longer feasible.

And I didn't mind—I mean, I didn't really care that I wouldn't be able to straighten my hair; I didn't care that my hair on my legs would be prickly, if not long and hairy; I didn't care that my eyebrows wouldn't be plucked or that I wouldn't be wearing any makeup; I didn't care about my personal appearance at all.

What bothered me the most was that for the next three years, I wouldn't even be able to see my own face.

CHAPTER 5

I wouldn't have expected to see Murk sitting among her villagers, laughing with her head thrown back, and sipping liquid from a sliced coconut. She'd always been so secretive—so mysteriously hidden in the depth of the Working Grounds' waterfall or hidden behind the closed door of her cabin at the far end of the Village.

Seeing her this way opened my eyes to the overlooked reality that she was just like the rest of us: a human being who'd been sentenced to spend years of her life on a remote island, fighting every day to survive among lawless women and predatory animals.

Being leader didn't make her immune to emotion or pleasure. I watched as she laughed with Trim, telling stories while pointing out past the Village walls, and for the first time since I'd been dropped onto Kormace Island, I realized how fortunate I was to have been found by Trim and to have been brought into a village led by such an admirable and worthy leader, someone capable of maintaining order while also ensuring comfort and overall happiness.

"This seat taken?"

I glanced up. It was Biggie. She was holding a half skull in one hand and a half melon in the other. "Here," she said, handing me the melon. She sat beside me atop a thick wooden log that had stabilized itself into the ground over the course of several years, I presumed.

"What is this?" I asked. I leaned over the melon bowl and inhaled. The stench made my nostrils flare even wider, and I immediately turned away.

"Oh come on, it ain't that bad," she said. She tilted her skull bowl toward her lips with both hands and sipped on the liquid. "Tegan makes it. It's home brewed."

"Alcohol?" I asked.

She smiled sideways before drinking some more.

"It smells rotten," I admitted.

"Kinda is," she said. "Won't hurt you, though. Ain't you ever done a tequila shot or a vodka shot? That shit don't taste like chocolate, but it sure feels good."

My mouth watered at the thought of chocolate.

I reluctantly tilted the melon toward my lips, allowing the warm fluid to enter past my bottom teeth and over the top of my tongue. The taste was overpowering—it tasted like rubbing alcohol with the subtlety of tropical fruit. I immediately spat it back into the melon bowl, only to then realize that everyone's eyes had turned my way.

"What's the matter, Archer? Can't handle Tegan's brew?" Eagle said.

Everyone burst out laughing. I stared at her for a moment even though all I wanted to do was glare or tell her to go fuck herself. I wasn't the one who'd severed her nerves or the reason she'd landed herself on Kormace Island to begin with. She was acting like a child.

As the fire crackled, I noticed a crooked smile take shape on her shadowed face. I wasn't sure whether I had remained quiet simply because confrontation wasn't in my nature or because Eagle was sitting directly beside Murk.

"Give her a break, Eag. Everyone has a hard time drinking the stuff at first." Rocket sat down by Eagle's side and nudged her on the arm.

Eagle scoffed, still eyeing me. "Not like that."

"Don't worry, I did the same thing," I heard.

There was a middle-aged woman standing behind me with both arms crossed over her chest and an overall careless way about her.

"Shit's not for everyone," she added.

I tried to smile at her, being that she'd come to my defense, but she walked away to join a group of women gathered on the other side of the fire. Eagle went on to mutter something to Rocket, but I wasn't able to hear. There were too many voices being thrown in all directions.

I looked around in search of Flander and Fisher, but it was too dark beyond the fire to see anyone's face. There were dozens of women gathered in honor of Eagle's bravery the day of the attack.

"You gonna drink that?" Biggie asked, leaning over me.

I looked down at my melon bowl, which was almost entirely full, and I shook my head. I couldn't see myself ever acquiring a taste for such a vile concoction.

"No use wasting." She reached over and pulled the drink out of my hands.

I leaned forward with both elbows on my knees, staring into the fire. I imagined myself suddenly waking up from an induced coma, only to be told by hospital staff that I'd suffered a severe head injury the night Gary attacked my mother. Maybe this was all just a dream—Kormace Island, the Hunters, the Northers, the Ogres—maybe none of them were real. Maybe, just maybe... they were all fictional characters from a television series that I'd somehow managed to incorporate into my vivid dreams.

* * *

"Can you believe that?" Melody asked. She was pointing at the daily newspaper, just below a title that read, "New Economical Prison."

She'd brought in the paper as she did every morning at St. Mariana's Thrift Store, and we were both leaning over the counter killing time on a rainy Sunday afternoon.

"I thought that was just a rumor," I said.

"Me too. Listen." She picked up the paper and pulled it closer to her black-rimmed glasses. "A new plan is currently in place to begin replacing maximum security prisons with government-owned islands for economic purposes and for civilian safety. According to our source, this plan is targeting only the most dangerous of criminals—those convicted of first-degree murder.

"'The plan is to replace certain concrete institutions with Mother Nature herself,' Mr. Milas, Attorney General of the Department of Justice, stated during a conference held at the Goliath Centre last week. 'This is the most economical way to proceed.'

"The length of sentencing remains unclear, and Mr. Milas has yet to provide any clear details as to when this plan is to be implemented."

Melody glanced up at me. "I've been hearing about this for years. I'm surprised they're actually going through with it."

I scoffed. "Or someone caught them sending prisoners away and now it's being leaked publicly."

She smirked. "Look at you... Conspiracy nut." She placed the newspaper back on the counter. "Either way, I think it's brilliant."

I laughed. "Why's that?"

She raised an eyebrow. "Do you really want to let our tax money feed murderers in prison? I completely agree with the guy. Drop 'em off on an island and let them fend for themselves."

* * *

"Fruit?"

I glanced up to find an older, orange-haired and freckle-faced woman standing directly in front of me, carrying kabobs of multicolored fruit in both hands.

I hesitated. I'd never been offered fruit on a stick before.

"There's mango, guava, banana, papaya, and acai berries," she said, eyeing the kabob as if trying to point at each individual fruit with her eyes.

"It's free?" I asked.

I remembered being brought to a hockey game by my mother when I was young, where men and women strolled through the aisles with bags of popcorn and cans of beer. I must have been six, maybe seven years old, and I remembered reaching for a bag of popcorn thinking it was free.

"Nothing's ever free," my mother had told me, "even if it's offered to you."

"Course it's free," the woman said. She plucked one of the kabobs like a rose from a bouquet and handed it to me.

I hadn't had the time to thank her, before Biggie's thick arm brushed past my face in reach of a skewer. She took it right out of the woman's hand, thanked her, and pulled off the first piece of fruit with her teeth.

"Thanks, Fran," Biggie said.

The woman, Fran, rolled her eyes and made her way around the fire, bending over gently and offering her handmade creations.

"That's Fran," Biggie said through a mouthful of chewed-up mango. "She's one of the Farmers. Likes to be creative when it comes to food."

"It's pretty," I said, poking at a piece of sliced guava. It had a beautiful green exterior, and its insides were a vibrant pinkish red—like the inside of a juicy watermelon. It wasn't what you'd find at the local grocery store or at the market. It was evident that this fruit hadn't been subjected to any chemicals or long-distance transportation.

I pulled it off of its finely carved branch and bit into it, careful not to crunch down on its seeds.

"Oh my God," was all I managed to say.

"Ain't nothing like Kormace fruit," Biggie said, finishing her last piece of banana. "You gonna eat that?" She pointed at my mango.

I instinctively pulled away like a rabid dog protecting a piece of broken bone, and Biggie burst out laughing.

"You're a true Islander now," she said, throwing an arm around my shoulders so hard I nearly dropped my fruit.

"I'll be right back," I said, feeling as though my bladder might explode.

The funny thing about many apocalyptic movies and TV shows is that they don't really incorporate the dirty details of basic comfort—which is something I had to learn the hard way on Kormace Island. Believe it or not, Murk had established rules when it came to releasing. Urination was to be done outside the Village walls and away from the Working Grounds.

* * *

"Just keep the Village in sight and do your thing," Rocket told me one of my first few days on Kormace Island. She then plucked an oversized leaf from the base of a tree. "These are probably your best bet for wiping. I wouldn't be too adventurous with the type of plant you grab, either... Might break out in a rash."

She then led me around the Village walls to where greenery turned into rock and flat surfaces became rough and slanted. At the edge of these rocks was a sudden drop.

"We call this the Cliff," she said.

I peered down into the abyss. I could see the tops of trees and I could hear the soothing sound of flowing water, but nothing more.

"Think of it as a natural garbage disposal pit," she said. "Bones, feces, fruit peel, bodies, you know... And you don't hover over it to take a shit, if that's what you're thinking."

I hesitated. "Bodies?"

Rocket shrugged almost nonchalantly, although I could tell she'd lost people she loved by the way she avoided my eyes. "People die, Brone. It's not like we have shovels to dig graves for every single one of them."

"What about funerals? A ceremony?" I asked, feeling like nothing more than a disposable object constructed of flesh and bone.

She shrugged again. "If they die in battle or on our territory, then of course we celebrate them. If they go missing, well, that's kind of hush-hush around here. Murk doesn't like rumors floating around, ya know? So if someone disappears, no one talks about them."

"And no one goes looking for them?"

She shook her head. "Not everyone who disappears gets killed. Some of them are used to lure us in by the Northers, which isn't worth the risk. Some women decide to live on their own—or, at least, try to—and others, well… They seem to think that Rainer has more to offer."

"That's the Northers' leader, right?" I asked.

Rocket smirked. "One and only. I hope she burns in hell."

* * *

I hated leaving the Village walls past sunset. I caught the Night Watcher's eyes as I made my way through the Village's entrance, and I knew that despite her standing there to keep watch over the Village, her presence did not guarantee my safety. She stood tall and stiff, carrying a beige tusk in her right hand, which I knew was the only weapon she had—a means of alerting everyone of oncoming danger.

A horn wouldn't save me from an attack or a kidnapping. I clenched my teeth as I rushed through a narrow path, guided only by old tracks dimly illuminated by the moon. I reached out, gently gliding my fingertips along the coarse, massive tree trunks as I moved forward.

"When you go, just move away from the Village. No one likes the smell of piss when they eat breakfast," Rocket had told me the day she brought me to the Cliff.

I glanced back. I could see an orange glow hovering above the Village walls, and I could hear women talking among themselves. I shot several glances in every direction, only to be reunited with darkness and wildlife noises—cracking of tree branches, rustling of leaves, insect cries, and the faraway sound of running water.

I lowered my pants and squatted by the base of a tree, emptying my bladder as quickly as possible. I managed to find a leaf and to refasten my pants around my waist, but the moment I moved toward the Village, I heard something...

My eyes widened into the blackness, as if opening them to their fullest would somehow allow me to see beyond human capability. I couldn't see anything, but there was movement nearby, and I feared that the sound of my own heart pounding would give away my location.

I fell into a crouched position and waited. I considered running back to the Village, but for all I knew, I'd be running away from a wild cat. It was better to stay still.

Silence returned. Maybe I was overreacting... Maybe it was nothing more than a rabbit or a wild turkey lurking nearby. I'd been so paranoid ever since Sunny's abduction that I imagined the slightest of sounds to be some horrid predatory beast.

But the sound that followed next proved to me that I wasn't overreacting... I was being followed. The noise had been faint but distinguishable nonetheless—heavy breathing.

CHAPTER 6

"You so much as breathe too loud, and I'll slit your fucking throat," she said, a filthy hand held tightly over my lips and the sharp point of a blade pressing into the base of my throat.

I lay on my back, my elbows digging into the jungle's moist earth; she sat on me with both legs on either side of my body. I couldn't see her face—not because of the darkness but because of the yellow serpentine mask covering her nose, her eyes, and the majority of her forehead. It almost looked as though she'd collected snake molt and glued it to a plain wooden mask.

Behind her stood another woman who wore a similar mask, only it appeared brown and much too large for her face. She fidgeted, constantly shifting her gaze toward the Village as if at any moment, the Night Watcher would blow the horn, warning everyone of the nearby threat.

The woman in the yellow mask leaned in closer, her raunchy breath warming the lower half my face.

"Every time you get paid, we'll expect a cut."

The woman behind her shuffled around. "Hurry up, H—Panther, I think someone's comin'."

Panther—I assumed it was her code name—turned around and waved a careless hand before returning her focus onto me. "Three pearls, weekly."

Three pearls? I only earned five pearls per week. And this woman expected me to hand over more than half of my earnings?

"That gonna be a problem?" Panther asked.

I quickly shook my head, feeling as though my heart might explode. I didn't have much of a choice.

The weight of her body began to take its toll, and all I wanted was to run away, but I couldn't move.

"You know where the Cliff is?" she asked.

I nodded, feeling the sharp point of her blade dig deeper into my neck.

"There's a boulder farther down with a palm tree beside it. Dig the pearls behind the boulder, got it?" I nodded.

"Panther, come on..." the other woman said.

"I know you get paid every seven days. In fact, pay day's coming up, so I'll expect to find me some treasure by the Cliff soon," Panther said. She shoved me into the dirt and climbed off of me. But she didn't walk away. Instead, she just stood there, hovering over me as would a predator over its tortured prey.

She pointed her blade at me, and I realized it

was actually a shiv made of bone. "You mention this to anyone, and waste won't be the only thing thrown over the Cliff."

And with that, she disappeared into the jungle. I wished I'd caught a glimpse of her eye color, her hair color, tattoos—anything. But it had been too dark. All I could see in my mind was the cracked snakeskin floating above my face.

I hurried back to the Village, both terrified and vulnerable. What was I supposed to do? Run to Trim? Tell her what happened? I didn't know who this woman was. For all I knew, she was Trim's friend. I thought of finding Ellie, but the last thing I wanted to do was put her at risk. This woman—Panther—was unidentifiable. Was she a Norther? An Ogre? Was she one of us? My heart pounded, and my legs trembled so bad I had to walk slowly to avoid collapsing to the ground.

I could hear Murk's voice in the distance, but it sounded so faint, so surreal as if being emitted through a large construction pipe, or a never-ending tunnel. She was praising Eagle, from what I could gather—recognizing her bravery, her selflessness, and so on. But the last thing I cared about was Eagle.

The only thing racing through my mind was the serpentine masks and the idea of being thrown to my death from atop the Cliff. How had this happened? The Village was supposed to be safe. Murk prided herself on keeping her women safe. Why was there no security outside the Village walls?

"Whoa, Brone, where're you going?" I heard.

I glanced up and realized that nothing had changed inside the Village's walls. Everyone was still celebrating—women were beating down on drums and dancing to the rhythm, drinking from their cups, smiling and laughing, and eating freshly cut fruit from wooden sticks.

"Hello?"

It was Fisher. She was standing in front of me with both hands on her waist and her head tilted to one side.

"I'm just tired. I need sleep," I said.

"You okay?" she asked.

I nodded and quickly moved past her, but her hand caught my arm.

"What happened?" she asked.

Fisher wasn't the empathetic type. She looked at me through narrowed eyes—not those of worry, but rather, concern.

"I... I," I stammered.

Was my demeanor so different that she had picked up on my fear? Fisher never seemed to worry about others' emotions. So what did she care, anyway?

She scratched the front of her throat and raised both eyebrows. "You're bleeding."

I mirrored her movement and gently pressed my finger against the base of my neck, feeling warmth and irritation; then I pulled my hand away. Blotches of dark red covered my fingertips.

"Well?" she pressed.

"Oh, this," I said. "I, um... I had to go... You

know. And, well," I said and tried to create a false reality in which I slipped trying to get back up and caught a sharp rock.

"I don't need to know," she quickly interrupted. "Just clean it out. The last thing you want is an infection. We don't have antibiotics here. If Trim sees you with that, you're in for a speech. Find some lemon, salt, whatever. Go see Tegan, and get that taken care of."

I nodded and continued toward my tent. The last thing I wanted was to go talk to anyone else. The cut could wait. I'd clean it out in the morning.

I distanced myself from the Village's celebration and hurried into the comfort of my tent. It wasn't much, with its dirt flooring, torn ceiling, and a stack of giant leaves I'd found while venturing to the Cliff several days after my arrival on Kormace Island—but it was where I felt comfortable.

"I hope you plan on checking those every night," Rocket had said, eyeing me curiously as I dragged a handful of leaves at a time into the Village. "Bugs like leaves. Just sayin'."

But that night, after having been ambushed by the women in masks, the last thing I wanted to do was rummage through piles of leaves in search of a critter. I hadn't spotted one in days, and I was willing to take my chances. I dropped heavily onto my side, appreciating the cool beneath me.

For the first time since I'd been dropped onto the island, I felt a hopelessness overshadow my state of surrealism—my need to believe that

Kormace Island was nothing more than a nightmare.

The reality of my situation had somehow been triggered, if not amplified, by my attack. I thought of my mother, and I could only pray she was okay. She'd endured so much. Would she try anything stupid? Would I return from Kormace only to find her name listed in the obituaries?

I thought of my body and how filthy and rugged it had become. I wondered if I would return home damaged and scarred, both physically and psychologically. Would I even survive my sentence? It was apparent that war was unfolding, and for all I knew, I could go to sleep one night and wake up to my throat being slit by a Norther.

Then, I thought of the life of comfort I'd once had—sleeping on a pillow-top bed and my down-filled pillows; sitting on our ancient, yet comfortable fabric sofa with a bowl of hot buttery popcorn; having the option to either warm or cool the apartment at any given moment; making a warm cup of coffee in the morning; wearing clean clothes every day; being smoothly shaven. My throat swelled, and I felt something I hadn't felt since being sentenced to Kormace Island—tears. At first, the warm droplets trickled down the sides of my cheeks, but this sadness was quickly overpowered by grief, and with grief came uncontrollable sobbing.

The feeling was so intense that I felt my heart clench every surrounding muscle and my throat swell to the point of causing labored breathing.

The crying resulted in a migraine, which brought forth yet another realization—my inability to obtain medication. This would also prove to be a challenge on this island. I couldn't just pop a few Tylenol to ease the pain or swallow some antacid liquid when I felt nauseated. And then I realized... As a woman, I had monthly visits. How were the Islanders dealing with this? Had they found a way to make tampons?

How was anyone supposed to be prepared for this? I would have rather gone to prison.

Why couldn't I stop thinking? I pulled one of my giant leaves closer to my chest, holding onto it as I'd once done every night with my fluffy pillow. The effect wasn't quite the same—the leaf was cool and thin—but it was better than nothing.

All I could do was hope for a better tomorrow.

CHAPTER 7

I didn't need a mirror to know my eyes were all pink and puffy when I woke up the next morning. I'd cried myself to sleep, which, ever since I was a little girl, had always resulted in my eyes swelling to an embarrassing grapefruit pink.

I avoided eye contact with as many women as possible on my way to breakfast, not wanting to be ridiculed or viewed at as weak. I followed the line to the fire pit with my head low. When it was my turn to be served, I extended my bowl, careful not to glance up.

"One scoop, or two?" Sumi asked.

I glanced up. She'd never cared about me or about what I wanted to eat. Why the change of heart? I hesitated.

"Two."

"You get one." She scooped a spoonful of slimy egg into my bowl then turned to her followers and said, "Told ya she was hiding somethin'. Looks like the city girl finally broke." Laughter erupted all around me, and I felt everyone's eyes on me.

"Lookin' a little pink there, Brone."

"Stace owes me three pearls. I bet two weeks, she bet one."

"Don't beat yourself up, kid."

"I'll take care o' ya, babe."

"Fuck off, Nym. The girl's mine."

Why was everyone talking to me? I tried to move past them, but I was trapped. There were distorted faces all around me—some smiling, others grimacing. I felt a hand on my shoulder, and I was pulled out of the crowd.

"Don't mind them," Flander said, flicking her wrist, "ain't like they got nothin' better to do."

"Did I miss something?" I asked. "My eyes are swollen... So what?"

"Just a game the women play," she said. "Every time there's a new drop, everyone bets on how long it'll take before the girl finally realizes how shitty her life is and finally breaks down for the first time. Don't always come quick, ya know. Took me four weeks when I first got 'ere. Think it's the shock... Nothing feels real at first, ya know?"

I nodded slowly. I definitely knew. I couldn't understand how these women purposely went out of their way to find amusement in someone else's misery. I couldn't imagine myself betting on a drop.

"Case you're wonderin'," Flander said, "the average is two weeks."

I smirked, even though I didn't find this funny. "So, I'm the average, then."

She smacked me on the shoulder and laughed. "Eat up, buttercup. We're goin' fishing today."

* * *

"I feel sorry for you," Rocket said, leaning in.

We were exiting the Working Grounds, with bows and spears in hand, on our way to the western shoreline.

I turned around to catch dozens of women with their eyes glued to me. They were smiling at me, but not in a genuine way. There was a thirst in their eyes—a sexual, predatory lust. I swallowed hard.

Rocket shook her head. "You're fair game now, Brone."

"Because I cried?" I asked, even though all I'd wanted to do was scream. Was I not allowed to cry? How juvenile were these women?

"Just the way things work around here," Rocket said. "You're not available until you break, 'cause once you break, it means you're one of us. Those are the rules. So most women won't even look at you until that happens. But now, in their eyes, you're fresh meat."

"But I'm not a lesbian..." I whispered.

Trim and Fisher, who must have been listening in on our entire conversation, burst out laughing up ahead of us.

"You are now," Fisher said, glancing back at me.

What was that supposed to mean?

Rocket must have noticed the look of disgust on my face because she nudged me in the shoulder and said, "Happens to guys too, you know... in prison. I miss a good fuck like any other woman here, but all we got's each other. You learn to like it"—she winked at me—"sometimes more than you thought you did."

I felt my face warm. I'd only ever had sex a handful of times at the age of sixteen with my boyfriend, and to be quite frank, it was everything my mother had told me it would be—painful and awkward. The last thing on my mind on Kormace Island was sex.

"This way," Trim ordered.

I saw a break of white in between the trees up ahead, and as we moved closer, I realized that the light was in fact not light at all—it was sand. We stepped out into the opening, and I was nearly blinded by how bright everything was. The sand was white as snow, and I could see it even through the ocean water.

"Welcome to the western shoreline," Biggie said, tapping me on the back so hard I nearly fell forward.

"Why couldn't they have dropped me off here?" I asked, but all I received in return was laughter.

I'd never travelled before, but the scenery before me could have been mistaken for a picture found on the cover of a travel magazine. A true paradise. A cool mist floated over the beach, sprinkling onto my chest and face. I listened to the sound of waves crashing on the tide and the sound of birds chirping as they flew in circular motions above the water.

It was a bit overwhelming, if not frightening, to gaze out into open water. The horizon was flat with not one hint of land in sight. I couldn't imagine how far we were from civilization. Were there other islands like Kormace? Other felons sentenced to the same fate?

"Brone, come on," I heard.

I glanced up to spot Trim walking into the ocean completely naked. Fisher quickly pulled off her top, revealing small but rounded breasts and a set of abs you'd expect to see on a man. The others quickly followed, tossing their leather garments onto the bed of sand and running wildly into the foamy water.

"Come on, Brone!"

I stared into the open water—at Trim, whose head was visible, but nothing else; at Biggie, who stomped her way into the water, her body jiggling at every step; at Fisher, who dove headfirst into the deep; at Rocket, who playfully lunged toward Flander; and finally, at Flander, who cursed as she fell backward, submerging herself entirely into the water.

Did they really expect me to join them? Naked? I awkwardly tugged at the bottom corner of my hand-sewn leather top.

"It's just skin!"

"No one here but us, Brone!"

I'd always been the type of girl to shy away in one of the enclosed changing rooms after gym class while all the other girls dressed and undressed around one another, gossiping about boys or about the newest sugar-free salad dressing available at the store. I'd always been so self-conscious of my body, even though I weighed a measly one hundred and fifteen pounds and I'd been gifted with a naturally muscular build.

It's just skin, I repeated in my head. I knew I had to get over myself. Life just wasn't the same anymore, and it wouldn't be for a very long time. I'd be hairy and filthy, and I'd smell of sour sweat and salt for the next few years. There was no use trying to maintain appearances or impress anyone for that matter. We were all living life on Kormace Island for the sole purpose of existing, of surviving—not for pleasantries.

With this new outlook in mind, I slid my top over my head, slipped out of my bottoms, and removed my brown cruddy sneakers, before running full force into the open water.

Although captive on a remote island, I felt liberated for the first time in my life.

"Wooooo!" Rocket slapped a handful of water at my face.

I splashed back, forgetting the island's brutality and the savagery just long enough to relish something I hadn't experienced for quite some time—fun.

But it wasn't long before Trim stepped out of the water and ordered us to do the same. I slid my clothes back on, covering my skin in a grainy layer of wet sand and fastened my quiver and bow onto my back.

"Here," Trim said, tossing a fishing spear to me.

To my surprise, I actually caught it.

"Time to fish," she said.

The others were handed their spears, and

together, we moved along the shoreline toward what appeared to be a small bay bordered by heavy rocks and darkened sand.

Trim was the first to step up onto one of the rocks and stab her spear into the water. She pulled back, revealing a large blue-tailed fish that flapped from side to side.

"And that's how it's done." She smirked, pulled the fish off the sharpened point of her spear, and tossed it into the sand beside my feet.

"Show off," Rocket muttered.

We circled the bay, stepping up onto the stones, and I gazed into the water, admiring the multitude of shapes and colors moving swiftly below us. Spears started piercing the water, and the fish moved about frantically. I just stood there with my spear gripped in both hands.

"Come on, Brone, help us out," Biggie said, wiping sweat from the tops of her eyebrows.

"Ain't rocket science," Flander said.

"I don't see you catching anything, Flander." Fisher laughed then swung down hard and tore a silver, yellow-backed fish from the water. "My favorite."

I pointed the sharp end of my spear toward the water. I'd been about to jab downward when I heard it—a high-pitched whistling that skimmed the lobe of my ear. I quickly glanced back to find a broken arrow lying at the base of a massive boulder.

"Retreat!" Trim shouted.

Another arrow came flying out from distant

trees, followed by another and another. Trim ran in the opposite direction toward the jungle, lunging over fallen tree trunks and fish carcasses. I kept up, fueled by adrenaline and survival instincts.

Everything was happening so fast, I didn't know what was going on.

We ran into the thick of the jungle, plowing our way through heavy verdure.

Trim led us south, away from the shoreline and away from our attackers.

"Trim!" Fisher hissed.

Trim turned around.

"I think we lost them." Fisher bent over, hands on her knees, fighting to catch her breath.

There was a moment of silence, before Trim's eyes met all of ours. "Stay on guard." Her eyes quickly shot down at my neck. "They got you."

Confused, I reached up, and with the tips of my fingers, grazed over the skin of my neck, only to feel the lumpiness of the cut I'd been given the night before—the one I'd forgotten to clean.

"Oh," I said. "Barely."

I wasn't prepared to tell any of them the truth. I couldn't trust anyone.

"Anyone else?" Trim asked.

"We're okay," Fisher said. Everyone nodded in unison.

"Who was that?" I asked.

"Fucking Northers," Rocket growled. She pressed the skin of her thumb into the point of her spear, and I could tell all she wanted to do was kill someone.

"How do you know?" I asked.

"The arrows. That's their specialty. And, well, they came from the North," Rocket said.

"Did anyone see anything?" Trim asked.

Everyone shook their heads.

"Didn't 'ave time," Flander said, scratching the top of her gray-haired head.

"Guys..."

"The fuck are they doing on the western shoreline?" Fisher asked.

"Guys..."

Trim sighed and shook her head. "I don't fucking know. This is the second attack in broad daylight."

"Yeah, and they're trying to start a full-blown war. They won't stop until they kill us all." Fisher clenched both fists and turned in circles like a shark in water.

"Can't we go after them?" I asked even though violence was the last thing I wanted. "I mean... hit them before they hit us again."

"Guys..."

"Murk won't allow it," Trim said. "She doesn't want war, and she can't risk losing us or any of her people."

"We're already at war!" Rocket said.

"Guys!"

In unison, everyone turned toward Biggie, who'd been attempting to capture our attention. "Stop talking." Her eyes were as round as golf balls, and her lips were curved downward as if she'd seen a ghost.

And in that moment, it was as if our surroundings instantly came into focus—as if a veil had been lifted, revealing a gruesome reality. There were strings of teeth dangling from tree branches all around us, some of which were large canines, but most of which were flat and obviously human.

There were fragmented pieces of skull and bone scattered across the earth beneath our feet, around which tall wooden torches were stabbed into the ground. The candles had melted entirely, and their leftover wax formed crooked, drooping lips.

There was something eerie about this place; it was as if life itself did not exist. For a moment, all sound from the jungle's wildlife faded, and the only thing I could hear was the shallow breathing of everyone around me.

"What is that?" Biggie moved toward the center, her eyes glued to the ground.

Beneath our feet was a circular drawing carved in mud, part of which had been smudged due to our footprints. It was a perfect circle with three gashes drawn evenly across its center. But what caught my attention was not the shape or its location, but rather, its color. It was stained in a deep red, which almost resembled black earth.

Trim's knuckles whitened around her fishing spear. "We're on Ogre territory."

Biggie's face contorted and her nostrils flared. "Do you smell that?"

I inhaled a deep breath through my nostrils, although I suddenly wished I hadn't. I couldn't understand how I'd failed to notice such a foul stench. It was like nothing I'd ever smelled before, and the more I breathed, the more nauseous I became. It smelled of decay, something far worse than sour milk, and moldy cheese combined.

A drop of red fell from above and onto Biggie's shoulder. She slowly tilted her head back, and I followed her eyes.

I wished I hadn't.

What I saw was beyond anything I'd ever imagined to find in the jungle. It was a naked female body tied by the ankles, dangling upside down from a massive branch overhead. Her throat had been slit straight across, and there were symbols carved into her chest and shoulders. Her skin was completely blanched and her face and neck swollen to the point of being unrecognizable. But her lifeless, dandelion eyes remained wide open.

I knew exactly who we were looking at—Sunny.

CHAPTER 8

"We continue to train our people." Murk lit the tip of a green cigar and leaned back in her chair.

Trim clenched both fists and stepped forward. "Did you not hear anything I just told you? They'll attack us again. We need to make a move."

"I did hear you, and my decision remains," Murk said.

I couldn't understand how she was being so calm about our attack and about our being ambushed and forced to retreat into enemy territory. I also couldn't understand how we'd manage to survive Ogre territory without an encounter.

Fisher stepped forward and knelt on one knee. "With all due respect, Chief, if we do nothing, we're sitting ducks just waiting to die."

Murk exhaled a cloud of white smoke, ashed her cigar onto the stone floor, then eyed us carefully. "You all know how this works. You Hunters are the only ones with enough experience to take on an attack against the Northers. If we lose our Hunters, we lose our food supply, and we destroy ourselves from the inside out."

"Our food supply is already being cut," Trim said. "We're already going to destroy ourselves from the inside out if we keep being intercepted during our hunts."

"Is this the first attack during a hunt?" Murk asked.

Trim nodded.

"Then we can't assume they'll attack at every hunt. Stay away from the western shoreline until further notice. There's fish in some of the fresh water around here."

No one countered her argument, and all that could be heard was the waterfall's heavy drop at the entrance of the cavern.

Murk slowly stood and met Trim's side. "How many Battlewomen do we have?"

Trim stiffened up with both hands on either side of her body. "Twenty, at most."

Murk scratched her chin. "And how many Archers?"

"Two. Three, if you include Brone," Trim said.

"I want six Archers at all times on our territory," Murk ordered.

"And where do you propose we find these Archers?" Trim asked.

"I'll let you handle that," Murk said. "No need for another Assessment. It'll only worry the women." Trim responded with a quick nod.

"From now on," Murk announced, her voice loudening, "no hunt is to be executed without proper caution, and no hunt is to be mentioned to anyone other than myself." She crossed both arms over her chest and parted her legs at shoulder's width. "If we're strategic about this, we'll never have to attack the Northers on their turf. Let them come to us... We'll be ready for them."

"And when they attack?" Trim asked.

Murk formed a slow-crushing fist below her chin. "Destroy them."

* * *

"How many Northers you think they got?" Biggie asked, rushing to Trim's side.

Trim walked briskly away from the waterfall with dozens of eyes following her. It was apparent trouble was lurking by the way Trim moved, and the women of the Village could sense it.

"I don't know..." she said. "Rainer took half our village when she left, and who knows how many drops she's taken from us."

"So equal or greater than our population," Fisher said matter-of-factly.

Trim didn't respond.

"Yeah," Flander added, "but what you're all forgettin' is that Rainer don't do civilization. She never believed in it. Which means all of 'er people are trained in battle. That's what she recruits 'em for."

Rocket hopped sideways, keeping up with Trim's pace. "This would be so much easier if we could burn their fucking homes to the ground."

"Agreed," Biggie said.

"Enough," Trim said. "You're all dismissed."

163

Everyone stopped following her.

"Give 'er time," Flander said. "She needs 'er space."

Fisher's eyebrows came together as she watched her leader exit the Working Grounds. "The last thing any of us needs right now is fucking space. We need to stick together."

"Yeah, well, that ship's sailed," Biggie said. She used her forearm to wipe sweat away from her chin then turned around and made her way toward the water.

"I'm with Biggie," Rocket said. "Need me some water time."

Fisher released a sigh—a growl, almost—and walked in the opposite direction. I stood awkwardly by Flander's side, pondering whether or not to also walk away.

"Looks like ya got the day off, kid." Flander stretched her back, cracked her fingers, then said, "I'm goin' to take a nap."

I caught Savia's eyes—the woman who'd been supposed to train me as Needlewoman. She was sitting underneath the shadow of a tree with a dry piece of leather in one hand and carved wood in the other. A pile of arrows lay beside her, and I could tell by the solemn look in her eyes that she knew exactly what was coming. I tried to smile, but my lips didn't move. So instead, I left the Working Grounds and made my way toward the Village.

I'd been about to enter my tent, when I heard Ellie's voice, "Hey, right on time."

I glanced back.

"I'm doing my rounds," she said. "Here." She offered a closed fist, so I placed an open palm underneath it and caught five pearls.

"Payday," she said.

"Oh, um... thanks," I said.

She stared at me for a moment, her almond eyes narrowing. "You okay? Looks like you've had a long day."

A long day was an understatement. I'd nearly been killed out on the western shoreline, and although grateful that I'd survived the attack, there was a part of me that wished the Norther who'd fired the arrow hadn't missed. I couldn't get Sunny's swollen, lifeless face out of my mind or the way she'd just dangled above us, poisoning the air with the rancid smell of decay. How was anyone supposed to live with such a memory? The image of Sunny being dragged away by a masked Ogre still haunted me, and now, I'd have a new memory to accompany it.

I felt queasy.

"Brone?"

I shook my head and forced a smile. "I'm okay."

"Come here," she said, pulling me in close.

I stiffened, feeling entirely ill-prepared for affection.

"Relax," she said. "You looked like you needed a hug."

Although uncomfortable, I enjoyed the sensation of her warm body against mine. It soothed me. I couldn't remember the last time I'd been touched, with the exclusion of Rocket, Biggie, or Flander slapping me across the shoulder or on the back.

She slowly pulled away and smiled, her plush pink lips curving on either side. "Better?" I nodded.

"Now use those pearls wisely," she said.

I opened my hand and stared down at the silky, multicolored pearls, suddenly remembering that only two of these actually belonged to me. I remembered the yellow serpentine mask hovering inches away from my face, and the last thing I wanted was to see that mask again. I'd do as instructed and drop three pearls near the Cliff.

Ellie reached up and stroked my cheek. "You'll be all right."

I didn't understand how she saw right through me, being that I'd always been the type to hide my emotions from the outside world, but she did. And I wished this were true—that everything would be all right. I wished that I could rewind my sentence and steer clear of Trim and her crew. I didn't want to be an Archer. I wasn't prepared to go to war. I wasn't prepared for any of this.

Maybe—just maybe—this inevitable war could be delayed just long enough for me to finish out my sentence. Attacks were unavoidable, but it wasn't unrealistic of me to hope for long gaps in between each attack. I didn't want to be a part of the merciless bloodshed. I just wanted to go home.

"Ellie?" I asked.

Her eyes lit up, and she waited in silence.

"How long do you have left to serve?"

I felt as though I'd offended her. The happy-go-lucky way about her faded, and what remained was unease and masked depression.

"Why're you asking me that?" she asked.

I shrugged. "I just... I'm just wondering... How do you know when your time is up? I mean, do you count the days? Does the government keep track of it? Where do you get picked up? When will I know when my sentence is up?"

And she just stared at me as would a child being explained the actual meaning of death for the first time. She parted her lips to speak, but nothing came out. I'd been about to ask her to answer me, but something told me I already knew the answer.

I felt a sickening nausea overwhelm me. No one was coming back for me—not in three years, not ever.

PART THREE

PROLOGUE

The gritty black-inked headlines kept flashing in my mind like an old black-and-white movie clip on a repeat cycle.

"New Sentencing System to Reduce Tax Dollars."

"The People Have Spoken, and They Don't Want Murderers Living in Their Country."

"New Approach to Criminal Law—What Do You Think?"

How was everyone so blind? How had I been so ignorant? How had I truly believed that a new system had been put in place—one where criminals convicted of murder were dropped off on a remote island, forced to serve time in the most wearing of ways, only to be picked up by helicopter at the end of their sentence and returned to civilization?

The government didn't keep track of their abandoned convicts—they didn't care. We were nothing but waste left to rot in an oversized garbage dump chosen by Mr. Milas, the Attorney

General of the Department of Justice.

I'd been living on Kormace Island for about a month, having already become a Hunter—one of the most sought-after positions among Murk's people—and having also made several enemies, but none of that mattered now.

I cracked my eyes open. I was lying in my tent, flat on my stomach, the side of my face pressed into the dirt floor.

I wanted to die.

The government wasn't coming back for me. I'd never see my family or friends again. What was the point? Why try to survive when I had nothing left to live for? I was about to close my eyes again, wanting nothing more than to melt into the dirt and selfishly disappear from the face of the Earth, when I heard it.

I snatched my bow from the top leaf of my bed and slipped out of my tent. Women rushed north of the Village toward the entryway, forming a disorderly herd. I couldn't see what was happening, but I heard it: the sound of pure agony—that of a woman being slowly tortured to the point she no doubt wished for death's release.

I noticed something else... someone else. A young woman with a long auburn-brown braid dangling over her shoulder and a beige, cotton-like dress came blasting out of one of the wooden cabins at the back of the Village. I knew precisely what this cabin was and who this woman was, even though I'd never actually laid eyes on her before. The cabin was our Hospital, or infirmary if you will, and the woman—Navi, our Medic.

As the crowd made its way toward the Hospital, I caught only glimpses of the woman whose hoarse voice echoed across every nearby tent. Her hands danced in all directions, and she screamed as women covered in splattered blood attempted to hold her down. Navi entered the crowd, but within moments, she ran back toward her Hospital and the crowd hurried to follow her.

I caught one last glimpse of the horrific scene before the woman was rushed to Navi's care: a face contorted with bared teeth, skin full of open gashes and puncture wounds, and black blood-stained material wrapped around the woman's leg, or at least the bit that was left of it.

CHAPTER 1

"Fresh out of the turkey's ass," Sumi said, slamming a spoonful of yellow mush into my bowl.

"I don't think it comes out of—" I tried, but she dumped another spoonful of colorful bits and pieces over my eggs, and I realized these were fruit. It wasn't every day that fruit was served with breakfast, so I kept my mouth shut.

"Extra sugar this morning," she said.

I forced a smile, but all she did was give me a dirty look. What was her problem, anyway? Ever since I'd landed on Kormace, Sumi had given me a hard time. She wasn't much to look at—a short, Asian woman with flat eyebrows and lips the color of her face. Her narrow black eyes often found their way to my feet before scanning me from top to bottom in the most conspicuous of ways. These eyes remained glued to me as I walked to my usual spot—a tree log positioned farthest away from the center fire, which was basically Sumi's oven.

I stared at the back cabin, wondering what had happened. I'd heard gossip floating around, but the story changed depending on who was delivering it. There was a trail of blood in the yellow grass leading all the way to the Hospital. I wondered if we'd ever get rain again. If we did, would it clean the blood from the grass blades?

"Funny finding you here," I heard.

The sound of her voice immediately comforted me. It was Ellie.

I glanced up at her with a smirk. "What a coincidence."

She smiled big and whipped her long dark brown hair behind her back. I couldn't help but return the smile. Nearly every morning, Ellie found her way to me at the log. It had become routine, our morning chats. She often vented about how frustrating it was to serve as the Village's bank— the woman responsible for currency, which was nothing more than shiny pearls—and how every woman believed she was entitled to more than the standard five-pearls-per-week salary.

Then she'd go off asking me about hunting and about being the Village's primary Archer. I was still unable to think of myself as the *primary* Archer. I'd only obtained this title because Eagle, our previous Archer, was maimed during an attack by the Northers, and due to my perfect vision, I was handed the position. It wasn't fair, really. There were other women far more capable of shooting an arrow. My only advantage was that I could actually see my target.

I questioned why Pin and Hamu hadn't been selected as Hunters. The Asian twins were skilled with their bows, but their tasks were limited to protecting the Village and its people. Maybe Murk had seen something in me—something of value.

"Oh, speaking of money," Ellie said, "here." She dropped my hard-earned pearls into the palm of my hand.

"We're friends, aren't we?" I asked, smiling sideways at her.

She laughed. "Don't even. You get five, just like everybody else."

I slipped the pearls into the pouch on my waist. Ellie didn't know it, but receiving my weekly pay was a negative experience for me. Not because I didn't enjoy being able to purchase useful items from the Merchant tents, but because I'd been bullied into an involuntary contract that forced me to hand over three pearls to two women whose identities I had yet to uncover. I'd considered telling Ellie, but I didn't want to involve her by putting her life at risk. There was no telling how dangerous these women were.

I even contemplated telling Trim, the leader of the Hunters, but I feared that being a rat may get me killed. I'd already been threatened to keep my mouth shut about the whole thing.

"So what happened?" I asked, gazing out toward the Hospital.

There were still a few women lingering around it, most likely the woman's friends who hoped to receive an update on her condition.

"Which version do you wanna hear?" Ellie leaned in so close I noticed the color of her butterfly tattoo—blue and yellow.

"The real one," I said.

"Leopard," she said simply.

I swallowed hard. "Were you there?"

"I helped bandage her leg. It wasn't pretty. She lost her calf, her knee, and part of her thigh." She shook her head. "You could see everything... the bone... Thankfully one of the entrance Guards ran toward the Cliff to help her when they heard her screaming."

I felt queasy. The Cliff. She'd been attacked all for having to use the "bathroom," so to speak. I'd never imagined the Cliff as a dangerous spot. It was so close to the Village walls. I stared at the grass, suddenly feeling nothing but despair again.

I would be exposed to the risk of excruciating pain every day for the rest of my life.

What a shitty life.

"Hey, you okay?" Ellie asked.

I tried to smile to hide what I was thinking, but I couldn't. I wanted to, especially for Ellie, because she'd been the one to tell me the truth about Kormace Island—about the sentencing duration being nothing more than a lie—and I knew she felt guilty.

She wrapped a hand around the back of my neck and squeezed gently. It felt so warm. "I'm truly sorry," she said. "Just hang in there, okay? We need you."

Just hang in there, I thought. That's exactly what I was doing—hanging by a thread. How much longer was I supposed to cope with this? How could I accept the fact that I was never going home? That my life was over?

* * *

"Good morning." Murk grinned knowingly down at me, and I felt like a child who'd been caught sleeping on a school day.

I quickly wiped the drool from the side of my chin and sat upright. I didn't understand why the leader of our people—our Chief—was just standing there, in *my* tent. Murk didn't *go* to people. People went to Murk.

"It's okay. Stay where you are." She moved in closer and sat on the ground.

I fidgeted, feeling exposed and vulnerable. Murk was the equivalent of a big boss, and I was the employee who never spoke and consistently came to work on time. So why was my boss here? I assumed her visit was to discuss my emotional absenteeism—to explain to me that if I didn't pick myself up, I'd be fired and thrown into the jungle to fend for myself.

"I'm sorry to hear you've learned the truth so early in your sentence," she said, her bright eyes glued to mine.

I hated to hear her say it—to hear that my sentence was, in fact, a death sentence. I remembered the look on Ellie's face when I confronted her about the duration of my term. She'd just stood, her lip twitching on one side as if debating the formulation of another lie.

I quickly looked away. Murk wasn't the type of person you were able to maintain eye contact with

179

for any length of time. There was an indescribable intensity to her—an intimidation factor that was useful given her rank in our society. My wandering eyes caught the sharp-toothed necklace she'd worn since the day I met her.

She followed my eyes and pinched one of the canine teeth between her thumb and index fingers. "You like?"

I nodded.

"First predator kill," she said and leaned backward against the palms of her hands. "Believe it or not, I used to be a Hunter back in the day."

This caught my attention. Murk, our Chief, had once been one of us? It was hard to envision, but it only made sense that the leader of our people had made her way to the top, as would the CEO of a multimillion-dollar industry—unless, of course, it was handed down by blood. This, I believe, is why I respected Murk as our leader. She'd earned her place.

"How long ago was that?" I asked.

She cocked a brow. "Long ago."

I glanced at her spiked silver hair, and I wondered if it had once held color while on Kormace Island. If so, how much time had passed? She must have sensed my curiosity because she let out a faint laugh and cocked her head to one side.

"You know," she said, "that's usually the first thing every woman wants to know... How long I've been here. You wouldn't believe me if I told you."

I smiled as if to say, 'Try me.'

A narrow crease formed in between her

eyebrows and her lips tightened. "There's a lot that happened behind closed government doors that no one knows about..." She sighed. "I was a foster kid, way back when... I was in and out of foster homes. No one wanted me. I was too angry. By the time I hit sixteen, I managed to get myself involved with the wrong people."

"What happened?" I was shocked at how easy it was to speak to her. For a moment, I forgot she was Chief.

She averted her gaze. I wondered if she regretted what she'd done.

"Wrong place, wrong time," she said. "Feds got involved. It was a mess."

I stared at her, unsure how to respond. Clearly, she didn't like to talk about it, so I figured it was best not to keep pushing. I'd heard so many rumors about Murk—from her being a mass murderer to her performing acts of terrorism. Maybe it was best I didn't know.

She sighed. "Funny, isn't it? The way life happens? I could have ended up anywhere in life, yet here I am... forty-two years later."

* * *

"I'll see you later, okay?" Ellie said. "Maybe at bath time."

Bath time, I thought. I couldn't recall the last time I'd bathed or showered (which, believe it or not, was considered a luxury given that you had to purchase handmade soap to shower). It was much easier to float in the waterfall's pool and let the salt do the cleaning for me.

I'd been so busy trying to perfect my archery skills and attempting to kill prey in order to feed our people that I completely gave up on hygiene. What did it matter, anyways? Clean or dirty, I was still going to die.

I remembered Murk's last words before she left my tent that one morning. "It's never going to be rainbows and sunshine here on the island. It's not easy, and I didn't come here to lie to your face—to tell you that everything will be okay. I came here to tell you what you already know: your life on the outside is over, and the sooner you accept that, the sooner you can go on living as part of our society."

She stood and slowly made her way toward the exit, then turned around. "I understand how you're feeling, Brone, I really do. As a woman who's been through what you're experiencing right now, I'm deeply sorry. As your Chief, however, I'm giving you three days to pull yourself together. If you can't contribute to this society, then your presence here is useless."

And with that, she left. Although her words initially angered me, it wasn't long before I realized Murk was just doing her job. She couldn't have women lazing around, refusing to contribute to the Village's sustenance.

If I couldn't linger on the fact that I'd be spending the rest of my miserable life secluded from advanced civilization, I'd simply have to hold on to an abstract ideology that one day, I'd find my way back home.

CHAPTER 2

"Do you see it?"

I stood closer to the fast-moving river, leaning forward to see what Rocket was pointing at. The water had a green tint to it, most likely the result of its forest surrounding, and from the looks of it, it was quite deep. I wondered where it led. Across the river was a jagged stone wall, and above this, countless slanted trees and bright green bushes leading up a mountain.

I noticed a lot of fish moving along with the current of the water. Their bodies were rounder than those of other fish I'd seen before, and there was an orange hue cast from underneath their bellies.

"So Murk was right," I said.

Since we'd been attacked on the western shoreline during a fishing trip, Murk had advised us to steer clear of this shoreline and to fish only from the jungle's fresh waters.

Rocket laughed. "Sure was."

I glanced back at the others, who had also

joined in on the laughter.

"What's so funny?" I asked.

Fisher smirked. "They're piranhas."

I carefully turned to catch another glimpse of the sharp-toothed fish, but something hard suddenly hit me in between the shoulder blades. I was propelled forward, mere inches from the water, before quickly being pulled back to safety.

Adrenaline burst through me. I swung backward in an attempt to knock my attacker, but what I found was not an attacker at all—it was Biggie, and she was laughing so hard she'd fallen over.

"Oh, man... Every time," she said through broken laughter. "Girl... You shoulda—"

I stared at her as she slapped her belly and pointed at me. How did she think this was funny? Fueled by pent-up anger, I tore an arrow from my quiver and lunged forward with all I had, knocking her flat on her back. I knew she was twice my size, but I didn't care.

"Fucking do that again," I said, my knuckles whitening around my arrow as I pressed its sharp point into her neck.

"Whoa, whoa, whoa," I heard.

Several hands grabbed me, and I was pulled off of Biggie, whose eyes I thought might just pop out of her head.

"You good?" Fisher asked, holding an open palm out to me.

The moment I realized what I'd done, my muscles loosened and I dropped the arrow. My hands trembled at my sides, and my legs shook so hard I thought they might give out.

"I... I'm sorry." I feared that Biggie might kill me.

But she didn't. In fact, she burst out into a full-blown belly laugh.

I shot a glance at Trim, whose lips slowly curved upward, and at the others, who'd joined in on the buffoonery. How was this funny?

Biggie rolled sideways onto her hands and knees and stood up, dusting pieces of dry mud from her knees and back. She moved in toward me, and I flexed my ab muscles, certain she'd tear a hole right through me. But she didn't swing or kick. Instead, she raised an open hand and waited for me to grab it.

I reluctantly reached forward, and the moment our hands met, she pulled me in hard against her chest and tapped me on the back, knocking the wind right out of me.

"You're finally feral," she said.

I stood there, dazed. Was I being celebrated for having finally snapped? I felt ashamed of what I'd done, yet I was being praised for it.

The others chimed in.

"Welcome home, Brone."

"Way to go, girl."

"You're one of us now... a savage."

"Good job, kid."

Trim stepped forward, and I noticed the smile disappear from her face. She reached out and squeezed my shoulder. "We've all done it, and we're proud of you for finally standing your ground, but I don't want to see that happen again."

I nodded quickly, my cheeks reddening, and the laughter subsided. I remembered Trim banishing that woman—Marlin—from the Village for having attacked a fellow Battlewoman.

I knew I'd been given a freebie, but I also knew I'd have to control my temper no matter how much rage or sorrow I kept tightly bottled up inside. Trim wouldn't tolerate a loose cannon in her crew.

"Over here," Rocket said, pointing toward the flowing water. I followed her index finger to where a school of silver-backed fish swam just beneath the current.

"Come on, hurry," Fisher waved a hand at Biggie, who dragged a large leather bag to the fishing spot.

From it, she pulled a mesh net of sorts—it looked like a giant spider web constructed of yellow grass blades or dry weeds.

Together, Fisher and Biggie cast the net into the water, allowing roughly a dozen fish to swim right into the trap, before pulling their catch out of the water and dropping it on the stone ground.

"I'll do it," Rocket said, moving in.

She reached into the net and pulled a fish out by its tail.

"May wanna turn around," she told me and smashed the fish's head hard against the ground. The sound of the impact made my stomach churn and I quickly turned away.

I wondered if I'd ever get used to seeing these women kill or tear animals apart. I knew that killing was our means of survival, but I couldn't bring myself to watch—especially not during the gutting process.

After Rocket finished smashing every fish in the net, Trim ordered, "Again," and the empty net was cast back into the water.

They did this several times until a large pile of lifeless, shiny-skinned fish formed by the water.

"All right, wrap them up," Trim said.

Biggie reached down and began tossing the dead fish into the net they'd used to catch them with in the first place. "Don't worry, Brone," Biggie said, winking up at me, "No piranhas in here."

I faked a smile, not finding any humor in her remark.

Once the fish were collected in the net, Trim filled her water bladder from the river, then said, "Let's go."

She led us away from the river and back toward the Village. I wasn't sure how far we'd journeyed in search of fish, but it must have been far because I felt a dull ache in my legs and feet. I glanced down at my rotting sneakers. I'd have to part with them soon, I knew. I just wasn't ready to wear leather slabs... or nothing at all.

"So what other animals live in this jungle?" I leaned in toward Rocket.

She smiled sideways at me. "Well, I'm sure there's a lot more than what we've seen so far. Couldn't name all of 'em..."

"Guys!" Trim glared back at us. "Stay close and be on guard. There could be Northers anywhere...

Or Ogres."

The last thing I wanted to think about was Ogres, but they were a threat, and as a Hunter, my job was to be on the lookout for potential threats. It still blew my mind that human beings could turn out so appallingly uncivilized, so cruel and inhuman. Did they even speak a word of English, these Ogres? Rocket had described them as the most barbaric of people you'd ever encounter—carnivorous women who lived like animals and behaved as monsters.

Then I thought about the Northers. Although more civilized than Ogres, they were, in a sense, worse. They were methodical in their attacks—eager to strike us down from every possible angle. Ogres, on the other hand, kept their distance from the Village and the Working Grounds. Sure, they'd slice you up into pieces and pile your remains by an altar, but only if you happened to set foot on their territory. They weren't out to gain power or land like the Northers.

A soft whistle caught my attention. I glanced up to find Trim making some sort of military signal with her index and middle finger. She pointed at her eyes, which looked more like brown slits, then straight ahead. I followed her hand, still unable to make out what she was pointing at.

I slowly drew an arrow from its quiver and rested it against my bowstring. Had she spotted an animal? My eyes narrowed and I moved forward, careful not to step on any fallen branches. What was she looking at? I eyed Trim for guidance, but all she did was quickly swirl her finger in a circular motion, and everyone instantly separated, scurrying away in opposite directions. Was I supposed to move? Why hadn't I been taught these hand gestures? I stood there, a loose grip on my bow and arrow, feeling like a complete moron. Everyone disappeared from view, and I moved to Trim's side, not knowing where else to go.

"They're sweeping," she whispered.

"What's going on?" I asked.

She pointed straight ahead toward a hollow at the base of a dramatically slanted tree. At first, I didn't see anything other than darkness in the hole. But then I caught a glimpse of blonde hair, so I looked closer, realizing there was someone curled up in a fetal position, her face buried between her knees.

CHAPTER 3

It was obvious she was new on the island by her brand-name clothing—something I'd been advised against keeping when I was first caught by Trim and the gang.

"What's your name?" Trim asked.

The girl grabbed her scraped knees and pulled them in closer. "Br... Breanne."

She had scraggly shoulder-length hair that hadn't been dyed in months. The tips of her hair were almost yellow, while the rest of her hair, including her roots, was dirty blonde. She had a quirky square-shaped nose that didn't suit her features at all. Her skin was white as snow, and she had coffee-colored eyes, which matched the dirt smeared across her clothing and neck. It looked like she'd fallen face-first into a puddle of mud.

"How long have you been here?" Trim asked.

"I... I don't know."

"We haven't heard a drop in days," Rocket said.

Trim glanced at her, then back at Breanne. "How long?" she repeated, her voice hardening.

The young girl was shaking—the last thing she needed was to be interrogated by the bad cop, but I didn't feel bad for her. Not because I didn't care, but because in comparison to the initial greeting I'd received (being knocked on the head), this woman's initial contact with the gang was a walk in the park.

"Days, weeks," she said. "I'm not sure."

"Have you eaten?" Trim asked.

Her sunken cheeks and pale blue lips were a clear indication she hadn't consumed adequate amounts of food or water for quite some time.

"Come on," Trim said. "We'll get you fed and cleaned up."

Fisher quickly grabbed Trim's arm.

"You know we always hear the drops," she whispered. "This could be a setup."

"She needs our help," Trim said.

Fisher didn't question her. She reached down and helped Breanne to her feet.

I was surprised to see Trim dismiss a potential threat to save a complete stranger's life. Trim—the leader of the Hunters—had been methodical and analytical from the moment she'd found me on shore. She'd never acted on emotion. Did she know this woman?

We led Breanne toward our Working Grounds, where women were busy with their daily chores: cooking, carving weapons, filtering water, drying leather, and hacking away at wood. Breanne received the same welcome as I did when I first set foot onto the Working Grounds—frowns formed above primitive eyes.

I felt sorry for her. I remembered how afraid I was and how I wanted nothing more than to vanish into thin air. I remembered feeling as though my state was merely a dream, as though I would awaken any moment, safe from the island's barbarism and filth.

But I didn't wake up. In fact, I spent most nights tossing and turning, wondering how my life had taken such an awful turn. How would I ever survive on this island? I'd contemplated this horrific thought over and over again, all the while visualizing my lifeless body being torn by hungry panthers, or worse...

"Brone, you're dismissed."

I glanced up. I realized that most of the Hunters had left our group, and only Trim and Fisher remained, leading Breanne to meet with Murk inside the waterfall. She was to be assessed for a position among our people—a job. I only prayed that for her sake she wouldn't be assigned the task of Battlewoman. No one deserved that. But Murk had made it clear that the Northers posed too great a risk for our people not to be prepared for battle, which meant there were plenty of openings.

I remembered her speech following the attack on our Village and how she'd said, "We need more Battlewomen to protect our people—to fight for what's ours and to defend what we've worked so hard for," before initializing another Assessment to recruit more Battlewomen.

Voices grew louder around me, and I watched as several women left their posts to gather closer to the waterfall's edge.

"I bet you two pearls Murk's gonna give'r Battlewoman," someone said beside me.

It was a tall lanky woman with shoulders curved forward in such an exaggerated fashion, I was reminded of the Hunchback of Notre Dame. She looked down at me when she caught me staring and said, "Whad'ya think?"

I'd been about to say, "I have no idea," even though I knew Murk's intention was to increase the size of her army, but a young Latina woman beside me stepped in. "Yo, count me in on that bet," she said. "Double or nothin'. I say she's givin' her Archer."

She threw her thick black hair over her shoulder and rubbed both hands together.

"That's the same damn thing, you twit," came a familiar voice.

It was Hammer—the woman who ran the Tools tent. She still had the same big belly as she did when I first met her.

The Latina woman pursed her lips and moved in on Hammer, her hips swaying from side to side. "How da hell is Archer and Battlewoman the same thing? You need me to build you a dictionary? They're two different fuckin' words."

I took a step back not wanting to get caught in the crossfire. To my surprise, Hammer threw her head back and laughed. "Relax, taco. What I'm sayin' is, they're all related. An Archer is technically a Battlewoman with a specialty. That's like saying Murk'll assign her Archer instead of Hunter. They're all connected, and it's confusing to try to differentiate the three terms."

"Whatevs," said the young Latina woman.

The tall one was curiously eyeing Hammer and the Latina woman. She then made eye contact with me, smirked, and said, "Women."

"How about you, sweetheart, what do you think?" I heard.

The voice had come from another woman beside me. She had blonde hair, which was braided back in cornrows against her head, and a necklace made of rope or dried plant. She stood stiff like a man, her chest puffed out and her freckled chin raised high. I didn't have time to say anything because she reached an open hand and said, "I'm Tulip."

I shook her hand, but she didn't let go. She just stood there, smiling at me from top to bottom, before adding, "You know...'Cause I'm good with flowers." She glanced down at my groin area and smirked sideways.

"Leave the poor girl alone," said the tall, hunched woman.

The Latina woman scoffed. "Don't pay no attention to blondie over here." She moved in closer, grabbed my wrist, bent forward, and gently kissed the back of my hand with her plush lips. "When you're ready for a real woman... name's Lola."

"Please," said Tulip. "Ain't nobody got time for

romance on Kormace. What the girl needs is a good screw."

I swallowed hard. I felt completely violated. I didn't want any one of them near me.

"Ain't that right, sexy?" Tulip asked, throwing her chin out at me.

I clenched my teeth and swallowed hard. I imagined myself pulling an arrow from my quiver and repeating what I'd done to Biggie, but Trim had warned me about attacking one of my own. I didn't want to end up banished from the Village. It wasn't worth it. But at the same time, if I didn't defend myself, women would come to realize that Brone, the pathetic Archer, was a pushover.

"Come on," Tulip went on, "I can fuck better than any man you've ever been with." She flicked her tongue in the air several times.

And although I wasn't the type to vocalize my thoughts—to confront conflict in any way, shape, or form—I knew if I didn't speak up, I'd never put an end to this behavior. I was an Archer, I repeated to myself. A Hunter. I was to be respected.

My heart was pounding out of my chest, and I stared at her, imagining what it would feel like to have both hands around her throat. I was so sick of bullies. I'd already been forced to pay a portion of my weekly salary to two masked women who'd jumped me while on my way to the Cliff. I couldn't keep allowing myself to be a victim. Then the thought of Gary, the reason I ended up on Kormace Island, entered my mind. I remembered the way he'd yell at my mother from across the living room, commanding that she bring him a cold beer, or the way he'd tell her that putting on makeup was a waste of time because no man would ever look at her anyways. I was glad he was dead. I was glad I killed him.

I shook my head. No, I hadn't meant this. I wasn't a killer. I hadn't done it on purpose.

Tulip reached for my hand, and that's when the words just came pouring out.

"Stay the fuck away from me if you know what's good for you." I glared at her, swinging away.

Her eyes went big for just a moment as if rejection was entirely new to her. She raised her hands to the sides of her face. "Whoa, whoa, sweetheart. No disrespect."

I just stared at her, my nostrils flared and my jaw clenched. I couldn't look away. I was furious. I knew she wasn't the sole reason for my anger, but I didn't care. All I needed was a punching bag.

"Hey, easy girl," I heard, but I wasn't sure who'd said it.

I suddenly realized that my hands were clenched into fists, and I knew that if I didn't compose myself, I'd do something I'd regret. So I walked away.

There was muttering behind me, words such as, "Crazy," "Bitch," and "Psycho," but all it did was put a smile on my face. My legs shook, and I felt like I was walking on an angle, but I was so proud of myself. I'd never talked back to anyone before— not like that, anyway. If I was going to spend the rest of my life living with uncivilized, pig-headed women, they had to know I wouldn't put up with their abuse.

* * *

"Yeah, keep looking, you goddamn pig. I wouldn't touch you with a ten-foot pole!" Melody shouted from across the street.

God, I loved my best friend.

There were two older men sitting on a cement block, sipping on their Styrofoam cup coffees and eyeing us like wild dogs gazing at two pieces of bloody steak. All I did was laugh. I didn't understand how Melody could be so blunt—so daringly vocal toward anyone who upset her even in the slightest.

"Fucking pigs," she muttered.

I smiled at her. I loved watching her flip out on people. "Were you always so feisty?"

She pushed her thick black glasses up her nose with her index finger—a geeky gesture she often did, which completely contradicted her aggressive demeanor—and shook her head. "Foster care teaches you to stand up for yourself. Not like anyone else is gonna do it for you."

She threw her arm around my shoulder and tossed her hair. "Except for me. I always got your back."

* * *

"Here they come!" I heard.

It was difficult to see ahead of me with all the bodies gathered at the side of the waterfall. I saw Trim come out—well, her frizzy brown hair—and I assumed Breanne was by her side. They came into full view as they walked up the narrow path to the right of the waterfall—the one I'd been led up when Trim had announced my new post to the women of the Village.

When they reached the top, Trim reached for the torch, just as she'd done with me, and pulled it out of the ground. She then raised it into the air above her shoulder and shouted, "Holland, Battlewoman!"

I assumed Holland was Breanne's last name.

There was an uproar among the women, and I couldn't tell whether they were cheering her on or rebelling against Murk's decision. Women jumped up and down, others pushed and shoved one another, but then something else happened. The shouting ceased, and instead, a low chant began to spread among the women: "Death to the Northers."

CHAPTER 4

"What is that?" I asked, pulling away from Rocket's green-stained thumb.

She smirked. "Camouflage."

I cocked an eyebrow. "I know what it's for... But what's it made of?"

"Dirt, plants... Nothing that once had a pulse, if that's what you're wondering. Now hold still."

I stared at the designs on her face: chalky green lines drawn vertically across both of her cheeks and a thick black bar painted straight across her eyes and over the bridge of her nose. The contrast made the white of her eyes look almost fluorescent.

"Does it actually help?" I asked. "You know, for camouflaging?"

"I like to think so." She dipped her thumb into a black substance and began smudging the color underneath my eyes. "Besides, it's good luck."

"Says who?"

"It just is," she said impatiently.

"Why don't we use paint on all of our hunts?" I

asked.

She dropped her hand and stared straight at me. "What's with the interrogation?"

I smiled. "Just curious."

"Lookin' good, Brone," I heard.

I shifted my eyes toward Biggie's voice, not wanting to upset Rocket by turning my face. She was standing beside Fisher, and I felt like the last kid in line to get their face painted at day camp.

I noticed that Fisher's paint didn't match the rest of ours. The line across her eyes was blood-red in color, which made her eyes look even darker than usual, and she had thin black lines running horizontally across her high cheekbones and nose. She must have sensed my curiosity because she smirked at me and said, "Red symbolizes strength. It tends to scare."

"Why would we want to scare? Don't we want to actually catch something?" I asked.

She laughed, but whether it was genuine or not was beyond me. Fisher was still impossible to read. She was definitely much nicer than the first time I'd met her, but she was still cold and unemotional.

"That's why we don't all wear red," she said, matter-of-factly.

"She likes to ask a lot of questions," Rocket said, glancing back at Fisher.

"Ain't nothing wrong with asking questions," Flander said, stepping in to watch Rocket's last few thumb strokes. "It's how you learn."

Although Flander's paint looked like everyone else's, it was much messier and more uneven. Had she attempted to do it herself?

"Enough chitchat," Trim said, appearing beside Fisher. "Let's move."

To my surprise, her face paint was unlike the others. There was no black line across her face, but instead, bright red smeared across both cheeks. It almost looked as though she'd just slaughtered a pig only to have its blood splatter across her face. I remembered seeing this pattern on Murk's face when I first met her. Having already been scolded for asking too many questions, I kept my mouth shut and held on to the assumption that this pattern and color represented leadership.

I fastened my quiver around my back and swung my bow over my shoulder. Trim led us out of the Working Grounds and into the thick of the jungle. But we didn't follow our usual course—we traveled alongside the Grounds and through the forest's edge where Battlewomen were training in the sand.

Although I feared for my life every time we set foot in the jungle, it was far more exciting than practicing target shooting for hours on end. My hands were now calloused and the skin of my inner forearms was scarred due to my bowstring.

"Where are we going?" I asked, walking alongside Trim.

"Quiet," she ordered.

I had a hard time separating friendship from hierarchy when it came to Trim. Although I'd grown comfortable around her, I sometimes felt as though she viewed me as nothing more than a pawn—a tool to be used only when required. Was friendship on Kormace Island even achievable? How could anyone care for another if we were all so self-involved? The only thing that mattered was survival—self-preservation.

But then I thought of Ellie, of Rocket, of Flander, and of everyone else. Although I'd only known them for a few months, I felt as though we were all in this together, almost as a family. I cared about them. Surely, friendship *was* possible.

"We don't go this way too often," Flander whispered.

I glanced back, hoping that maybe someone else might fill me in on where we were headed, but all I received were raised eyebrows and shrugged shoulders. We made our way up a slanted path, and I realized we were climbing the side of the Working Grounds' waterfall. I'd never given much thought to what lay beyond the waterfall or above it, for that matter. All I'd ever been able to see beyond our home base was the silhouette of a mountain hiding under countless layers of green, brown, gray, and yellow.

The sound of the water became faint behind us as we ventured away from the Grounds. I wondered if I'd finally see the waterfall's source. Was there a lake above it? Was it even safe? How did Trim know she wasn't leading us directly into Ogre territory?

I remembered Sunny—one of the first women I'd met when I arrived on Kormace Island. What I remembered most, aside from her rotten teeth, were her flower-like yellow eyes, which were unlike anything I'd seen before. But the last time I'd seen those eyes, there was barely any color left to them. They'd darkened to a cloudy brown behind swollen eyelids; her body just hung there naked and beaten over some sort of ceremonial circle.

And then I remembered her abduction. Through blurry vision, I watched as she was dragged away by a masked figure into a blended green sea of shrubs and trees. How many more Ogres were there on Kormace? Was it just the one? Were there several?

I shook these thoughts away when we finally reached a dead end—a wall made of natural rock.

"Fisher." Trim knelt on one knee and with both hands, formed a flat surface to use as a stepping platform.

It was evident by how swiftly Fisher bounced upward from Trim's hands that they'd done this before. She caught the ledge of the wall and dangled by both hands before pulling herself up. Her back muscles bulged and her legs kicked at the wall, yet she made it look so easy.

"Ready," Fisher said, staring down at the rest of us.

"Flander, you're next," Trim said.

Flander stepped into Trim's hand and jumped. Trim's thick arms swelled as she propelled her into the air. It was almost like watching a circus act. Flander caught the ledge with her fingertips, and Fisher reached down to pull her up.

Biggie then stepped forward. Rocket faced

205

Trim, and together, they threw Biggie upward. It didn't make sense to me how they'd even managed to throw her up, even if the others were waiting at the top of the wall to help her climb. She was a big girl, and stealth was not her forte.

I was next, then Rocket, and lastly, Trim, who stepped back to catch a running start. Fisher reached out a hand to pull her up, but Trim ignored her and climbed up on her own as if she'd done it a hundred times before.

"This way," she ordered.

This part of the jungle didn't look any different from any other part we'd traveled through before. It was nothing more than thick greenery, a multitude of vivid-colored plants, and dried-up mud.

"It's getting worse," Rocket said, sliding her fingertips alongside the ragged edge of a yellowing leaf.

Flander sighed. "It'll rain soon, kid."

I hadn't given much thought to rain since landing on Kormace. It had drizzled a few times when I'd been lying in my tent listening to the raindrops splatter atop the roof's stretched leather, but that had been the extent of it. I hadn't even realized that the leaves were starting to die or that animals were scarce. Was this what they called dry season? Was there even supposed to be dry season here on Kormace?

I quickly glanced up at the sound of something unusual—it was an inconsistent combination of crow-like cries and high-pitched squawks. Its source wasn't hard to spot with its oversized orange beak and beautiful tuxedo-colored feathers. I'd seen a toucan only one other time when my mother took me to a tropical-themed traveling show that so happened to stop in our city. But to see that type of bird up close without any barriers at all was absolutely breathtaking.

Although in awe, I felt like it was laughing at us, amused by the idea that human beings were stupid enough to venture out this far into the jungle.

"Craw, craw," it went on, throwing its massive beak into the air and peering down at us from behind small black and blue eyes.

"That right there's Molly." Trim pointed her chin toward the toucan.

It had a name?

"Used to see her all the time here," Trim said. "She's missing part of her foot. That's how I know it's her."

Sure enough, part of its blue talon, or one of its toes, was missing.

"This is Trim's old home," Flander said, leaning in toward me. It was hard to look at her without laughing. Her makeup, or face paint, had been sloppy to begin with, but due to the jungle's heat, it had already begun leaking down both sides of her cheeks.

"What do you mean? Before you joined the Village?" I asked, looking at Trim.

She nodded.

"Craw, craw, carooo," we heard behind us as we continued on ahead.

We stepped out into a vast opening—a field, almost—that led to the side of a mountain. The field was yellow with dying plants and tall, dried-up grass, and the path toward the side of the mountain was filled with gray bark trees and fallen boulders.

At the end of this path, something peculiar caught my eye... something man-made. There were mold-encrusted pieces of wood fastened at the high top of a tree forming a platform and uneven walls. I couldn't understand how anyone had climbed so high to build a fort. Wrapped around one of the upper branches was a rope or intertwined vines, dangling all the way down the tree's massive trunk and twirled up like a snake on the ground.

"Home, sweet h—" Trim said, but her eyes narrowed on something and she suddenly stopped moving.

CHAPTER 5

We tiptoed behind Trim as she ran toward the wooden fort. It was clear by the way she moved, as if on a hunt, that someone was lurking nearby. Her old home was now inhabited.

She didn't say a word—just told us to remain quiet and to follow closely. When we reached the bottom of the tree, we pressed our backs against the trunk and waited for further commands.

"No one's home," Trim said.

"How do you know?" Fisher whispered.

Trim stepped out and wrapped her fingers around the fort's rope. "Whoever lives here needs to be able to climb back up."

"Couldn't 'ave gone very far," Flander said, peering out into the mountain's forest. "Ain't too smart to leave your door open like this."

"Flander's right," Biggie said, "we should probably—"

The sound of something cracking echoed nearby and birds flew into the air. Everyone's eyes shifted toward the sound, and I instinctively reached for my bow and arrow.

Fisher was hunched forward with a white blade in one hand and a sharp stone in the other. Everyone moved in like a group of wolves on the verge of feeding after weeks of starvation.

But the sound that followed next was not one we could have anticipated.

"Please don't hurt me."

The voice was soft and childlike. I nearly lowered my bow but stopped myself when I noticed everyone else maintained their aggressive stance.

"Show yourself," Trim ordered.

The sound of rustling leaves and breaking tree branches erupted nearby, and something small came stepping out from behind a tree. It was a young girl. She held both hands up by her face as if to say, 'I surrender.'

I exchanged a confused look with Rocket, who appeared to be mulling over the same thought as me: what was a minor doing on Kormace Island? This girl was nowhere near the age of eighteen, the minimum age restriction for convict banishment.

She was wearing something that almost looked like an oversized green bikini made of dry seaweed. Her face was covered in dirt, either intentionally or due to lack of hygiene. She had bright red hair that fell at shoulder's length and matching freckles across the bridge of her nose and cheeks.

Rocket was the first to step forward, which seemed to frighten the girl because she quickly stepped back and jumped behind the protruding root of a tree, prepared to make a run for it. I knew that trying to outrun Rocket was a silly idea, but I didn't blame the kid for being afraid.

"It's okay," Rocket said softly. She knelt on one knee and playfully tilted her head. "What's your name?"

"Sandy... Sandy Macintosh," the little girl said.

"Sandy," Rocket repeated. "I'm Rocket." She pressed a hand against her chest and smiled. "That right there is Trim." She pointed at Trim, who was standing farther back with the rest of us, and pointed at each of us individually. "That's Fisher, that's Brone, that's Biggie, and that's Flander."

Sandy nodded but didn't speak.

"If you could be anyone, Sandy, who would it be?"

Sandy's leaf-colored eyes stretched open big as if in disbelief that it was even acceptable to dream of being someone else. "Anyone?"

Rocket smiled. "Anyone."

"I'd be Elektra!" She jumped out from behind the tree and began kicking her legs up into the air and throwing tight fists at invisible enemies.

Rocket laughed. "The superhero?"

But Sandy didn't hear her. She made fighting noises while stabbing enemies with her imaginary sword.

"Sandy?" Rocket said.

The young girl dropped her weapons and stared at Rocket.

"How would you like us to call you Elektra from

now on?" Rocket asked.

Sandy grinned from ear to ear and puffed her chest out. It was apparent that the name change alone made her feel like the actual superhero.

"Elektra, can we chat for a few minutes? Would that be okay?" Rocket asked.

I'd never imagined Rocket as the motherly type—nurturing and patient. She'd always been so playful and impulsive. In my eyes, she was just a kid herself, even though she was probably in her late twenties or early thirties.

Elektra nodded and moved in slowly. There were scabbed cuts across her arms and legs, and her hair was matted everywhere. How had this young girl survived all by herself in the jungle?

"How old are you, Elektra?" Rocket asked.

Elektra shot a shy glance at the rest of us, before focusing her attention on Rocket and whispering, "Nine."

There was a heavy silence, but Rocket forced a smile. "Wow, nine. You're a big girl."

Elektra's pale chapped lips curved into a smile.

"How long have you been out here?" Rocket dropped into a seated position with both legs crossed out in front of her.

Elektra mimicked her and sat on the ground beside a bush of purple-colored flowers.

"I don't know," she said. "A while."

"A few nights, you think?" Rocket asked.

"Lots of nights. I stopped counting."

"When did you stop counting?" Rocket asked. "At how many nights?"

Elektra played with her fingers and bit into her lip. "Two hundred and four," she said. "That was my foster parents' address before they got rid of me. I didn't wanna lose the number in my head, so I stopped there."

Rocket quickly shot a glance at Trim. "And how did you get here, Elektra?"

Elektra pointed up at the sky. "Helicopter."

I felt my stomach sink. How could they have dropped a nine-year-old onto Kormace Island? She was just a kid, and Kormace was a death sentence.

Biggie stepped forward. "We can't just leave her here."

"Whoa..." Elektra said, tilting her head back to see Biggie. "You're big."

Biggie grinned, revealing pearly white teeth. Given that there was no toothpaste on the island, it was a mystery how she'd maintained such a nice smile. The majority of teeth I'd seen on Kormace were either yellow and brown, coated with plaque, chipped, or missing entirely.

I licked the front of my teeth, suddenly feeling repulsed by my own dental hygiene. I'd learned to scratch at the plaque build-up with my fingernails and to chew the occasional peppermint leaf for freshness, but it wasn't enough. I'd heard a few women talk about turmeric as an all-natural decalcifying ingredient; it was cultivated in the Working Grounds, but I never got around to buying some. I was too busy trying to survive.

"S'why they call me Biggie." Biggie pressed her

chubby hand over her chest.

Elektra giggled and stretched her lips into a buck-tooth smile. But without warning, her brows came together and she began frantically pounding her fists against the soil beneath her.

"Elektra?" Rocket asked.

There was no getting through to her. Elektra grimaced, her eyes fixed on the ground. She continued pounding, her face darkening a deeper shade of red with every swing she took. She released short, growl-like sounds, but nothing more.

"Elektra?" Rocket asked again.

"What's wrong with her?" Fisher asked.

Trim stepped forward, but it was apparent that dealing with children was not her strong suit. "I don't know... Is she having a tantrum?"

"That ain't no tantrum," Flander said. "Girl's clearly got issues, and I reckon that's why she's 'ere in the first place."

Rocket quickly stood with both fists clenched and faced Flander. "That's not good enough. Why would they drop her off here because she's got a few problems? It's called medical care. It's called medicine!"

"How should I know?" Flander said. "I ain't the government. Maybe she did somethin' real bad. Maybe..."

Rocket threw an open hand in my direction. "Doesn't matter what she did! Eighteen is the youngest they're supposed to drop!"

"Rocket's right," Fisher interjected. "Law says

minors don't get dropped on the island."

Biggie scoffed. "Law also states they come back to pick us up after our sentence. Ain't nobody comin' back for us."

Trim stepped inside the circle we'd created. "No one's right or wrong here. The law *does* state that minors aren't being subjected to banishment, but it also wouldn't be the first time the government lies about something."

Rocket's bright eyes bulged from their sockets. "This doesn't make any sense!"

"Rocket!" Fisher growled, but the sound of laughter interrupted her.

Elektra was back on her feet, twirling in all directions with her hands above her head as if preparing for a ballet competition.

"We can't leave her here..." Rocket said.

Fisher crossed her arms and cocked an eyebrow. "You gonna be the one to babysit?"

"Enough," Trim ordered. "It isn't up to us— it's up to Murk."

"Only if Murk has a choice to make in the first place," Fisher said.

Trim bit her lip and scrunched her nose, contemplating Fisher's words. After all, what did we even know about this kid? Was she worth the risk? The old me felt guilty for even toying with the idea of leaving her behind, but the new me—the one who lived only to survive—realized that this young girl could potentially pose a threat, not only to us as individuals, but also, to the entire Village as a whole. She was too young to understand the

215

importance of regulations, and from what I could gather, too unstable to follow them even if she did understand them.

And what would she do, anyways? Cultivate? Sew clothing together? She certainly wouldn't be a Battlewoman, regardless of her passion for fighting.

"Pull out an arrow, Brone," Rocket said, but her gaze was fixed on Trim.

Was this some sort of joke? I stared at Trim, but she offered no guidance.

"Go on," Rocket said, "and aim for her heart because leaving her here is the same thing as killi—"

"Enough," Trim said. She turned away and began marching into the open field. "This isn't my decision," she said, her voice fading. "It's Murk's."

"You heard the boss," Rocket said, glaring at Fisher. "Girl comes with us."

She turned to face Elektra, who'd stopped moving altogether. She was gazing out into the field, watching Trim cut through tall grass with her blade.

"She's brave," Elektra said, her eyes round as if she'd seen a ghost.

"Who is, sweetheart?" Rocket asked.

Elektra pointed toward Trim. "That's where Shere Khan always hides."

"Shere Khan? As in, from *The Jungle Book*?" I asked, stepping forward.

She nodded.

"Ain't that the tiger—" Flander started.

"Trim!" Fisher said in a panic.

I whipped out an arrow and bolted toward the field by Fisher's side. The others quickly followed, except for Rocket, who wrapped her arms around Elektra to comfort her.

I wanted to shout Trim's name—warn her to get out of the field, but I knew that shouting would only capture the tiger's attention if it was anywhere nearby.

Trim continued to aggressively swing her blade from side to side, dicing bits of dead grass into hundreds of pieces. My eyes shifted in every direction and my heart raced as if I were actually being chased myself.

"Trim!" Fisher hissed as we moved in closer.

The sound of Trim's blade must have masked Fisher's call because she continued deeper into the field. It wasn't like Trim to walk away from her people—to take off in such a selfish manner. Not only was it dangerous, it was completely foolish. She needed her Hunters, just as her Hunters needed their leader.

"Trim!" Fisher tried again.

Trim stood straight and glanced back, her cheeks a bright red and her forehead glistening with sweat.

"Took you long enough," she said, but her cocky smile quickly warped into a frown when she saw Fisher's frantic hand signals.

I didn't speak sign language or understand her coded gestures, but the distressed look on her face and the way her hands aggressively tore through the air made it apparent that the gist of her message was *danger*.

Trim dropped into a crouched position with her blade up in one hand and a handful of grass in the other. Everyone followed suit, bearing their weapons and repositioning themselves in a strategic manner.

Biggie backed into all of us with both arms out and away from her body as if her size alone were her weapon. Flander pulled two sharp pointed pieces of bone from her waist holster and held them at eye level.

I held my arrow against the elastic of my bow, even though I knew that an arrow would prove completely useless in the event of a blind attack—especially one led by several hundred pounds of pure muscle.

We waited, listening to the sounds of the wind slipping through the meadow, birds crying overhead, and Flander grinding her teeth from side to side—something I'd notice her do during our hunts.

The silence was torturous. I knew that at any moment, one of us could be dragged into the field by jaws so powerful they could take off an entire leg. And then I thought of the woman who'd been attacked by a panther and lost her leg. I remembered her screams and the way she'd frantically thrown her arms into the air while being dragged to the Hospital because the pain was so excruciating.

I shook these thoughts away. I couldn't allow

fear to cripple me.

We pressed our backs together, forming a defensive stance, and stood there for what felt like hours, anticipating a gruesome attack.

CHAPTER 6

"Golly, you're lucky you weren't eaten alive!" Elektra said, whipping a piece of broken branch from side to side.

I glared at her, feeling like she was a source of impending chaos. Nothing good would come of having a child live among wild women. Not only was she useless, she was a complete pain in the ass.

We stepped out from the field, untouched and unharmed. Was Shere Khan even real? Had Elektra just made it up for a good laugh? Don't get me wrong—I was relieved we'd made it out of the field, but at the same time, I wondered if our panic had all been for nothing. I wasn't sure what bothered me most: knowing that Elektra would be coming back with us or the thought of being mauled by a wildcat.

"Let's go. And stay close," Rocket said, glancing at Elektra.

But Elektra didn't budge. She simply stood there, holding on to two broken branches at her sides.

"Elektra?" Rocket asked.

"Where are you going?" Elektra asked.

Rocket smirked. "Home. And you're coming with us."

Without warning, Elektra threw both branches to the ground and released a high-pitched squeal. She turned around, ran to the tree fort, and lunged at the dangling vine. From a distance, had I not known Elektra was a child, I'd have assumed she was a monkey. With both feet pressed against the massive trunk, she pulled herself upward by quickly alternating her grip on the vine one hand at a time.

I'd never seen a kid climb anything so fast in my life.

Fisher scoffed. "Way to go, genius. Did you honestly think she'd leave just like that? Kid's been living here for God knows how long. Might just be a tree fort to you, but this is *her* home."

"Do you have a better idea?" Rocket asked. "If you're so smart, why don't you fix this?"

Fisher threw her hands in the air. "I don't want the kid coming with us at all. I sure as hell ain't helping any of you convince her otherwise."

"I don't care what you want!" Rocket said. "You heard Trim! It's Murk's de—"

But a deep, hoarse roar quieted them both instantly. I slowly turned toward the sound, my heart pounding so hard I thought it might stop.

It was just standing there, its fierce yellow eyes gazing into us as if trying to determine whether we were a threat, food, or both.

"Nobody move..." Trim said slowly. "And don't break eye contact."

We all stood stiff like statues.

It was hard to maintain eye contact with a beast of such intimidating size. It was bigger than any animal I'd ever seen: its head alone was the size of a Rottweiler, its massive body the size of a Harley Davidson. It had a white chest, a white ruff of fur around its thick neck, and its stripes were dark brown.

I flinched when the tiger pawed into the air and released another loud growl. Its jaw opened slightly, revealing large canine teeth, and I imagined how painful it would be if they were to sink into my muscles or crack through my bones. Months ago, my biggest fear was the thought of accidentally touching a spider hidden underneath the handles of my recycling bin, and today, I was in a standoff with a real-life tiger.

It stepped forward and released another powerful roar. Although all I wanted to do was back up or run up into the tree, I'd been instructed to stand still. Surely, Trim knew what she was doing... I hoped.

Had she ever encountered a tiger before? My eyes shifted from the cat to Trim, who stood still, her fists clenched and shoulders drawn back as if to portray a false image of confidence, of fearlessness and strength.

I mimicked her stance, even though I was the exact opposite of fearless. The animal stepped closer again and growled, only this time, it swung its paw out at us with its claws extracted.

I instinctively jumped back, regretting it immediately. The tiger threw its head sideways and stretched its jaw wide open, roaring so loud I felt the sound's vibration run through the tips of my fingers.

I'd been about to reach for my bow despite Trim's orders, thinking it was better to attempt a fight than be attacked, when I heard a bizarre sound come from the thick of the jungle. At first, I thought someone was under attack, but as it drew nearer, I realized that the shrieking and growling were completely intentional.

It was coming from a woman swinging from a vine—something you'd only expect to see in the movie *Tarzan*—covered in greenery and hidden behind a tiger mask constructed of black, orange, and white feathers. She threw both arms out on either side of her and released the most demonic of noises—growling, hissing, screeching, and grunting. Underneath her arms hung more feathers and loose pieces of animal skin, giving her a larger and more daunting appearance.

She lunged toward the tiger, flailing her arms above her head and barking cacophonous nonsense. Surely this masked woman had done this before, because to everyone's surprise, the tiger bolted back into the field.

I caught a glimpse of the woman's black eyes behind the mask where two holes had been cut out. She stared at me for a moment, before swinging around and sprinting back into the jungle. I watched as the feathers on her back bounced up and down and as the colors of her gear blended with the surrounding trees.

My legs trembled and my back was drenched in sweat. This woman had saved our lives.

"What the hell was that?" Fisher gasped to catch her breath.

"Do you really care?" Rocket asked. "Whatever it was, it just saved our lives."

"Well, I think we should care," I said, and everyone's eyes turned to me. It wasn't in my nature to speak up or voice my opinion, so when I did, everyone listened.

"What'ya sayin', Brone?" Flander asked.

I stepped forward. "Well, all I'm trying to say is... How well do you guys know Kormace? I mean, you hunt around the Village and the Working Grounds, for the most part. Have you ever gone farther out? Shouldn't we know what's around us? What we're up against?"

"Brone's right," Fisher said, stepping forward as if prepared to battle anyone who challenged her. "We don't know anything beyond our comfort zone."

"Having a comfort zone keeps us safe," Trim said.

"Safe, maybe. But for how long?" Fisher said. "I mean, look at what just happened. Who's to say there aren't more women like her? Who's to say the other ones won't kill us instead of spare us? What was she, anyway? She didn't look like an Ogre

225

to me."

"That wasn't no Ogre," Biggie said.

I gawked at Biggie.

Trim shook her head. "Biggie's right. That was a Rogue."

"A Rogue?" I asked.

"Yeah, something I used to be," Trim said. "No rules, no civilization, no law. It was nice for a while"—she stared up at the tree fort and grimaced—"but you can't survive on your own in the wild. You can't survive away from civilization, away from other human beings. Isolation makes you feral—it makes you begin to think and act like an animal."

Biggie laughed, her deep voice resonating against the forest trees. "'Cause we ain't all already like that, right?"

But Trim didn't smile. Instead, she gave Biggie a solemn look and said, "You'll never understand it until you've lived it."

I glanced up at Elektra who was lying flat on her stomach, watching us with her chin pressed in the palms of her hands. This little girl would die if we didn't take her to Murk. I didn't want to be an animal. I didn't want to be completely feral, some heartless animal who lives only to survive.

"No child should have to go through that," I said.

Rocket cocked an eyebrow, almost as if stunned by my newly found boldness. "Exactly," she agreed.

"Call her down," Trim ordered. "We're taking

her to Murk."

CHAPTER 7

"She's just a kid."

"Look at that little thing."

"My God, she shouldn't be here."

There were hundreds of eyes as round as golf balls on Elektra as we entered the Working Grounds. Everyone circled around her, so much so that Trim had to order them to back off.

I noticed Elektra reach for Rocket's hand and Rocket wrap her arms around her.

"Where'd you find her?"

"She staying here?"

There were so many voices surrounding us that I worried Elektra might have another episode, being that her earlier fit was likely triggered by stress. The last thing we needed was for everyone to witness her instability and to want to cast her back into the wild.

"Hi there, sweet child."

"Look at the face," one woman said, and she reached to squeeze Elektra's cheek.

Elektra shouted and pulled away, digging her

face into Rocket's side.

"Enough!" Trim shouted, but the women didn't listen.

There were too many of them—blurred faces twirling around us in every direction. It was as if the presence of a child had caused them to forget the meaning of hierarchy, of law.

"Come 'ere, kid," Biggie said. She quickly reached down and grabbed Elektra underneath the arms, then pulled her up over her shoulders and out of everyone's reach.

"Wow!" Elektra said, gazing out toward the waterfall. She tapped Biggie on the head several times and giggled.

It helped, but it wasn't enough. There were women reaching up by Biggie's face just to touch Elektra's feet. They were acting like a bunch of animals.

Fisher quickly pulled a blade out from her leg holster and pointed it at everyone circling Biggie. "Get back to your fucking jobs before I slit your throats. You know better than to disobey Trim when she gives an order."

Some women scattered as if they'd only just realized we were the Hunters, but a few others backed off only far enough to evade Fisher's blade, all the while remaining in a circle.

"What's the meaning of this?"

I would have recognized that authoritative voice anywhere—even if distorted by the jumbled sounds emerging from the Working Grounds.

Murk stood at the edge of the waterfall,

droplets of water glistening on her shoulders and face, her silver hair wet and messily combed to one side.

Everyone dispersed, returning to their posts to attend to their daily chores. Trim stepped forward and knelt on one knee.

"Chief," she said.

"Get up," Murk ordered. "Bring the girl inside." She disappeared into the waterfall.

As Trim led us into the waterfall through a narrow path along sharp, uneven rocks, Elektra burst out laughing. She'd managed to stretch her arm far enough to reach some of the falling water, which forced her hand down hard against Biggie's shoulder.

She did this as many times as possible before we were out of reach from the water. To my surprise, Biggie glanced up and grinned. I couldn't help but smile, too—it had been so long since I'd heard someone laugh this hard over something so minute. It was nice to be reminded that despite living like animals, we were still human beings, and by nature, we all had a sense of humor. I wondered if mine would ever return.

"So dark in here," Elektra said as we moved through the damp cave. The scent was familiar—it smelled of cool water with a hint of mildew or mold. Although the thought of mold repulsed me, there was something refreshing about walking through the cave. Maybe I enjoyed it so much because it was peaceful, not because of its scent, but because I'd somehow associated it with a feeling of tranquility. Water droplets fell from the cave's ceiling, the only thing I could hear aside from our footsteps. The wet stone around us looked black, and farther down a faint light was cast across the floor and up against the wall. I knew we were approaching Murk's quarters—I'd only visited twice, but both times, her space had been filled with countless torches, their flames dancing from side to side, filling the room with an orange hue.

"Wow," Elektra said as we reached the end of the cave.

Murk sat on the ground at the far end of the room, facing away from us and toward the back wall. A string of white smoke climbed into the air beside her, forming uneven loops and circles. Sketched in white across the wall was an unusual design; it appeared to be a gazelle or a deer jumping upward and away from a flock of poorly drawn birds. Murk just sat there, staring at the artwork, and I questioned if she'd been the one to draw it. I also wondered if it signified anything.

Trim cleared her throat. "Chief."

"Astonishing, isn't it?" Murk said. Her back was as straight as a piece of plywood—the stiffest posture I'd ever seen.

"Looks great." Trim glanced at us sideways.

I'd always noticed a certain eccentricity in Murk. She spoke as if everything meant something—as if every action and every word signified something so great that it could not be comprehended by the average human mind. I didn't know whether to feel stupid or whether the Village was being ruled by a lunatic. Pride aside, I preferred the former; my lack of knowledge did not affect the Village as a whole, but Murk's lack of sanity, did.

"Do you see it?" Murk asked.

Trim stepped forward. "See what, Chief?"

It was apparent she was accustomed to dealing with Murk's bizarre moods. I stared at the smoke that drifted into the air, wondering exactly what it was she was smoking.

"Freedom," Murk said, tilting her head back as she analyzed the artwork. "Fear."

She stood quickly and clasped both hands together. "Birds are symbolic of freedom." She pointed at the white lines shaped into birds on the cave's stone wall. "The gazelle represents awareness and speed." She moved closer to the drawing and gently pressed the tips of her fingers against the chalk. "The truth is, there's no such thing as freedom," she said coldly.

Trim cleared her throat, and Murk looked back. "Who's this?" she asked, eyeing Elektra.

Elektra squeezed her arms around Biggie's head.

"She was dropped on the island, Chief," Trim said.

Murk stepped away from the wall and toward Elektra. "A child... on Kormace Island..." She rubbed her chin. "How is that even possible?"

Trim shook her head. "We have no idea, Chief. We're all confused."

Murk paced back and forth several times, glancing at Elektra every few steps.

"Will there still be an Assessment?" Trim asked.

Murk stopped moving. "No need."

I swallowed hard. Was she about to cast Elektra back into the wild? Although I'd originally thought it best to leave the kid behind, I'd come to realize she was still a human being—an innocent girl in need of help if she was going to survive Kormace. We couldn't just throw her back into the jungle to fend for herself.

"Chief?" Trim asked.

"Battlewoman," Murk said, before turning back toward the wall.

"Cooooool!" Elektra shouted.

"Battlewoman?" Rocket asked, but Trim nudged her in the ribs.

Murk glanced back, her eyes resembling those of a dog offering a courtesy warning before a bite. This wasn't the Murk I'd come to know. She had always seemed dominant and strong, but there had also always been a kindness in her, an unbreakable love for her people. In that moment, all I saw was coldness. I hoped she had a valid reason for assigning Elektra the task of Battlewoman—for putting a child in harm's way.

"Dismissed," Murk said.

I only hoped she knew what she was doing. The moment we left, Rocket began spewing her thoughts like an audio clip on fast-forward.

"Shut up!" Biggie hissed. Her eyes were huge, and she threw her head toward Murk's quarters as if to say, 'She can probably still hear you.'

Rocket sealed her lips, but the moment we exited the waterfall, she threw her arms into the air and went off again. "Battlewoman? What the—"

"Language," Flander said calmly.

Rocket eyed Elektra before exploding. "What is she thinking?" She drew in a noisy breath and exhaled sharply. "She's just a kid! She can't protect us. She shouldn't have to protect us."

We walked the same path I'd been led up when Trim had first announced my assigned task of Needlewoman. There was a sinking feeling in my stomach—not because of the memories brought on by this symbolic walk, but because I feared the women below us might start a riot upon hearing Elektra's assigned task. After all, some of these women were mothers or even grandmothers. They wouldn't sit by and allow a nine-year-old child to fight against exterior threats.

"I think what Murk did is smart," Fisher said nonchalantly.

"Smart?" Rocket scoffed. "Are you fuc—are you kidding me?"

"Think about it," Fisher said. "What better way to protect the kid than to train her to fight?"

"She's not old enough to fight!" Rocket said.

"Trim decides who fights," Fisher said. "It's not like all Battlewomen ever get to fight. Most of them are spares."

Spares, I thought. It sounded like a synonym for disposable.

"Yeah, until the Northers attack us full force.

Then she'll be expected to fight," Rocket said.

"Look, it's not like—" Fisher started, but Trim waved a hand to silence her as we approached the torch at the top of the cliff.

Just then, it dawned on me that all Hunters were present for the announcement. Traditionally, it was only Trim who announced the newcomer's task. Perhaps Trim was too distraught to even realize we'd followed her all the way up. Or, maybe she felt safer having us by her side, knowing that the women would not react well to her announcement.

She pulled the torch out of the dirt and into the air, before shouting, "Elektra, Battlewoman!"

There was an eerie silence—so much so, that for a moment, I thought perhaps I'd imagined the announcement. But then, all at once, an uproar shook the Grounds. Women shouted in rage, pointing accusing fingers at us Hunters as if we'd somehow had a part in this decision.

"Enough!" Trim shouted, but her voice couldn't be heard over the crowd of angry women.

I wondered how many of these women were mothers—how many had lost their children after being sentenced to this island. I watched as they threw their arms into the air, their teeth bared and their eyes round like a pack of hungry wolves. Although Trim held a position of authority, we were completely outnumbered. What was stopping them from turning on us? It wouldn't have been the first time that an entire society turned on their leaders.

236

"Silence!" Trim shouted again, but the outcry didn't stop.

"Shut up!" Fisher's muscles tensed—she hated it when anyone disobeyed Trim. I admired her loyalty.

I flinched at the sound of a loud crack against the wall behind me. A rock rolled by my feet, and then another, and I realized we were being stoned. How was this happening? Were they truly this upset over Murk's decision to train Elektra to be a Battlewoman?

"Shit!" Biggie quickly threw a hand over her right eye, where a thick line of blood slid through the crease of her fingers.

What I did next was not something I'd ever envisioned myself doing. I'd always followed Trim—always obeyed her orders and acted only when commanded. But in that moment, I knew that if action were not taken, we'd be severely injured, if not killed, over a riot fueled by intense emotion.

I quickly drew an arrow from my quiver and readied my bow toward the women standing below me. I aimed it at a young, native-looking girl who held a rock in her hand.

Silence returned almost instantly. We were the Hunters—their protectors and bringers of food. Who were they to turn on us? I clenched my jaw, prepared to release my arrow. Although I knew I'd proven my point, I craved the kill. I wasn't a murderer, but I'd also never felt so angry in my life. I wanted to prove myself—to prove to everyone that we, the Hunters, were not willing to accept any form of bullying.

One kill, I thought. Just one kill, and never again would anyone question authority.

I felt a gentle hand on my shoulder, but I was unable to release my stare. The woman dropped the rock and cowered backward, and I loved it. I loved the feeling of power, the feeling of utmost dominance over an entire group of people who'd just attempted to attack us—to betray their own.

"Brone."

I ignored my name. I stretched the elastic of my bow even farther, prepared to shoot the woman directly in the chest. I wouldn't miss. I was too focused.

"Brone!"

I'd been about to release the arrow when I heard Trim's voice.

"Stand down," she ordered.

Like a dog trained to obey basic commands, I immediately lowered my bow and stepped back, feeling as though I'd been shaken from a trance. My hands trembled, causing my bow to shake from side to side, and a familiar guilt sank into the pit of my stomach. How had I allowed myself to lose control again?

"For years," Trim shouted, "we've worked together as a society to survive. We've done this by assigning everyone jobs—by making sure that everyone's contributing to the society."

She glanced back at Elektra, who was hiding behind Biggie's leg, before continuing. "Elektra was assigned the task of Battlewoman by Murk. If any of you want to question that, you're questioning Murk. When has our leader ever led us wrong?" She paused for a moment, eyeing everyone beneath her. They stared up in silence, using their hands to block the afternoon sun from their eyes. "If you have faith in your leader, then have faith that Murk's decision was not blindly made."

I stared at Trim as she spoke, her chest heaving and her shoulders drawn back, and I wondered if she spoke of what she believed or of what she hoped was true. Did she actually think Murk's decision had been thoroughly thought out? I'd seen how quickly Murk had assigned Elektra the task of Battlewoman, and I began to question it myself.

"This isn't a dictatorship," Trim said coldly. "If you don't agree with something, you voice your opinion..." She angrily eyed everyone. "But this!" She threw a finger at Biggie's injured eye. "This is unacceptable! Not only have you attacked your leaders today—you bit the hand that feeds you! This is a complete betrayal of your own people."

"You," Trim shouted, pointing her finger at the young native girl I'd nearly killed and aiming her finger at a few others. "And you! You! And you!" Her voice grew hoarse. "Step forward!"

Four women stepped out of the crowd, forming a horizontal line ahead of everyone.

"On your knees," Trim ordered through clenched teeth.

They did as commanded and even went as far

239

as to bow their heads.

"You are hereby banished from the Village." Trim stared at them, her chin raised high.

They threw their heads back in a panic and jumped to their feet.

"No, please!" one of them shouted.

"Trim, we're begging you!" said another.

"We're sorry!"

"Enough!" Trim bellowed. "You know the rules. Get out."

One of the women burst into tears, but the oldest-looking of the bunch—a woman with bright red hair and piercing green eyes—glared up at Trim. I felt the animosity, the hatred.

"You'll be real sorry for this!" the woman shouted.

"Was that a fucking threat?" Fisher growled. She darted down the pathway we'd climbed, but Trim shouted her name and ordered her to stand down. I wasn't even sure Fisher heard the order.

The woman smirked up at Fisher, who was now reaching the ground. "And you," she said, "you'll be seeing your dead girlfriend real soon."

Fisher shot Trim a look at the top of the cliff, almost as if to apologize in advance for disobeying a direct order. She bolted through the sand like a lion about to catch its kill. Several women scattered at the sight of Fisher's charge, but the redhead stayed put, smirking so arrogantly I had to assume she didn't value her life.

This look, however, quickly turned upside down the moment she saw Fisher pull a blade from her holster. She didn't have time to dodge. Within seconds, Fisher lunged through the air and tackled the woman onto the sand.

There were shouts all around; some women encouraged the fight and some pleaded for it to end. But it wasn't a fight. It was a vicious attack. The red-haired woman didn't have a chance to defend herself. A circle of women formed around the scene, making it difficult for us to see what was going on.

"Come on," Trim said quickly, and we ran down after Fisher.

There was a loud shriek immediately followed by silence.

"Move!" Trim shouted, pushing through the women surrounding the fight.

But when we finally reached Fisher, it was too late. She stood up, her skin and clothing stained red. Her blade hung at her side, thick red blood slipping off its sharp point and onto the sand.

There was a deafening silence, and I feared now more than ever the women would revolt against us. But they didn't. In fact, several women fell back, and others avoided eye contact with us altogether.

Fisher stood there, her chest expanding with every rapid breath. Beside her, in the sand, was the still body of the woman who'd threatened Trim. Her face, which was pressed into the sand, was surrounded by a quickly forming pool of blood.

There was no doubt she was dead.

Fisher reached down and grabbed the dead

woman's hair at the back of her head, then pulled upward, revealing a thick gash at the base of her throat. The cut widened, splitting farther open and spewing dark blood in all directions.

"This may not be a dictatorship"—Fisher eyed everyone with ferocity—"but it sure as fuck ain't no democracy, either."

CHAPTER 8

I stared into the fire, reliving the moment over and over again so vividly I could have sworn I saw it come to life in the flames. I remembered the shriek and knowing at that moment someone had died. How had this happened? Why were people dying so pointlessly? We were barely surviving on Kormace Island as it was. Why not band together?

But then I remembered that as human beings, personalities, beliefs, and values varied so drastically from one person to the next that the ideology of large populations coexisting without conflict was inconceivable.

I recalled back in high school—one of the worst times of my life—when I watched cliques argue over insignificant drama. Back then I thought surely, once we reached adulthood, maturity would set in. But as I sat by that fire, aware of my surroundings—among women of all different ages, races, and religious beliefs—I realized we were nothing more than educated animals.

The Hunters had unintentionally gained

control around the fire. Women spread out across the Village, sitting in the dirt or on patches of colorless grass as far away from us as possible. Even Sumi and her cooking crew joined the others after having served everyone supper.

I didn't blame them. The moment Fisher slit that woman's throat was the moment she unwillingly declared an unofficial separation between the women of the Village and the Hunters. We were dangerous in their eyes. I hoped the fear would maintain control rather than persuade rebels to take a stand against us.

Bickering instantly erupted around us, and I noticed everyone's eyes turned toward the Village's entrance. I followed their eyes, only to find Fisher walking toward us. She sat down heavily beside Flander without a word.

"So?" Flander asked, breaking the silence. "You banished, or what?"

Fisher shook her head. "It ain't turning on your own if the other woman ain't even part of the society anymore."

"What's that supposed to mean?" Rocket asked, poking her utensil at the piece of fish in her bowl.

"It means the woman she killed wasn't one of us," Trim said. "I'd already officially banished her."

"Must be nice," Rocket scoffed. "Kill someone and just get away with it."

"Nice?" Fisher said. "The hell is wrong with you? You think I'm happy about what I did?"

"All right, enough." Trim waved a hand.

"What'd Sumi make today?" Fisher asked,

eyeing our bowls.

"Fish," I said, scooping cold fish into my mouth.

There wasn't much of it, but I wasn't in any position to complain. It was food, and if there was one thing I was thankful for on this island, it was the food. Despite our limited resources and food supply, Sumi always managed to cook up tasty dishes, even if they were cold by the time we got around to eating.

"I don't like fish," Elektra said, poking at her supper.

Biggie burst out laughing. "Girl, you'd better start liking fish if you wanna survive this place. Ain't nobody gonna serve you mac n' cheese or French fries."

"French fries..." Rocket said dreamily.

"Macaroni..." Flander said. "I always did make the best mac n' cheese on the block."

Fisher laughed. "How would you know? D'you go around knocking on everyone's door? Challenging them to a competition?"

"I just know." Flander stiffened up. "I put half a brick 'o cheese in mine and a secret ingredient."

"Jesus," Rocket said, "I hope the secret ingredient was laxative."

"Is this seat taken?"

I glanced up and met her mocha-colored eyes. I recognized that face and that hair—blonde tips and dark roots. She smiled at me and at the empty space between Fisher and me.

"Holland," she said. "You guys found me—"

"We know who you are," Fisher said. "What do

you want?"

Holland's smile faded, and she stepped back.

"Fisher!" Rocket hissed. "Don't be such a cunt."

"She killed someone t'day," Flander said, staring at Holland and throwing Fisher a look. "Ain't in the best of moods."

"Flander!" Rocket said.

"What?" Flander shrugged. "Everyone saw it. And for those who didn't, well, they know 'bout it by now. So much goddamn gossip 'round here."

"It's okay," Holland said. "I was there. I heard the threats she made. You made the right decision."

I stared at her. The right decision? It hadn't been a decision. It had been an impulsive act based on anger and hatred. Fisher hadn't *decided* to kill the woman the way people decide to put down animals who pose a threat to human beings.

Who was this Holland, anyways? I noticed Trim eyeing her curiously, just as she'd done the first time we'd found her in the jungle.

"You related to the Bishops at all?" Trim finally asked. "South Dakota?"

Holland shifted her eyes to one side, confused by Trim's question. "Sorry, I'm not sure—"

"Never mind," Trim said quickly.

And there it was—the reason for Trim's special treatment toward Holland. I'd been given a blow to the head when the Hunters had first found me, and Holland had been given immediate attention. How was that fair? This was proof that even the strongest leaders' judgment could be clouded by emotion or personal beliefs.

"Have a seat," Fisher said, eyeing the log across from us.

I glanced up across the fire, where an entire log—usually crowded by a group of Mexican women—was completely vacant. Holland sat down at the edge closest to us. Elektra jumped up to her feet and extended a straight arm out in front of Holland.

"I'm Elektra," she said happily.

Holland grinned and shook her hand. "Got a strong grip on you. I'm Holland."

"I'm a Fighter." Elektra sliced through the air with open palms.

"A Battlewoman," Flander corrected her through a mouthful of fish.

"She isn't exactly a woman," Rocket said. "Let the kid be whatever she wants to be."

Fisher scoffed. "And who's gonna train the kid to fight, huh? And be responsible when she gets killed?"

"I am," I heard.

Everyone turned around to find Eagle standing behind us. To my surprise, she stood without a crutch and without Ellie by her side to help her maneuver.

"Eag!" Rocket jumped up and threw her arms around Eagle's neck.

"Easy," Eagle said, a crooked smile on her face, "still healing."

"Man, where've you been?" Rocket asked.

Eagle shrugged. "Night shift. You know how it

is."

She limped over the log and sat down beside Trim. It was evident she'd been isolated from daytime civilization for quite some time. Her skin had lightened to a beige, and her short scraggly hair had grown several inches and hung just below her eyebrows.

"I'm Elektra." Elektra stood in front of Eagle with that same stiff arm.

Eagle smiled—something I didn't see often—and shook her hand. "Eagle."

"Eagle!" Elektra shouted. "Like the bird?"

"Like the bird." Eagle looked at her steadily. "I hear you're pretty strong. I can make you even stronger if you're up for a challenge."

"I sure am!" Elektra shouted.

"Good. We start at sunrise," Eagle said matter-of-factly.

"Ain't you workin' the graveyard shift?" Biggie asked.

Eagle's lips curved at one side. "Not anymore. Now that I'm off the crutch, Murk assigned me to train the Battlewomen."

Although I already knew Eagle wasn't my biggest fan, I resented the idea of other women being trained by the best of the best when I'd received mediocre training through some measly words of advice and hours of strenuous practice. I'd been taught to shoot an arrow—but only well enough to hit my target. Eagle was far more skilled than I was even with her injuries, and although she rubbed me the wrong way, I hoped one day she'd be willing to teach me everything she knew.

"Looks like you guys are popular today." Eagle eyed the crowd of women surrounding us at a distance.

"Fisher's fault." Flander pointed a thumb in her direction.

"To be fair, Fisher did defend her honor—and all of yours," Holland said.

Everyone stared at her.

"Who's this?" Eagle asked.

My thoughts exactly.

"That's Holland," Trim said. "One of our Battlewomen."

Eagle nodded slowly but didn't say anything.

"So why you here, anyways?" Fisher asked, nudging Holland.

"I told you, I think what you did—"

"No," Fisher said, "what'd you do? Why you on the island?"

"Oh," Holland said. "Um... isn't that kind of private?"

"Ain't no privacy here," Biggie said, her eyeballs round and wide. "Who'd you kill?"

"Guys," Trim said, glancing sideways at Elektra, and everyone went quiet.

How long was this supposed to last? How long was this kid going to follow us around? I felt like we'd been assigned the task of Babysitter. It was humiliating. We were supposed to be Hunters—and yet, here we were, mincing words to avoid tarnishing some kid's innocence, even though her very presence on Kormace Island proved she was the complete opposite of innocent.

What had she done to end up here, anyway? Kill her parents? Why wasn't anyone questioning her about her background? She clearly had mental problems.

"So what's this girl talking about, anyways?" Eagle asked. "What'd you do to defend your honor?"

"She made someone fall asleep"—Elektra proudly crossed both arms over her chest—"because the lady was rude."

Eagle smirked.

"Yeah, asleep." Biggie slid her thumbnail across her throat.

Eagle nodded. "Gotcha. And where's the woman sleeping now?"

"Biggie and I took care of it," Trim said. "Let's just say she'll be making friends with lions and tigers and bears."

"Oh my!" Elektra shouted, before bursting out into a fit of laughter.

I hadn't found the reference funny. Her face darkened, and small veins bulged out on her temples as she laughed. But the laughter gradually turned into sobbing, and she fell to the ground with both hands over her eyes.

Fisher rolled her eyes. "Here we go."

"Sweetheart," Rocket said softly. She dropped onto her knees beside Elektra and pushed her hair behind her ear, but it only aggravated her further. Elektra began slapping herself across the head repeatedly, babbling on about something that no one could understand.

Like a doctor conveniently present during a medical crisis at a shopping center, Eagle jumped up and rushed behind Elektra. She wrapped both arms around her, securing her wrists against her chest, and held her close.

"Shhhh," she said. "You're okay. When you calm down, I'll let you go."

I was stunned. Not because she'd reacted so quickly and confidently, but because it was evident that she'd done this before. I hadn't pegged her as the comforting type. There was a side to Eagle that I had yet to know. It was so difficult to remember the women on this island were just that—women. They were instinctively nurturing despite their barbaric ways. I became queasy. I'd always wanted to be a mother. There had always been a yearning inside me—an indescribable need—to care for an innocent life. And now, I would never have that.

I forced myself out of my trance because I knew if I allowed myself to feel my emotions to their fullest extent, I may never recover. I preferred to maintain a certain level of denial.

I refocused my attention on Eagle, who still held Elektra tightly in her arms. Elektra screamed, and many eyes were directed our way, but Eagle's grip didn't loosen.

"It's okay," she continued. "No one's gonna hurt you."

Elektra finally stopped fighting. She inhaled a deep breath and released a long sigh.

"Good," Eagle said, before letting her go. "How

about you go look over there and find yourself a nice solid stick? I'll carve it for ya and I'll teach ya how to fight with it."

Elektra's lips stretched into a grin, and she bolted toward the back of the Village, where several tall trees cast a shadow over the cabins. I stared at the third cabin to the right. I knew Murk's house, which sat right in the middle, and the Hospital, located on the left. But what was the other cabin used for?

Flander leaned in against me and followed my gaze. "That right there's a prayer house. Somethin' you may wanna consider using."

A prayer house? Why would I need to pray? Any so-called God that would allow for a world to exist in which human beings were cast to die on an island by a corrupt government was not a God I wanted to pray to. My life had been taken from me, and there was absolutely nothing I could do about it. What would praying do for me now?

* * *

"Keep your knees closed like a lady," my mother said, smiling down at me.

I sat on an uncomfortable wooden bench in my Sunday dress and my black see-through tights, staring at the little leather bibles in racks at the back of every church bench.

The pastor spoke of fairness and equality, but I barely listened. My mother always brought a sketchpad for me to doodle in, so that's what I did—I doodled during the sermons. Most kids did, actually. It wasn't realistic to expect a child to pay attention to a man speaking in the distance about God and the bible. I found it boring.

But then I heard something that caught my attention—the word *justice*. I wasn't sure why the sound of this word had caused me to look up. From a young age, I'd always found the world cruel and unfair. The idea of justice and absolute fairness had always seemed too unobtainable.

"Justice," the pastor repeated. He brushed through the pages, then raised a finger into the air. "Ecclesiastes 3:17. 'I said to myself, God will bring into judgment both the righteous and the wicked, for there will be a time for every activity, a time to judge every deed.'"

I wondered if my dad would be punished for leaving us.

* * *

"Whoa..." Holland stared at Elektra in the distance. "What's wrong with her?"

Rocket shook her head, almost defensive. "She's a good kid."

Eagle sighed. "Asperger's."

"Ass burgers? What the—?" Fisher said.

"AsPERgers," Eagle enunciated. "Or autism. Hard to tell. My nephew, Kyle, had it. He was four years old last time I saw him." She gazed out in Elektra's direction, a look of sadness in her eyes. "It's tough."

There was a moment of silence until Biggie clapped her hands together, causing my shoulders to jerk forward, and said, "Well, she's in good hands now."

I assumed this was her way of saying that the buck had been passed off to Eagle. Although I didn't think it fair to delegate such a demanding responsibility solely to one person, I had a feeling Eagle may have been the right individual for the job. She was familiar with Elektra's condition, and it was apparent she missed her nephew. Maybe, just maybe, Elektra would fill that void.

"Piss off, Hammer!" I heard several feet away.

Hammer—the butch woman from the Tools tent—was laughing away while a thin, Filipino-looking woman swatted at her, urging her to leave her alone. I wasn't sure whether Hammer was flirting with her or purposely antagonizing her or both. What I did notice, however, was the duo these two women made.

I suddenly remembered being ambushed in the jungle by the two women in serpentine masks— one larger and one smaller; the larger of the two women had been the one to pin me down on my back. I was still paying pearls on a weekly basis just to avoid a violent confrontation. Was Hammer responsible? I remembered the smaller woman— the one in the brown mask—and how she'd nearly given away her partner's name, "H...," before correcting herself and referring to the larger woman as "Panther."

I clenched my jaw. How had I not seen it? Hammer had hated me from day one when she'd tried to rip me off in the Tools tent, only to be scolded by Ellie and forced to offer me a fair price. I knew Ellie shouldn't have become involved. How were they still getting away with this? Why was I so pathetic as to allow two women to dictate the amount of pearls I received? I was a Hunter, yet here I was, still being bullied into giving away more than half my pay.

I bit the inside of my cheek just to maintain a certain level of sanity. There was a part of me that wanted to draw an arrow and shoot her right in the back, but I knew this was idiotic. I had to be methodical. I had to plan.

But one thing was for sure—enough was enough.

I'd catch them in the act, and I'd make them fucking pay for it.

CHAPTER 9

I blinked repeatedly, hoping my dry, tired eyes might produce enough moisture to stay open for a few minutes longer. All it took was one moment of confrontation—one moment to prove myself as something other than a victim.

Although the concept of time was irrelevant on the island, I knew it had been at least several hours since sundown. I sat in silence near the edge of the Cliff, my bow and quiver fastened to my back, and my eyes fixated on the tree under which my pearls were resting.

The smell of urine and feces filled my nostrils, and I felt like I was sitting in a port-o-potty, which didn't make any sense. Rocket had clearly explained that *waste* should be wrapped in a leaf and thrown over the Cliff. Had some missed their shot? Or were some women so lazy as to defecate wherever it suited them?

Goddamn animals. Hadn't their parents taught them any better?

* * *

"Don't you ever wonder?" Melody asked, removing her glasses and staring at me with such intensity that I became uncomfortable. "I mean, he's still your dad, and he's out there... Somewhere."

"My mom doesn't like to talk about it," I said, hoping this might end the conversation.

But it didn't.

"Just because someone doesn't like to talk about something, doesn't mean they shouldn't."

I wasn't sure whether she was coming to me as a concerned friend or deflecting feelings of her own. I knew she wasn't over her father's passing even though it had been seven years since it happened. I still remembered the night she'd called me through broken sobs and told me to turn on the news, where headlines read, "Police Officer Shot and Killed by Masked Robber."

The worst part was, they'd never found the guy. I couldn't imagine what that felt like: knowing your father's killer was still out in the world and living his life after he'd destroyed the lives of so many.

"Look, I've tried—" I started, but the store's welcome bell jingled.

"Welcome to Saint Marianna's Thrift Store," Melody said, a huge smile on her face. "If you need help finding anything, just say the word."

She turned back to face me, her smile quickly turning upside down. "You were saying?"

I shot a glance up at the young woman who'd just entered the store, then shook my head.

I didn't understand why Melody was so intrigued by my biological father all of a sudden.

She'd mentioned him before, but only briefly. She'd never actually interrogated me about how I felt regarding the abandonment.

I hated that she'd asked me because I went home that evening mulling over every possibility in my mind. Had he died? Did he hate me? I thought about this often, but hearing Melody mention his existence only added salt to the wound.

Of course I was curious. Of course I wanted to know why he'd left and whether or not he still thought about us.

Did he even know anything about me?

* * *

I woke up to the sound of happy birds chirping away in the overhead trees and the feeling of dry mud caked to the side of my face and in my hair. I brushed my fingers against my cheek, causing little pieces of it to break away and roll onto the ground.

My pearls, I thought suddenly.

I jumped into a seated position. The sun had come up, and the air was cool and dry. When I'd first arrived on Kormace, the air had always been so sticky—warm and muggy. A few strands of grass poked out of the dirt by my feet, but they were yellow and withered, almost to a crisp. How long was this drought going to last? Was our water supply at risk? Without water—without our waterfall—we wouldn't survive. And the thought of relocating over a hundred women in a jungle inhabited by savages and carnivorous predators was inconceivable. And what about the animals? What about our food? It was already becoming scarce.

I shook these thoughts away, stood, and approached the famous tree under which I'd been giving away my earnings on a weekly basis. They just sat there, looking so beautiful in comparison to the mold-encrusted rocks resting alongside them. Why hadn't my bullies picked them up? Why would these two women risk losing money by not collecting their taxes immediately after payment? I pictured Hammer's thick squared-off face and her stupid buzz-cut hair, and all I wanted to do was punch her.

I should have known.

I suddenly became conscious of the bow fastened to my back, and I realized I wasn't the new girl anymore; I was a Hunter. Maybe they'd realized I was more dangerous to them than they were to me. Or maybe they were smarter than I thought, and they avoided collecting their pearls the night of payment, knowing far too well that should I decide to retaliate, I would wait for them after payment drop-off.

I debated coming back every night until I caught the culprits red-handed, but the itch on my face and my stiffening neck muscles persuaded me to reconsider this idea. For all I knew, they'd only be back days from now. And how was I to know how many women were truly involved? What if there were more than just the two? What if I didn't stand a chance at all, even with my arrows?

Fueled by my pride and a new sense of self-worth, I reached down, picked up the pearls, and gently placed them back into my pouch. I was taking a risk, but I didn't care. There was one thought that stood above all else—I wasn't Lydia anymore; I was Brone, and if I wanted others to remember that name, I'd have to prove myself as a fighter, not a victim.

I hurried along a row of trees, as far away from the Cliff's edge as possible, and returned to the jungle's unkempt path toward the Village. I caught a whiff of something rank as I moved forward, but it wasn't long before I realized the smell wasn't just following me, it was me. I'd have to bathe sooner or later.

What time was it, anyway? Had I missed breakfast? It was usually served at the crack of dawn, and I could tell by the sun's position that at least two hours had passed since sunrise. I'd been so caught up in my own mind that I didn't even see her until she came rushing around a massive tree trunk.

"Shit, sorry," Holland muttered, dodging me just in time to avoid our noses from touching.

"Hey," I said awkwardly. I assumed her breakfast wasn't settling well by the way she rushed in direction of the Cliff. "You okay?"

"Y... Yeah," she said, a forced smile on her thin lips. "Really just have to go, if you know what I mean." She tugged at the corner tip of her shirt before swinging around and rushing through the trees, disappearing around the forest path's bend.

What a goof, I thought. I didn't trust that girl.

I continued down the path on high alert. I'd

grown accustomed to being mindful of my surroundings at all times, no matter the time of day. I considered walking past the Village and going straight into the Grounds, but my stomach was growling so loud I decided it wouldn't hurt to check in to see if there were any leftovers. I'd have eaten dirty eggshells if they were offered to me.

But as I approached the Village, something felt off. I listened to the sound of dried-up vegetation crackle underneath my feet as I moved forward, and I prayed to hear the sound of a voice—any voice—in the distance. But there was nothing.

Even when everyone was stationed at the Working Grounds during the day, there were always a few women roaming in the Village: the elders, the sick, the disabled, and the Guards. And that's when I realized it—there were no Guards. The front entrance was completely open and unguarded. Murk had assigned both Guards and Night Watchers to keep a close eye on the Village walls at all times, yet there I stood, mere feet away from free passage into the Village.

I swallowed hard, the bottom of my throat sticking together. I'd never paid much attention to my gut, but ever since being dropped on Kormace Island, I'd come to realize through unfavorable events that my gut was the only thing I could trust. I cautiously reached for my bow and crouched as I ran toward the Village's outer wall, placing an arrow against my bowstring and pulling back slightly. I moved in toward the entrance, my breath quickening with every step. Maybe I was just being paranoid. I hoped to God that's all it was.

I crept along the few final feet of weed-entwined wall separating the Village from the jungle, my body hunched over in hunting mode. I pulled back harder on my arrow, preparing to fire, and quickly swung around the Village wall and into the opening.

And then I saw it.

Please be dreaming, I begged.

I dropped my bow in the grass by my feet and froze in place, gazing out into the Village at countless seemingly lifeless bodies that lay around the breakfast fire.

PART FOUR

PROLOGUE

First, I heard the screams.

Then, I watched in horror as the woman lying next to me reached for her throat, gurgling mouthfuls of gooey black blood while trying to remove an arrow from her jugular. But it was only a matter of seconds before her gray-brown eyes glossed over and her head fell against the ground, her hollow stare fixed on me.

Women of the Village woke from their poisoned state. They stayed in upright positions, rubbing their heads and red eyes in confusion as smoke rose around them.

"Brone?"

It was Fisher.

She tried to stand but lost her balance and fell on her hands and knees. It was painful to see the biggest badass I knew—the toughest of the Hunters—struggling to stand on her own two feet.

"What... What's going—" she tried, but another arrow cut through the wind and stabbed the dirt inches from her feet before bursting into a ball of fire.

"We have to go," I said.

"But Trim," she said. "And... and the others."

I glanced back at the entrance where I'd stood only minutes ago. At first, it had appeared as though there were only a few women responsible for the attack. But as they drew in, stepping out from the hefty gray smoke, I realized there were far more of them than we were prepared to fight.

The Northers.

They wore grimy, devilish masks on the bottom halves of their faces—assumedly masks with makeshift antismoke-inhalation mechanisms—and chalky white paint smeared across their foreheads and around their blackened eyes. Some wore feathered necklaces, and others, necklaces made of small pieces of bone. As they moved forward, prepared to massacre every woman in sight, they pumped weapons into the air: katana-looking blades made of either wood or bone, knives, spears, and solid sticks. I could hear them chanting something gruesome from behind their monstrous masks, but I couldn't understand a word of it.

I'd never actually come face-to-face with a Norther, but I'd always been told they were meticulous in their attacks. They'd poisoned us using a pawn on the inside, then attacked us with fire during Kormace Island's drought, knowing that our dry land was completely vulnerable.

My lungs ached as the smoke spread, and it was difficult to make out anyone more than five feet away.

"We don't have time." I scanned the area. Women scurried in every direction in an attempt to outrun our invaders, but it was useless. They'd sealed off the entrance, trapping us inside the walls like a bunch of animals on the verge of slaughter.

I didn't want to abandon the Hunters—the women I'd come to know as friends—but searching for them in the midst of an attack would only put us in harm's way. Something hot suddenly grazed the skin on my arm, and I looked back to find a firelit arrow pointed into the ground as it combusted and spread a hot blaze across the crispy grass and up the side of a tent's wooden structure.

I could now only see the Northers' silhouettes as they moved in, raising their weapons above their heads and swinging down against innocent women who were trying to crawl away from them. The sound of women screaming and pleading for their lives was gut-wrenching. My stomach knotted, and I swallowed hard to keep the vomit down.

How was this happening? All I wanted to do was fight and defend our people, but I was completely helpless. I'd dropped my bow at the entrance upon first witnessing the countless bodies that lay motionless across the land, and moments later, the Northers had begun their attack. For all I knew, my own bow had been picked up and was now being used to slaughter our people.

I thought of Ellie, my best friend on Kormace Island, and wondered if she was hurt. If there was one person I wanted to find, it was her. But I couldn't.

I remembered the cabins at the back of the Village. There was a hole in the vine-braided wall behind them. Ellie had pointed it out to me when she gave me a tour of the area, only to then shake her head and tell me, "They were supposed to fix that a long time ago," as if our Builders—the women responsible for construction in our society—were as unreliable as the low-budget contractors you'd hire when trying to save a buck or two.

"This way." I grabbed Fisher by the arm.

Suddenly, warm blood splattered across my face and chest. A Norther was standing right in front of me, a swordlike weapon in one hand and in the other, a head choppily cut at the neck hanging by its tangled golden-brown hair. She must not have noticed me because she threw the head to the ground and swung her blade in the opposite direction at someone else. I pulled on Fisher's arm even harder and ran toward the cabins. All I could do was pray that the others would make it out alive. In that moment, the only thing I could think about was survival. I had to get out.

I looked back one last time, blinking hard to moisten my irritated eyes, when I saw her. She walked through the smoke, splitting it right down the middle with her broad, fur-covered shoulders.

Although she too wore a mask over her mouth and white paint across the upper half of her face, there was something different about her. She wore bulky, knee-high boots and what appeared to be some kind of cape hanging from the fur on her shoulders. It flapped behind her back as she walked, her chin raised high. Her cold black eyes scanned the massacred bodies around her as if evaluating her people's performance. Blood was splattered across every inch of her visible skin, and she held two massive battle axes, which were completely stained in red. What struck me as odd was that she wasn't using her weapons. Instead, she moved quickly, stepping over bodies and kicking away pleading hands, making it evident that she was on the hunt for someone specific.

I knew precisely who this woman was even though I'd never seen her before—Rainer, the leader of the Northers.

CHAPTER 1

I sat upright, feeling like I'd woken from a coma. Dozens of seagulls circled above me, dancing to the sound of waves crashing against the shore.

Where was I?

I rubbed my eyes, immediately regretting doing so as debris and sand particles scratched my heavy eyelids.

What happened?

I remembered the bodies, the fire, the screaming; the sensation that I was dreaming... as though I'd begun to float outside of my body; the sight of blood and not knowing who it belonged to. And I recalled thinking, *This is it.*

How did I get here?

I searched the open water, seeing nothing but a perfectly straight blue line across the horizon. The sky was brighter than I'd ever seen it, but all I felt was gloom. There was dull aching on the surface of my shins and thighs where my skin had turned a bright red. I wasn't sure how long I'd been lying here, but it was long enough for the sun to cause some damage. I didn't even want to imagine what my face looked like.

Behind me was a mess of greenery, and around me, fallen tree branches and rotting logs. I was on a shoreline, but I couldn't figure out where. There was no beach—only a few meters of sanded area around me in the shape of a square.

I could still smell the smoke as if it had glued itself to the inside of my nostrils. My throat burned and my lungs felt like they'd been poisoned.

And then I remembered it: the entire Village had been attacked by the Northers.

"Get up."

I rubbed my eyes and squinted at someone's silhouette towering over me, the sun's warm glow forming a yellow aura around their head. I knew that voice.

"I said get up, Brone."

It was Fisher. Of course—we must have escaped together. Why couldn't I remember the details? Had I blacked out?

"I let you sleep long enough. You saved me, I saved you. We're even."

I raised an open palm to shade my eyes from the scorching sun, hoping to catch a glimpse of her face. "You saved me?"

She scoffed. "You're weak, Brone. You collapsed after climbing out of the hole in the wall."

"I did?"

She ignored me and turned toward the jungle, whipping her long black ponytail over one shoulder and throwing her nose upward. Out of all my fellow Hunters I'd come to think of as friends, how had I ended up with Fisher? Sure, she was young, brave, and incredibly well skilled in battle, but she was also arrogant, detached, and frightfully impulsive. I'd come to see her as a pit bull—short, muscular, lean, and feared by most due to poor reputation. I couldn't determine her ethnicity—she had dark features and her skin was golden brown, but most women on the island had dark skin due to the strong sun that blazed on the Working Grounds—the area in which women spent the entirety of their days working hard to maintain our civilization by filtering water, crafting weapons, growing fresh fruits and vegetables, curing meat, sewing clothing, and training for battle.

"Who else got out?" I forced myself onto my feet, limping to catch up to her. I must have twisted my ankle while running away from the attack.

Again, she ignored me. She was so unpredictable. Only days ago, I'd watched her slit a woman's throat for mentioning her dead girlfriend.

Had my friends survived? Our friends? I needed to know if they were alive...

Ellie: a young, vibrant beauty with wavy brown hair and chocolate-colored eyes with whom I spent hours every morning around the breakfast fire just talking. She reminded me of my best friend back home—Melody—only much less in-your-face and far more patient.

Biggie: a charismatic soul bigger than life to suit her body type—big, bold, and spacious. I missed her twisted sense of humor even when her pranks landed me mere inches away from a school of piranhas, and I missed the way she'd throw her head back when she belly-laughed, revealing a set of perfectly white teeth that almost glowed in contrast with her dark brown skin.

Flander: a sixty-something-year-old woman with silver hair and leathery skin whose age didn't define her. She was tough, but she was fair. She always had an answer to my annoying questions when others shot me glares, and her undefinable yet charming country accent drew me in every time she spoke.

Rocket: a young, small-framed woman with forest-green eyes and caramel-colored dreadlocks, who exuded gallantry and prided herself on her speed. She could outrun anyone, hence her name, and always made a point to tell anyone she met that she was fast, *like a rocket.*

Eagle: a tall, silver-haired fox who shot an arrow like no other. She was injured when I first arrived on the island, and as a result, I was given her position even though I still didn't measure up to her remarkable eye. She resented me for having taken her place, but if enough time were to pass, maybe she'd eventually teach me a trick or two.

Elektra: an annoying, high-energy, nine-year-old kid we found during one of our hunts. She reminded me of the character in *Brave*—red haired and freckle-faced with a courageous spirit.

According to Eagle, the kid suffered from Asperger's, which came to explain her neurotic tantrums and unstable mood. Although she rubbed me the wrong way, she was still just a kid, and I hoped she was okay.

Trim: the leader of the Hunters. She was tall and thin, but very muscular. I remembered being introduced to her for the first time and wondering whether her name had been inspired by her dark frizzy hair and bushy unibrow. She wasn't much to look at, with her long pointed nose and blemished skin, but I respected her entirely and obeyed her every order. I wondered how far we'd get without her.

And lastly, Murk, our Chief. Had she made it out alive? I was afraid to imagine a future without her in it. I remembered first meeting her inside of the Grounds' waterfall, which was apparently her quarters. She had silver hair, almost white in comparison to her suntanned face, and piercing blue eyes. There had been something so genuine about her, so real. I remember feeling as though her eyes could see right through me, could read my every thought. I had yet to understand her ways, but she'd always been fair to her people and never led us astray. For that, she had my loyalty.

"Fisher!" I hissed.

"What?" She turned around quickly, her brows high on her forehead and her eyes resembling those of a rabid dog.

"Please..." I followed her, clenching my teeth at every step. "Just tell me what you know. Did you see them? Biggie, Trim—"

She cut me off, "No, Brone, I didn't see any of them, okay? For all we know, they're dead."

CHAPTER 2

I couldn't believe they were dead—I wouldn't.

I poked a rotten tree branch into the little fire Fisher had managed to build by hunching over a pile of dried leaves and quickly rolling a thin, cylindrical piece of wood back and forth in between both palms.

Despite my hatred for fire, I knew we needed it if we were going to survive. Even so, guilt hit me with every jab. Fire had taken away our home, yet here we were, building another one simply for the sake of warmth as nightfall approached.

"Do you think we'll find them?" I was afraid of the answer she might give me.

Fisher's eyebrows came together as she aggressively carved the tip of her hunting spear. "We'll find them."

Would we? Were they even alive?

I couldn't imagine living on Kormace Island without the women I'd grown to think of as family. Then I thought of Elektra. She was just a kid who'd somehow managed to be dropped onto Kormace

Island despite the government's regulations against minors being sentenced to banishment. She didn't deserve any of this.

I sat quietly, staring into the dirt under my feet, beads of sweat sliding along my hairline. How long would we make it like this, Fisher and I? We needed to remain as a pack like we always had if we were going to survive.

"Which way do you think they went?" I asked.

Fisher threw her spear into the ground and flared her nostrils. Her mood complemented her appearance—ash-stained skin, bagged eyes, and chaotic hair, which was something I'd never seen being that Fisher always wore her hair in a tight ponytail.

"I don't fuckin' know!" Her shoulders bounced up and down as she quickly inhaled and exhaled, almost hyperventilating. "*Por el amor de Dios...*" she muttered

"You speak Spanish?" I asked. Her English was impeccable. I'd have never guessed.

She shot me a glance but ignored my question. I'd once been afraid of her, but as the months had gone by, I'd come to realize she was exactly the kind of friend I wanted to have on this island, even if she did frustrate me at times. She was honest, up front, and loyal to the point of suicide if it meant protecting someone she cared about.

Although she'd never admit it, I knew I fell into her "friend" category. I remembered when she'd noticed the cut on my neck—the one inflicted by masked women under Murk's reign, who I had yet to locate—and how she'd told me to get it cleaned up. I remembered the way she'd snapped on other convicts when I received shouts of insults for having replaced Eagle, the original Archer who'd been injured during battle.

In her own way, Fisher cared. And I cared, too. I was fortunate to have her by my side. We were in this together—alone, but together.

"I'm sure they're not far," I said.

She didn't say anything. Instead, she reached to the ground beside her, scooped up a dead rodent, and pulled a knife out from her waist holster. I looked away as she dug her knife into its fur and began tearing its skin off. As hungry as I was, I didn't want to watch the meal preparation process, just as any paying customer of a sidewalk food truck wouldn't want to see a cow slaughtered before being blended into the shape of a hotdog.

"We'll find them," I added.

There was no knowing whether these words were true. I'd only intended to reassure Fisher because I could tell her anger was fueled by fear and grief. For all we knew, some of the Hunters—if not all of them—had been killed during the attack. I couldn't bear the thought of it, but I had to be realistic.

And then, as if being struck by some invisible force, I remembered so vividly what happened moments after I walked into the Village—after I saw women lying still around the breakfast fire.

* * *

I stared at the bodies for what felt like hours, not

quite comprehending what was going on. My legs shook and my heart raced so fast, I was certain it would stop. I began seeing halos, and everything around me seemed like a dream—a nightmare.

And then I saw Fisher, and I immediately ran to her.

"Fisher?" I asked.

I only spotted her because she'd sat upright, her ponytail shifted to the side and a look of bewilderment on her face. Everyone else around her lay so still.

"Fisher!" I called out again, running to her side.

Her dark eyes met mine, but her focus immediately shifted to the women lying around her. She tried to stand, but she lost her balance and fell atop another woman.

"What... what happ..." she tried.

I grabbed her arm and helped her up. Her first instinct was to reach for her blade, but I blocked her hand with mine and shook my head. She was swaying from side to side—a knife would do her more harm than good.

"I don't know what's going on," I said. "I think it's poison. I missed breakfast, and I'm fine. That's the only thing that makes sense."

Her eyes narrowed on me and she pulled away.

"You did this..."

"Fisher! I'm trying to help!" I said.

She took a step back, but tripped over a body and fell to her side.

"Watch it!" someone said.

Someone else had woken up. What was going

on? Why had everyone lost consciousness? Had the attacker miscalculated their dose of poison? Had their intention in fact been to kill everyone?

"You!" Fisher said again.

"I was out trying to catch someone who's been threatening me for months!" I hissed. "I didn't fucking do this! I spent all night sleeping in the mud at the edge of the Cliff!" I pointed a stiff finger to the dried-up sludge in my hair and stared at her with my eyes wide open.

She seemed to believe me because she rolled onto her hands and knees and stood up. "Where's Trim? Where's everyone else?"

"I don't know," I said, gazing out into the Village. "Where were they when you had breakfast?"

"I don't... I don't remember," she said. "The last thing I remember—"

"What's... What's goin' on?"

"What happened?"

Several other women sat up, scratching their heads and rubbing their eyes. I couldn't see any of the Hunters—Trim, Flander, Biggie, Rocket. I couldn't see anyone I knew, for that matter.

I'd been about to start venturing in between the tents in search of my friends when the first arrow landed by Fisher's foot, and then another into the roof of Murk's cabin, immediately lighting it on fire. The few women who'd woken up began screaming and trying to stand up straight, causing other women to wake during the chaos.

Dozens of other fire arrows came raining down

into the Village, lighting tents on fire and spreading wildfire across the dried-up grass. There were shouts and pleas while some women tried to wake their friends, but all I could think about were the Hunters.

* * *

"How many arrows you got left?" Fisher asked, gnawing on a small leg bone and biting off the little bit of meat that was left.

I peered over my shoulder to catch a glimpse of my quiver. "Eight, I think."

"You're welcome, by the way," she said.

"For what?"

"For snatching you Hamu's bow. Not like she'll be needing it anymore."

Hamu, I remembered. Pin and Hamu—the Asian sisters Murk had assigned as Archers. I swallowed hard, the thought of Hamu's lifeless body clouding my mind. Although I barely knew her, or Pin, I'd trained by their sides for months. I wondered if they'd both been killed during the attack.

The bow in my hand was instantly hot against my skin. I stared down at it, analyzing every groove, every stain, every scratch. It wasn't my bow, but it would do. And then I wondered—would I be dead if I hadn't dropped my bow before the attack? Would I have tried to resist the attack, only to be killed? I was sick to my stomach knowing that those who had tried to fight had been slaughtered, while I, Lydia Brone, had escaped because I'd lost my weapon when it was my duty to defend our

284

people.

Fisher took another bite of the rodent. "Use those arrows wisely. And when you do, try to get them back."

It wouldn't have been the first time I pulled an arrow out of a carcass to salvage our resources. I thought of Salvia, the gentle-faced woman who'd overseen the Needlewomen—something I'd been assigned upon first landing on Kormace Island before being stripped of this title and reassigned as a Battlewoman, or a Hunter (as Rocket had told me, these titles were pretty much interchangeable)—and wondered if she was okay. I hadn't spent much time getting to know her, but she'd seemed like the calm grandmother figure who always knew precisely what was going on even though she hardly spoke a word.

Without the Needlewomen here with us to dry out leather, carve arrows, or sew clothing, we were limited on supplies. What were we supposed to do? Butcher an animal, skin it, and spread its skin out for the sun to dry? I'd seen the Needlewomen at work—the process of preparing leather was far more intricate than letting fresh skin dry up under the heat of the sun. There was a preservation technique involved, followed by soaking, and whatever else it was they did.

Soaking...

Water.

I swallowed hard, feeling like my throat was filled with sand.

We didn't have any water—at least, not any

fresh water. The island was surrounded by salt water, with limited bodies of fresh water inside the jungle itself. I thought of the Working Grounds, where the waterfall was located. The massive flow of water filled a bay large enough to sustain several hundred women. Women assigned the task of Farmers were responsible for not only food preparation and cultivation, but also, the distillation of salt water into fresh water.

I remembered the first time I'd laid eyes on the Grounds. I'd been captured by the Hunters after having been tossed out of a military helicopter and forced to swim the length of a dozen Olympian-size swimming pools to make it to shore.

I'd been led through an opening in the jungle, where a beautiful green pool of water sat. Around this water, countless women glistened under the heat of the sun, seemingly on the verge of heat exhaustion as they performed a variety of tasks such as food cultivation and water distillation, woodwork, the creation of leather, meat preservation, and target practice. But what I remembered most about that day was the feeling of cool water droplets floating away from the waterfall and landing on my cracked, dehydrated lips. I remembered thinking that I'd have amputated one of my own limbs just to get a sip of water.

What were we supposed to do now? Find a source of fresh water? It was too risky. Everyone wanted fresh water.

And then it dawned on me. That was precisely

what we had to do. Not only to hydrate, but to find anyone who'd survived the attack. If there were survivors, they would need access to fresh water, too.

CHAPTER 3

"You sure you've done this before?" I asked.

Fisher grunted.

She held the coconut in between the pads of her feet and hammered her knife into its eyes using a sturdy piece of wood. It seemed to penetrate.

I stared at the green shells around her. I wasn't sure how she'd managed to hack away the outer shell using nothing but a bone-constructed knife, but I was grateful. I licked my lips at the thought of cool coconut water. It was as though I hadn't had anything to drink in weeks.

She leaned her head back and placed the holes over her open mouth, allowing a straight line of coconut water to come pouring out.

I swallowed—or at least, I think I did.

"Damn, that's good," she said.

Was she doing it on purpose? Was she trying to torture me?

For a moment, I contemplated jumping her to get a few drops of water. But I didn't need to because she handed me the fruit.

I threw my head back and drank the fluid. It poured out very slowly, making me want to press my lips against the fuzzy brown shell and suck the water right out, but it was better than nothing. When the liquid finally dried up, I shook the coconut, hoping for one last drop of water. But nothing came out.

"Okay, okay," Fisher said impatiently. "Hand it over."

She then went on to hit the shell repeatedly with her block of wood, while rolling it in between her hands.

"Gotcha, you son of a..." she mumbled.

The fruit instantly split at its center, revealing two bowl-shaped halves filled with a thick layer of white meat.

"Here," she said.

I dug my teeth into the meat as best as I could and pulled back, collecting little bits of fresh coconut in the spaces between my top teeth.

"You really need to get one of these," Fisher said, slicing her knife through her piece.

How long had it taken her to carve bone into a shiv, anyways? I didn't ask. All I cared about in that moment was the coconut sliding down my throat. I'd have eaten the shell if it wasn't for the fact that I'd probably lose my teeth.

"There any more?" I asked, licking the bottom of my bowl.

Fisher shook her head. "Bet you miss Sumi right about now."

Not so much. I didn't miss our Cook. She'd always been so rude to me, and I'd never understood why. Sure, her food was delicious, and it made our sentence feel a little less like hell on earth, but the service was horrid. When I first set foot in the Village, she attempted to deny me a serving, even though main meals are supposed to be free of charge.

Fisher must have noticed the look of disgust on my face, because she smirked and said, "I take it you two weren't friends?"

"Friends?" I scoffed. "Sumi's had it out for me ever since I got here."

"That's just Sumi. She's not so bad. And the reason she's so crabby all the time is because she hates cooking and wanted to be assigned as a Hunter."

I glared at her. "I wasn't even a Hunter when I first got here, and she was still acting like a five-year-old."

Fisher shrugged. "She also doesn't like newbies. She's been on this island for years, and she's always been responsible for feeding hundreds of women every day. You, being a newbie, added to her list of women to feed. She's just bitter."

That made sense. I stared at the coconut shell in her hands, but she tossed it to the side and said, "We need to move."

I stood up but nearly fell over when the sole of my shoe slipped to the side, completely unattached from the sneaker.

"I think it's time to say good-bye." Fisher looked

down at my shoes and smirked at me as if I were some child holding onto a stuffing-less, one-eyed teddy bear.

I sighed. My sneakers were the last things I had left from the real world. I'd done a good job at maintaining their health. Every evening, after a long day of hunting across the jungle's moist floor, I would pull them off and allow them to dry inside my tent. Rocket had warned me that having wet feet was a sure way of developing trench foot—or immersion foot—which was both disgusting and extremely painful. Knowing this, I was always careful, hoping that I'd never have to part with my beloved shoes, but I couldn't deny the fact that they were now causing more harm than good.

"Keep the laces, toss the rest," Fisher said.

Laces. Why had I never thought of this? Rope was a valued object on Kormace Island. I could have traded it for pearls or used it to build some kind of fishing contraption.

"And what am I supposed to walk in?" I asked.

Fisher laughed and stuck out one of her feet. It was completely bare with chunky yellow toenails and calluses so thick it looked like she'd glued artificial skin to the bottom of her foot for protection.

I grimaced.

I didn't want my feet looking like that. I slid off my shoes, realizing that I'd already developed calluses everywhere. I couldn't remember the last time I'd taken the time to actually look at my feet. In fact, I couldn't remember the last time I'd even thought about my appearance. I supposed this was because survival was more important than looking good.

"How is that even safe?" I imagined stepping on a fat-tailed scorpion or a poison dart frog.

"It ain't," she admitted. "But until we find the resources to protect our feet, this is what we're stuck with." She wiggled her gnarly toes inches above the ground, flicking a few crisp leaves up into the air. "And if anyone asks, I never said that. Trim would have my head if she knew I was huntin' without shoes."

I hated the thought of exposing my feet to the jungle's poisonous critters, but I didn't have a choice. These rotten sneakers would only slow us down. I pulled the laces out of the loops and tied them around my wrists to form bracelets.

"Well, you'd better rest those feet," Fisher said. "Tomorrow's gonna be a long day."

I craned my neck back and looked up at the darkening sky through the gaps of intertwining tree branches.

"Find yourself somethin' to sleep on." She leaned her back against the trunk of a tree. "You're in no shape with that ankle of yours. We'll start looking for survivors at dawn."

Her eyelids became heavy, and her head rocked back and forth in a fight to stay awake.

"I'll keep watch," I mumbled, more so to myself than to her.

I sat on a patch of dry dirt, drawing lines into it with my index finger. I pulled myself back against the root of a tree, feeling something squish underneath my right palm. I raised my hand to find a yellow translucent mushroom flattened into a pile of orange mush. It looked disgusting, but I knew it was edible. I'd seen Sumi chop a few of these into one of her dishes several weeks ago.

I tore the squiggly fungus out of the ground and inspected it for insects before chewing into it. Although not a gourmet meal, it was food, and that was all I could ask for.

I listened to the static sound of insects all around me—a constant white noise I'd learned to ignore. Birds whistled in the distance, and branches rustled above me, drawing my attention to the treetops. The sky had darkened to an indigo blue, eliminating the jungle's vivid colors.

It seemed like only minutes had passed before the sky turned black, and the only thing I saw was a red glow at the tip of the fire log. I hated the smell of it—the smell of carnage and desolation.

It may have been my imagination, but every sound somehow seemed amplified as if I were standing in an empty auditorium. Every coo; every chirp; every distant snarl. I widened my eyes and tightened the grip on my bow, scanning every inch of black around me. I couldn't tell the ground from the trees, and then I thought of the Village, where the moonlit sky illuminated our rooftops.

God, I missed that place.

I swallowed hard at the realization that it was gone—all of it. I thought of my bed, the one I'd constructed out of giant banana leaves, and the privacy of my tent; of the waterfall's saltwater pool, and how women would float naked on their backs, allowing the salt to cleanse them of the jungle's impurities; and of medicine and about Navi. If we were attacked overnight, there'd be no one to help us. And what about sleep? Would I have to sleep on the jungle floor every night, amid wild animals and possibly Ogres? My stomach growled, and I thought of Sumi's tasty dishes she cooked with fish, nuts, wild boar, turkey eggs, or fresh fruit. What were we supposed to do now? Eat coconuts, fungus, and rodents for the rest of our lives?

I aimed my eyes in Fisher's direction, even though I could hardly see her, and I realized how lucky I was to have someone completely willing and capable of killing an animal, skinning it, and tearing it apart for us to eat.

If I were on my own, I'd probably attempt to survive on fruit alone and develop diabetes.

I inhaled slowly, listening to the sound of my own breath in the dark and seeing flashes of women being slaughtered before me as if my mind was a projector and the jungle's darkness, a wide-projection screen. I couldn't stop thinking about the attack.

I flinched at the sound of a woman screaming for her life as she begged one of the Northers not to swing a mighty blow, but no one was there. The only sound to be heard was the millions of insects humming in unison.

* * *

Someone tugged on my arm, shaking my limp body

from side to side. I opened my eyes to find Fisher's shaded figure crouched beside me. I parted my lips to speak, but she whipped a hand over my mouth and placed a finger over hers.

What was going on?

I tried to sit up, but Fisher's hand moved over my chest and held me down.

"I think she went this way," I heard.

I followed the voice, but I couldn't see anyone. It was too dark. How long had I been sleeping, anyways? I must have fallen asleep while keeping watch, which made me feel completely incompetent.

Tree branches and dehydrated flora cracked as the voices distanced themselves from us, and Fisher's hand slowly let go.

"Who was that?" I mouthed.

Fisher glared at me, her eyes warning me to keep my mouth shut until she gave the command to speak. She'd always had the potential for leadership, which made me wonder—if anything had happened to Trim, would Fisher step up? Because I sure as hell wouldn't. I wasn't cut out to be a leader—or anything else that required people to depend on me.

"I'll kill them all," she finally whispered.

Those words and the hatred in her eyes told me we'd come in close contact with Northers. I wanted them dead as badly as she did. They'd taken everything from us: our home, our people, our civilization. And now, they were out hunting for survivors of the attack.

I stared into the cracks of darkness ahead of me and imagined myself lunging out and slitting one of their throats. I'd never been one for violence, but this island was changing me. It was turning me into precisely what I promised myself I'd never become—a savage.

But I didn't want to be this person. I didn't want to fight, yet I had no choice. Why was there even war when all that truly mattered was survival? How did killing another group or clan benefit anyone? Was Rainer to blame for her people's actions?

Thinking about it was useless. Whether Rainer was responsible or not, her people were just that— people. They had minds of their own. If they were too incompetent to think for themselves and realize that slaughtering someone was wrong, then they were nothing more than biological shells. I, for one, wouldn't waste time trying to play hero by reprogramming these women's brains.

It was simple, really. Kormace Island could only be survived by following one very basic rule: kill or be killed.

CHAPTER 4

"Hey, what's wrong?" I asked.

Fisher was crouched over, digging her fingernails into the dirt at her feet and clutching herself below her belly.

"Nothing," she said.

"Doesn't look like nothing. Are you okay?"

She clenched her teeth and nodded as hundreds of little goose bumps crept up her arms and neck. Dawn was setting in, and broken streaks of orange light stretched into the forest. We had agreed that at the break of dawn, we would be setting out in search of other survivors near bodies of fresh water.

"I'm fine," she lied.

I stared at her. She wasn't fine. It looked like she'd eaten poison or something.

"I just need a minute," she said.

She slowly crawled onto her stomach, resting her face in the dirt, and closed her eyes. A drop of sweat slid down the side of her temple and along the curve of her thick bottom lip.

I waited, nervously scanning our surroundings every few seconds. If the Northers had truly decided to launch a widespread hunt for survivors, it was only a matter of time before we encountered one of them. We had to find the others before the Northers found us.

Minutes felt like hours as Fisher lay there, and I began to wonder if she'd fallen asleep.

"Fisher," I said.

Her eyes shot open and she reached for her knife in a panic.

I sighed. She'd fallen asleep.

"What's wrong with you?" I asked.

She slowly sat up, wincing. "It's just endo," she said.

"Endo—what?"

"Endometriosis," she said. "You don't stop getting your period just 'cause you're in the middle of fucking nowhere."

I was well aware that as women, we were all cursed with a monthly visit. This curse had proven challenging given the fact that Kormace Island didn't supply tampons or pads. Fortunately, Tegan had constructed a pad-like cloth with the use of cotton that could be purchased in her merchant tent.

But I couldn't understand what this endo-something had to do with Fisher's period. My face must have given away my confusion, because Fisher flicked her wrist and said, "Think of it as a bunch of spider webs stuck to your uterus."

I grimaced. That was disgusting.

"Exactly." She smirked at what must have been the look of horror on my face.

"It hurts?" I asked.

"Like fuckin' hell." She inhaled a deep breath through widened nostrils. "I miss Tegan."

I think *everyone* missed Tegan. Not only was she basically the Village's bartender, she was responsible for creating and selling medicinal remedies and hygienic products such as soaps, ointments, and natural toothpaste.

How was anyone supposed to survive without her? I sure as hell didn't know how to make soap. I wouldn't even know where to begin. And toothpaste? I sucked on my teeth, feeling the thick buildup of plaque and the layer of grime that coated the top of my tongue. I didn't even want to imagine what was hiding in between my teeth. I'd seen women floss using strands of their hair, but that didn't work for me. I tried it once, only to end up with pieces of broken hair caught between my teeth.

"She had something for the pain?" I asked.

Fisher nodded. "Some herb. Anti-inflam."

"Would you recognize it if you saw it?" I asked, eyeing a row of flowering shrubs.

She shook her head. "Tegan went through a whole drying process. It just looked like a cup of green tea by the time it was ready to be ingested..." She stared at her feet, her body leaning forward. "I used to take birth control. You know, in the real world." She looked at me, but only briefly as she always did. "You got any medical problems?"

I shook my head, realizing how fortunate I was to be free of any ailments.

"Count yourself lucky," she said. "I've seen it all—diabetes, thyroid problems, heart problems, arthritis, fibromyalgia... And that doesn't even begin to cover it all. Then there's mental illness, but Murk wasn't too tolerant of that."

"What do you mean?"

She shrugged. "We've abandoned a few drops along the way if we noticed something was off. Don't get me wrong, I ain't got any issues with mental illness. But the way Murk sees it—well, it's a liability, you know? If there aren't any meds to stabilize them, we can't risk having them in our Village."

That sounded terrible. These people—these grandmothers, mothers, sisters, daughters—were human beings. I couldn't imagine walking away from someone simply because they were wired differently from me. But, at the same time, I understood Murk's stance on this. Emotions aside, mental instability posed a threat, and as Chief, Murk's primary role was to protect her people.

"Young girl died just before you were dropped off," Fisher said.

"From what?"

"No idea."

I stared at her, not understanding the purpose of her story.

"That's the problem, though. Navi's good at what she does. She's good at healing—at being our people's Medic. But she ain't a real doctor. She doesn't always have the answers. You have no idea how many lives are lost, and we can't figure out why. Could be so many things, you know? Hormone levels, heart failure, infection..."

"Do you think Navi—"

"Is dead? Probably."

I was stunned by the coldness in her voice, but it wasn't unlike Fisher to be so matter-of-fact.

"Medics have a natural need to help others," she said. "There's no way she ran while women were being injured left and right."

"What if they're all dead?" I asked. "The ones with specialties? What're we gonna do?"

Fisher smirked, but I could tell by the look of hopelessness in her eyes that it was forced. "I don't know."

She stood up straight, stiffening her back, and let out a long breath. "Do me a favor?"

"Yeah?"

"If you see any cannabis leaves, let me know."

"As in pot?" I asked.

"Yeah, as in *pot*," she mocked. "It helps with the pain. Murk never allowed it, but she's not here right now, is she?"

"What's it look like?" I asked.

Fisher stopped midway in a stretch and simply stared at me as if I'd just announced to her that a man named Donald Trump had been elected president of the United States back in 2016.

"You're too square, Brone. And you *murdered* someone?"

I bit my tongue. I hadn't *murdered* him. It was *manslaughter*. But, Fisher was all I had, and I wasn't about to get into a petty fight over semantics. She waved both hands in front of her face. "You know what? Forget it. If I see any, I'll pluck them. Don't worry about it. Grab your bow and let's go."

I did as Fisher told me and followed her as she slowly moved forward, her shoulders round and her knees bent. The pain must have been excruciating; she was the last person you'd hear complain about pain.

"Do you know where you're going?" I asked.

She stopped moving and glanced back at me. For a second, I worried she might tear me a new one or accuse me of being nothing more than a fickle-minded brat incapable of trusting anything beyond the tip of her own nose.

But there was a solemn look in her dark eyes. "No, not really." She sighed. "I remember there being a bay of fresh water west of the island, but to be honest, I have no idea where we are."

"How far did we run from the Village?" I asked.

Fisher shrugged. "Couple hours, at least."

"In which direction?"

"South."

I'd never been good with geography. I remembered my cheeks warming upon hearing Mr. Grant's speech in seventh-grade geography class about how "China wasn't a continent." He'd kept eyeballing me at the back of the class, making it completely obvious that I'd been the one to pencil in this answer on my midterm exam.

"In the morning we feast, and at night, we rest," I mumbled.

Fisher cocked an eyebrow.

"Helps me remember." My mom's crooked smile when she taught me this little rhyme for the first time filled my mind.

"Jesus, Brone. I'm a Hunter, and I've been living on Kormace for years. I know the sun rises in the east, which is why we're walking away from it. I don't need some little rhyme to tell me that."

"Then what's the problem? If we're headed west..."

Her eyes went huge, and she straightened her hunched posture. "Do you have any idea how big Kormace is? It's not like we're going to find the bay I'm looking for just by walking west."

"Well we don't have a—" I started, but a strong smell of burning immediately caught my attention.

Fisher must have smelled it, too because she quickly turned around and followed my eyes. "You have got to be fucking kidding me."

CHAPTER 5

In the far distance, a bumpy wall of black and white smoke slithered quickly around the bases of trees and through hanging vines. Behind the smoke were orange flames so bright I thought for a moment the sun had shattered and fallen to earth.

And then I felt the heat. A hot, scorching wind brushed around the contours of my face, causing my eyes to dry and water.

"Brone!"

I looked back. Fisher was already running the other way, while I stood there in awe, gazing at the wildfire—such a breathtaking force spreading nothing but death.

"Brone!"

The skin on my face and neck had become uncomfortably hot. I shook myself from my trance and bolted toward Fisher, hopping over uneven soil and tangled webs of vegetation. An array of blurry greens and yellows dominated my sight as I ran through the forest, following closely behind her.

For the first time since I'd been dropped on Kormace Island, the thought of being killed by Northers, Ogres, or by a big cat didn't scare me. If there was one thing worse than our enemies, it was the idea of Kormace Island burning to the ground. My enemies now had no relevance—we were all going to die anyways.

I didn't bother asking Fisher where she was running. It was obvious she was moving away from the fire, but more specifically, toward shore. Our only means of survival was to set foot where the fire couldn't reach us—in the ocean.

I couldn't believe how fast the fire was traveling. Heat hit my back as I ran, adrenaline bursting through me. I prayed the fire wouldn't catch up to us. I didn't even want to imagine what it would feel like to be burned alive.

"Jesus Christ!" Fisher hissed ahead of me. She held her knife tightly at her side. It was only when she lunged sideways—when she broke our momentum and our direction—that I saw it.

At the base of an old rotten tree sat a woman beside a skull-headed pillar. Behind her was an oval-shaped shelter constructed of tree bark and leaves. The woman wore black fur over her bare shoulders and a gray rodent's skin over her head, its boneless legs hanging by her ears. The skin folds and ugly crevasses of her naked body were visible through her open fur cardigan, and she sat there, staring at me from behind dark, soulless eyes. Dirt and rusty blood stained her chest, neck, and chin.

I hadn't meant to stop running, but the sight had both frightened and intrigued me. Was she an Ogre? Was I standing mere feet away from a living, breathing Ogre? Was the blood on her chin that of a human's? I contemplated drawing an arrow and killing her where she sat. If she was an Ogre, there was no guarantee that she wouldn't try to kill me. Then I remembered Sunny and the way her body had been dragged away by one of these carnivorous monstrosities only to be strapped upside down and sacrificed to whatever god it was they believed in.

Her eyes quickly shot behind me; no doubt she noticed the rapidly approaching fire. She stiffened and her eyes widened. Although I was filled with hate and vengeance following the Northers' attack, this woman had nothing to do with the destruction of the Village. As I stared into her round eyes, seeing a speck of orange reflected from the fire, I realized they were filled with fear.

"Brone!" Fisher shouted in the distance, urging me to ignore the woman.

The woman's eyes quickly shifted between the fire and me as if she were waiting for my permission to move, hoping I wouldn't kill her the moment she tried to save herself.

But I couldn't move. I stood there at a crossroads between humanity and instinctual self-preservation. Kill or be killed, I told myself.

The woman flinched at the sound of a tree cracking and collapsing onto the forest floor. There was something childlike about her frightened features. It was as if she'd been born and raised on Kormace—an animal in a human shell. Was this the result of isolation?

I couldn't bring myself to take a life simply for the sake of eliminating a potential threat, even though I'd convinced myself there was no other way to survive the island. Her death would have been unnecessary. She wasn't trying to hurt me.

"Run!" I shouted.

The woman scampered away from her habitat and disappeared into the thick of the forest. I caught up with Fisher, my back so hot it seemed as though I'd been burned by steam. I could tell by the look on her face that she wanted to beat me for having wasted time, but that alone would have required more time that we didn't have.

She clenched her jaw and continued her sprint. Having spent several months running through the jungle in search of food, I was accustomed to long distances on jagged terrain. But as my lungs burned and my thigh muscles tightened, I understood I was either experiencing the symptoms of inadequate food and water intake or Kormace Island was as big as I'd been told it was— or both.

"How much farther?" I breathed, fighting to keep pace.

"No idea." Fisher gasped to catch her breath, which was a sight entirely new to me. "Keep moving."

I quickly glanced back at the fire, but what caught my attention was not the disintegrating herbage amid fiery flames. From behind clumpy gray clouds of smoke came the sight of bodies running away from the flames—both human and animal. From the treetops, dozens of chimpanzees swung rapidly in the opposite direction of the fire. Something small and fuzzy brushed against my ankle, and in the distance, handfuls of women ran together, barely visible within the murky air around them.

Maybe I knew them, maybe I didn't. Were they even Murk's people? I looked up at the sound of birds cawing as they circled above the jungle, almost in a pleading manner, almost as if wishing the chaos to end. We weren't the only ones who'd been attacked. The entire animal kingdom was being demolished.

I continued toward Fisher, tree branches snapping and rattling overhead as monkeys swept by. When I thought I might finally collapse, I saw a break of light blast through the trees in the distance—a glimmer of hope.

"Almost there," Fisher breathed.

I mustered the little bit of strength I had left and sprinted to the end of the forest, passing Fisher and beelining straight toward shore. But when I reached the end—when I was finally able to see the ocean's flat, daunting horizon in its entirety—I was taken aback by the dozens of women gathered near the water.

I recognized a few faces, but most importantly, their handmade leather attire. These were Murk's women. They must have fled during the attack before the fire spread.

What I then noticed was the sky. It was unlike anything I'd ever seen before. Clumpy black clouds floated low, casting similar-shaped patches of shade to darken the sand at the women's feet. The wind whistled eerily, blowing my hair back and out of my face.

I shifted my attention to the women and scanned their faces.

Please, God, please.

Surely, one of the Hunters was among them. Rocket, Biggie, Flander, Trim... My heart ached at the realization that my friends were nowhere to be seen. Aside from a few women I'd seen only briefly at the Working Grounds, I didn't know any of them.

A deep, phlegmy cough came from behind me and I turned around. It was Hammer—the woman who'd owned the Tools tent. She'd also been the one to threaten me at knifepoint.

I clenched my jaw.

"Jesus!" she shouted, pulling at her clothing as if trying to prevent it from melting to her skin. She tore off her shirt, revealing several large rolls and sagging breasts. She rubbed her hands through her short, sweat-drenched hair then wiped her face with the inside of her elbow.

"Think I just lost ten pounds," she said, marching out into the open with pretentious confidence.

A yellow, half-faced serpentine mask flashed in my mind. I remembered being held down on the bed of the jungle and forced to agree to pay up my hard-earned money—my pearls—on a weekly basis. I'd been like a mouse stuck inside the jaw of a bored housecat—completely helpless and poisoned by my attacker's rotten breath.

I bit the inside of my cheek and stared at Hammer as she walked out on shore, a smug look on her narrow-eyed face.

Where was her sidekick? Her partner in crime? When I'd been ambushed in the jungle, another woman with a brown mask had stood in the distance, keeping watch. I remembered her nearly slipping up and referring to the woman as, "H— Panther."

But the final nail in their coffins was hammered—no pun intended—the night before the attack. I was sitting with the Hunters around the Village fire when I heard a shrill voice begging Hammer to leave her alone. Side by side, the two women made quite the duo as they had the night they pinned me to the ground. After that moment, all the puzzle pieces fell into place: Hammer's hatred for me ever since her failed attempt at ripping me off in the Tools tent; the big belly pressed up against mine during the ambush; and the short, messily spiked hair sticking out over the serpentine mask.

And then something else hit me. The night before the attack, when I saw Hammer standing beside the short woman, I finally put two and two together. I'd gone off to the Cliff (where I'd been instructed to drop off my pearls) with an unquenchable thirst for revenge, hoping to catch and confront the women collecting their cut. Because of this, I'd fallen asleep in the dirt that night, only to wake up the next morning to the sight of countless women lying lifelessly around the breakfast fire.

Had I been present during breakfast, I could have helped, somehow. I could have spotted the culprit—the woman responsible for poisoning our people—or I could put a stop to the entire attack. Although this outcome was highly unlikely, I couldn't help but put the blame on Hammer. I hated her, and all I wanted to do was kill her.

The next thing I knew, I'd dropped my bow and was sprinting toward her like a marathon runner on their last few meters before the finish line. That familiar, floating sensation took over as if I'd been cast out of my own body and replaced by something carnal.

At first, her eyes narrowed and an arrogant smile distorted her fat face. Although I was small in comparison to her, I didn't hesitate. I ran through the sand, kicking clumped grains into the air behind me. She stood there, unmoving, her arms crossed over her sagging chest.

Keep smiling, you cocky bitch.

There was a glimmer of doubt in her eyes seconds before I lunged straight for her throat. The velocity of my attack propelled her into the air and flat on her back. I landed on top of her, the two of us sliding a few feet into the sand as if I were sitting on a snow sled.

I raised both fists into the air and began beating

down against her face one punch at a time. She tried to block me, but that didn't stop me. I punched anything I could. Blood splattered onto my knuckles, and a sick sense of satisfaction filled me. Her arms dropped to the sides of her face, and she lay there motionless. But I couldn't stop. I hated her... hated everyone... hated this fucking place.

"Stop it!" someone said in the distance, but it sounded like a voice underwater.

I kept bashing her face as if this would somehow make all of Kormace Island disappear and take me back home.

My hand stopped in midair and warm fingers squeezed my wrist. I quickly swung back, attempting to throw a punch at whoever was responsible for getting in my way but missed. Someone grabbed my other wrist and dragged me across the sand, turning me onto my stomach.

"That's enough," Fisher said.

"It's her fault!" I shouted, struggling to get out from underneath the weight of her body.

"I know you're pissed," Fisher said, "but whatever she did, it isn't worth it."

"Yes, it is!" I shouted, sand sticking to my lips.

"Brone!" Fisher growled, her knee digging deeper into my back. "Hammer's the one who builds our weapons. We need her."

"I don't fucking care!"

"Well I do," she said, her grip still tight.

I breathed quickly, wanting nothing more than to tear off Fisher's face for having intervened.

"When you calm down, I'll let you go," she said.

I lay there, fuming, for what seemed like an eternity. The sound of soft footsteps began to circle us, and shadows appeared around me.

When I finally came to, a sickening nausea filled my stomach. I wanted to vomit, and not because Fisher's knee was digging into me, but because I may have beaten a woman to death.

What had I become?

I stared at my hand. My knuckles were inflamed and covered in blood.

Fisher's hold loosened when my stomach, beneath her knee, began to contract. I stood up just in time. Stomach acid came pouring out.

I wiped my mouth and glanced back at Hammer, who lay on her back, motionless. Her face, neck, and chest were smeared with blood and completely swollen—so much so that her face was almost unrecognizable. I watched, my heart racing as a few women squatted beside her, feeling for a pulse.

Please don't be dead. Please don't be dead.

"She's alive," someone said.

I sighed, relieved that I didn't have another life on my hands. I couldn't even remember what I'd done. I remembered feeling hatred and wanting to kill her, but beyond that, I couldn't recall what had happened.

Fisher released a pained grumble.

"Goddamnit." She squeezed her belly and grimaced, dark red blood staining the insides of her pants and dripping down to her ankles.

CHAPTER 6

Had I hurt her?

I watched in horror as she ripped off her pants and rubbed sand onto her bare legs trying to erase the mess.

She must have sensed my worry because she looked up at me. "You didn't do anything, Brone. It's my fucking period."

I released a long breath. The last thing I ever wanted to do was harm someone I cared about. Fisher stood, and the women who'd circled us backed away a few steps. I didn't blame them for being afraid of Fisher. The last time a crowd was gathered like this, Fisher was standing over the woman whose throat she'd slit wide open.

Everyone feared her, but as I slowly stood, they cowered even further. I felt like a mannequin—on display for everyone to look at. I stood there, my body hunched and my veiny bloodstained arms dangling at my sides. I could feel the messiness of my hair atop my head. I must have looked like a complete savage.

Had I just ruined any chance I had at integrating with these women?

A sudden *crack* echoed around us, shaking the earth beneath our feet. Fisher's eyes rolled up at the sky where black clouds appeared to be doubling in size with every minute. I glanced back at the jungle, where lumpy gray smoke burst through the trees and out into the open. It crackled and snapped as it ate its way through the forest.

The stormy clouds had lowered so much, I thought they might collide with the forest's treetops.

And then there was a ghostly silence—a moment of absolute awe as though we were standing underneath an epic battle between Poseidon and Hades. My gaze followed the forest's edge, where creatures and women came bolting out, some coughing and others collapsing onto the sand. There were hundreds of them now, emerging from the jungle and running toward the open water.

Flames suddenly blasted out from the trees, licking the air and dancing fiercely. I took a step back. A cool gust of wind aggravated the flames, expanding them farther up toward the sky. There was another *crack* from above and then another and another.

The clouds above us finally gave out, releasing rain so heavy it was as though I'd set foot underneath the Working Grounds' waterfall. The winter-like breeze that had gently brushed my skin quickly transformed into a powerful force, pushing me back several feet.

"Holy mother of..." one woman said, her eyes fixed on the ocean. Its water resembled a massive reservoir of oil—black and glossy.

I wasn't sure which to fear more—the storm or the wildfire.

The wind picked up again, so hard this time that water from the ocean came swooping toward us. I squinted my eyes and turned away to catch my breath. A loud, static-like sound spit through the air, bending palm trees to the ground, their leaves flapping against one another.

Waves began forming and rising as they approached the land. They came crashing down hard enough to propel wet sand into the air.

"R...!" Fisher shouted, but it was impossible to hear anything over the deafening sound of the tropical storm.

I couldn't see anything anymore—not one single shape. A hand grabbed me. The next thing I knew, Fisher's face was almost touching mine, and we were crouching down beside a body.

"Help me pull Hammer!" she shouted.

Several other panicked voices shouted around me, but I couldn't make any of it out. I grabbed Hammer by the armpit and tugged back as hard as I could, feeling her body slide through the sand, which quickly became greasy mud.

The moment we reached the forest's edge, Fisher dropped Hammer to the ground and slapped her across the face. Hammer's eyes shot open, and in a frenzy, she jumped to her feet, her droopy breasts flapping from side to side.

"Come on!" Fisher said.

Several other women had followed us, apparently submitting to Fisher's natural leadership.

From above, rain poured through the treetops and trickled its way down onto our heads. Water spilled from my hair and onto my face, and I spat out a mouthful.

I did my best to follow Fisher's lead, shifting through the forest's soggy bed. A loud splatter behind me indicated someone had fallen. Quickly glancing back, I spotted a young woman clasping both hands around her ankle and baring her teeth in agony.

"Someone help her!" I shouted.

Two women rushed to either side of her and scooped her up. The injured woman hopped forward with one leg only, her face contorted with pain. They brought her to a patch of dry soil underneath a tree that almost looked like the head of a mushroom. Its leaves—or at least, what was left of them—formed a wide, dome-like shelter from the rain.

Everyone stopped moving. I wouldn't be one to complain; I needed the rest, even if only for a few minutes.

"Better heal fast. We're not standing around here for long." Fisher crossed her arms and inhaled a long breath.

No one dared argue.

Hammer tilted her round head back, her eyes fixated on the deathly sight around us.

My eyes met hers and she flinched. I couldn't help but stare at the still-growing bulge over her right eye and the uneven split that separated her bottom lip in two. Blood covered her chin and neck, and for a second, I was nauseated until she opened her mouth to talk.

"What're you lookin' at?" She took a small step back as if I wouldn't notice, and I remembered why I'd gone after her in the first place—she'd been my bully all along.

I widened my eyes and threateningly jerked forward, not quite understanding where this sudden confidence came from.

"Yo, man," she went off in a panic, "it wasn't personal. You were the newbie, and me, well, I have a problem taking advantage of the new ones. I'm sorry, Brone. Won't happen again."

"I know, sweetheart…" someone said, pulling my attention from Hammer.

The young girl who'd injured her ankle was sitting in a fetal position against the tree, shivering. One of the women who'd helped her was crouching by her side, rubbing her shoulder. I'd seen their faces before, but I wouldn't have guessed their names in a million years.

"Careful." Fisher quickly pressed a firm hand on my back, but it was too late.

There was a *crunch* underneath the heel of my foot before I noticed the body lying there. On the ground was a burned corpse trapped underneath a massive fallen tree that had presumably been the cause of this person's horrific death. The body was obviously female—I knew this not because everyone on the island was female, but by her petite frame twisted in such a frightened manner, and by the few remaining strands of long blonde hair mixed with clumps of black dirt and white ash. Half of her face was a disarray of slimy red flesh, and one of her crippled hands was so badly burned I could see bone.

How long had she been dead? Hours? Minutes? Seconds? I stared at her face—an unrecognizable jumble of partial features glistening underneath a layer of rainwater.

She was gone—at peace from this grisly nightmare.

Did I know her?

There was a whimper behind me, and I turned around to see a woman clasping both hands over her mouth as if forming a blockade to prevent vomit from spilling out.

"There'll be more," Fisher said coldly. "Keep your eyes open."

"Fisher," I said, gazing at the heavy rain in the distance. The storm was moving quickly, and soon, it would be directly over our heads.

Her glassy, marble-like eyes followed mine and she quickly nodded. "We have to keep moving."

"And where are we going?" someone asked.

The voice belonged to a brown-skinned woman who was as tall as Biggie, only slimmer. She had puffy black hair, soft eyes, and a small pointed nose. Upon first glance, I'd have assumed her to be the gentle-giant type, but the way she eyed Fisher proved otherwise.

"What makes you our leader?" she went on.

Fisher scoffed and faced her, shoulders slouched and eyelids low. She was either in too much pain to care or simply too tired. Only then did I realize how many women had followed us. I counted nine of them—Hammer; the three women, including the injured one, who were all sitting underneath the shelter tree; and four others who were standing behind the dark-skinned woman, cautiously observing Fisher's reaction.

"Do whatever the hell you want," Fisher said. "But whatever it is, I suggest you do it fast because that right there"—she pointed at the oncoming darkness—"ain't a regular storm."

The woman's eyes narrowed on Fisher and then at the dreary sky. "And where are you taking us?"

"I'm aiming for the Working Grounds," Fisher said. "We'll be safe inside the waterfall."

A cold droplet of water exploded on the bridge of my nose, and then another and another.

"We have to move, now!" I shouted, my voice fading behind the sound of massive rainfall.

The power-struggle was set aside, and the women followed closely behind as Fisher ran in the opposite direction of the storm.

"Keep your bow in hand." Fisher eyed me sideways as we splashed through a shallow stream that had already begun to flood over.

I glanced at her but didn't respond. The risk of being attacked by Northers still existed—even in a storm. Had their attack backfired on them? Literally speaking? Had the fire spread to their territory? I clenched my jaw, hoping it had. They all deserved to die.

I had no idea in which direction we were moving. Everything was either black, brown, or gray. This wasn't the Kormace Island I knew. Despite the hidden dangers and lurking enemies, the jungle I'd known prior to the attack was one of untellable beauty and magnificence. Now, as I looked around, I saw nothing but death and gloom. There were no birds chirping; no monkeys playing; no insects singing.

The Northers had taken away the little bit of goodness left in a nightmare filled with cruelty and savagery. How was anyone supposed to survive that? It would have been less torturous to die.

The sound of wood bark being hacked off a tree trunk shook me from my thoughts.

"Get down!" Fisher shouted. Another arrow whistled past her waving arm.

The women did as told and dropped to their bellies. Fisher pushed me hard behind a barren tree.

"Right there," she said, pointing straight ahead. The Norther stood alone with a bow in her hands and a skull mask over her face. She wore padded clothing, or fur, over her shoulders and chest.

She took aim at our women, who'd dropped for cover, and released. The arrow flew straight, before snapping in half against a tree.

"I'll distract. You fire," Fisher said.

I didn't have time to object. Fisher bolted perpendicular to our attacker with her knife in hand. I watched as the Norther's masked face turned slightly, following Fisher's movements. She raised her bow and pulled back.

I wiped my wet hands against the leather of my top and drew an arrow. I could sense the women's eyes on me, pleading me to save them. I'd killed animals at this distance before, but I'd never fired an arrow at a human being.

But there was no time to think.

Fisher was risking her life, and the Norther was preparing for a clear shot. I swung around the tree and raised my bow, arrow aimed at her chest, and quickly released. But the sound that followed next made my stomach sink.

Crack.

The arrow had landed at the base of the trees, most likely the result of the rain weighing down on my arrow. The Norther's eyes turned on me, as did her aim. I swung back around the tree just in time for her arrow to stab into bark at the height of my head.

Fisher must have noticed what happened, because she quickly altered her path, beelining straight for the Norther.

What the hell was she thinking?

The Norther pulled back and hid behind two trees attached at their base, their trunks separated only by a narrow gap, before drawing another arrow and pointing it at Fisher.

My clear shot was gone, and Fisher was being completely idiotic. She was going to get herself killed.

Without a second thought, I set my arrow and drew back, eyes fixed on the narrow gap between the trees so intently that everything around me seemed to fade. I envisioned my arrow sliding through the crack and through the Norther's neck.

With that thought in mind, I released.

At first, nothing happened. But then, the darkness behind the two conjoined trees was replaced by open space. I watched as the Norther fell to her knees, and then flat onto the ground. The women around me slowly stood, eyeing the wounded Norther from a distance like a bunch of beaten dogs.

"She's down," I said.

I was shocked by my hit, but I was more frustrated by the fact that these women had done nothing to try to help. But then I realized that not all of Murk's people had been trained for battle. For all I knew, these women were Farmers, Builders, or Needlewomen. Maybe they'd never held a real weapon in their lives.

Fisher approached the Norther's body. She reached down, but I couldn't see what she was doing. She then stood and waved at us, confirming that passage was safe.

"Let's move," I said.

Although satisfied and overwhelmingly proud of my shot, my stomach churned.

My first kill on the island, I thought. I'd taken a life. A real, human life. I swallowed hard and avoided eye contact with Fisher as we caught up. My legs were shaking, although not nearly as much as they did when I'd witnessed an attack for the first time.

"Nice shot, kid!" Fisher said, throwing an arm around my neck. She handed me a handful of arrows—one bloody, and the others clean. "Salvage these."

It was obvious most belonged to our attacker. I slid the arrows into my quiver, nodded, and forced a smile. What had I done? Although I wished the Northers nothing but death, I'd never actually imagined that I'd be the one to grant it.

"Hey." Fisher loosely swung her knife in front of us. There was a swirly streak of dark blood along its sharp edge, and she slid the flat side of the blade against her thigh to clean it. "You didn't kill her. I did."

I caught a glimpse of the body. The Norther was lying on her side, her mask removed, revealing a multitude of straight scars carved in her chin and across her lips. Her neck was slit at the base—Fisher's doing, I knew—but my arrow wasn't there anymore.

"Where'd I hit her?" I asked.

Fisher grabbed me by the shoulders and pulled my attention away from the body. "Does it matter? You saved me."

I stared at her, noting the urgency in her voice. What was she protecting me from?

"Check it out," Fisher said.

I nearly fell onto my back when she swung back around, her black eyes hovering above a skull-carved mask.

CHAPTER 7

"Why should she get to wear it?"

"Nyla, stop it."

"Yo, I'm just sayin'. You guys need to start speaking up. You can't have one person dictate your life."

"She's not dictating..."

"They did save us, you know."

"Yeah, so? She'd be the first to kill you if you ev—"

"Would you guys shut the fuck up?" Fisher tore the mask off her face and swung around. "I'm leading the way, so I'm wearin' the gear." She patted the brown fur on her shoulders, which was all wet, bloody, and uncombed. "If we run into another Norther, I'm the first one they're gonna see."

No one spoke.

"Glad we're clear," she said, before repositioning the mask.

"You know what the worst part is in all of this?" Fisher asked me, her voice muffled behind the mask.

I cocked an eyebrow.

"All the wasted weed."

I tried to smile, but I had nothing left in me. I also knew that behind Fisher's attempt at making a joke, she was tormented inside. She'd lost everyone she cared about. There was no telling whether they were even still alive.

"Jay needs a break," someone said.

"Who's Jay?" Fisher said, whipping around so fast a trail of water slapped me across the face.

I watched as the young injured woman—Jay, apparently—hopped through the forest's muck, then dropped down onto a fallen tree.

"Just a few minutes," said the woman who'd been helping her.

Fisher stared at her. "You have *one* minute."

I leaned back against a giant, ash-stained tree root, which would have normally been covered in moss, and tilted my head back. I hadn't paid much attention to my body, but the moment I relaxed, I realized that my feet, my legs, and my back were throbbing. My stomach felt like it had shriveled to the size of a raisin, and my chapped lips remained intact only due to the water dripping down my face.

I parted my lips, feeling cool droplets fall into my pasty mouth.

Water.

The other women must have noticed me drinking because everyone tilted their heads back as if they'd only now realized it was raining. Fisher brushed her wet hair back and stuck out her tongue.

And then something incredibly strange happened—someone laughed. I wasn't sure who it had come from, but then, another laugh followed.

Had I missed something?

Hammer threw her head back and joined in on the laughter. I eyed Fisher curiously, but I couldn't help smile. What was so funny?

Hammer walked out into the open and threw her arms out like a four-year-old girl caught in the rain without an umbrella. She spun around in circles, allowing the water to soak her beaten face.

Several other women joined in, their glistening faces smiling up at the sky. It was like watching starved animals who were given food for the first time in days. Emotion radiated from their bodies—so much so that my smile stretched into a grin.

But the celebration was short-lived. The eldest of the women—a gray-featured, flabby-armed woman—was the first to drop to her knees, causing mud to splatter in all directions. She threw both hands over her eyes and began to sob.

Hammer pulled at her hair, her face reddening and pudgy knuckles tightening, then let out a deep bellow.

The laughter developed into a low-pitch lament, followed by wailing and crying. Fisher avoided eye contact altogether, crossing her arms over her chest and swallowing hard. I stood there, my eyes clouded by a mixture of tears and rainwater, witnessing one of the most mortifying moments in my life—the aftermath of the attack.

It was almost as if reality had finally set in. The wildfire had stopped, and for a single moment, there was nothing to fear, nothing to run from. It made room for reality to slip in.

These grown women were on their knees, covered in dirt and blood, mourning all they'd lost. It was sickening to think that all this pain had been inflicted by one group of individuals—and for what? What did they get out of killing our people? It couldn't have been territory because they'd burned half the island, if not all of it, to the ground.

I thought of the Norther I'd fired my arrow at—the one Fisher had assured me I didn't actually kill—and suddenly, the idea that Fisher may have lied satisfied me. I hoped I'd taken that Norther's life for all that her people had done to mine.

And then, out of nowhere, my mother's face popped into my head.

What would Mom think if she knew I was having these thoughts? If she knew I was happy about killing someone? I should be ashamed.

But I shook the guilt away by convincing myself that my mother's opinion had no relevance. She'd never understand what it was like to live on Kormace Island.

Kill or be killed, I repeated to myself.

"This is because of you," I heard.

Nyla—the dominant, dark-skinned woman—stepped forward, her head tilted forward, her ebony eyes filled with contempt. She was staring at Fisher with such hatred that I feared for her life.

332

"What was that?" Fisher said, tearing her knife from her holster.

Nyla pointed a stiff finger at her, eyes round and nostrils flared. "Your job was to protect us! To protect these women!" Her voice hoarsened. She aimed her finger at the women on their knees who stared in silence. "So tell me—why the fuck are you here? Why aren't you dead, like the rest of your precious Hunters?" Saliva came spewing out of her mouth, and her shoulders bounced up and down as she breathed.

Fisher's grip tightened around her weapon.

My surroundings blurred. Was it true? Were the rest of the Hunters dead? I swallowed hard and held onto the notion that Nyla was lying, that she didn't know what she was talking about. They couldn't be dead. They just couldn't be.

The next thing I knew, Nyla had pinned Fisher up against a tree and the women around us were shouting and roaring a bunch of nonsense. She'd somehow managed to grab Fisher's hands and was now forcing Fisher to hold her blade against her own neck.

Fisher grunted something, but her throat was being crushed and I couldn't make it out. I moved in to help her, but two of Nyla's followers stepped forward, prepared to take me on.

I couldn't believe it. They were turning on us.

And as if things couldn't get any worse, the storm finally caught up, a torrential downpour blinding us almost instantly. Nyla's feet slipped, as did Fisher's, but her grip didn't loosen. Instead, she used this momentum and pulled Fisher down into the mud, then pressed a knee into her chest.

Fisher squirmed and kicked, but Nyla was too heavy.

Without thinking, I pulled an arrow out of my quiver and lunged at Nyla, stabbing the arrow's pointed tip into her thigh. She threw her head back and screamed—a sound almost unheard amid the pouring rain—and immediately let go of Fisher.

I sadistically twisted the arrow as best as I could, my grip slipping, then tore it out of her muscle. If she was going to turn on us, I'd make sure she couldn't follow us. Nyla swung her long arm backward, hitting me hard across the face. I was propelled into the air and landed on my back in a pool of brown mush.

One of her followers came charging at me with a massive rock above her head, her mouth wide open and her eyes bulging. She must have been yelling, but I couldn't hear anything. I didn't have the time or ability to move—it was too slippery. She was aiming right for my face. I raised both hands and squinted, convincing myself that two shattered forearms were better than a disfigured face.

But nothing happened.

I peeked through the gaps of my interlocked arms and immediately sat upright. Fisher was standing face-to-face with my attacker, almost as if on the verge of kissing her. I tilted my head, not quite understanding what was going on.

But the moment Fisher took a step back, I

noticed her blade slide out of the woman's belly. She dropped the rock and collapsed to her knees, brown muck splattering into the air.

"If you're with us, you're not against us!" Fisher shouted, her mouth nearly filling with water at every word. "We keep moving. Now!"

CHAPTER 8

"It was my sister's," Fisher said, playing with her bone-constructed shiv. The rope attaching the blade to the wood was completely frayed, but it did its job. There was a diamond-shaped emerald, or stone, woven into the rope as some sort of decorative piece. Small groves were evenly spread across one side of the yellow-stained blade, and that's when I realized it wasn't a bone at all—it was a tooth.

"She was killed before I got here. I found her body near shore when we went looking for a drop. She was stabbed to death." Fisher pressed her thumb into the blade's grooves, scanned the dead forest, then shook her head and forced a smile. "She had twenty-two stab wounds. What kind of a person stabs someone twenty-two times?"

I didn't know what to say. I stared at the shiv, envisioning someone with similar attributes to those of Fisher's—only pale and chalky-looking—lying there in her own blood.

"I'm sorry," I said.

I considered reaching to touch her shoulder, but I wasn't great at providing consolation and I presumed Fisher wasn't any better at receiving it.

She shrugged, still working to keep a fake smile on her face. "It's my fault. I was her big sister. I was supposed to protect her..." She eyed the women who'd followed us to shelter, seemingly affected by Nyla's angry words: *Your job was to protect us!*

"But instead," she scoffed, "I'm the one who got her involved with dealing in the first place."

I stared at the ground. I couldn't imagine the amount of guilt she was feeling. No wonder Fisher was so cold all the time—she'd lost everything.

She wiped her nose with the back of her hand in the toughest way possible, then stood. "Anyways, what's done is done. Can't be livin' with regrets." She turned her attention to one of our followers, who was keeping guard at the entrance of our shelter. "Yo, Franklin, how's it looking out there?"

The woman—Franklin—solemnly shook her head.

"Fuck," Fisher growled, then hugged herself and rubbed her upper arms. "Too damn wet to make a fire, too."

Several eyes looked up at her as if she'd spat venom at their faces.

"Fire isn't the reason for all this," I said, glaring at them. "The Northers are."

"Brone's right," Fisher said. "We still need to survive. And if we're going to do that, we need food, water, and shelter—and that includes

338

warmth."

Up until now, I'd forgotten what it was like to be cold. It didn't help that my suede attire was damp and heavy, causing goose bumps to spread across my arms and back. I'd grown so accustomed to the island's hot, steamy air that the idea of temperature didn't faze me.

When I first arrived on Kormace, it felt as though I'd walked into a sauna. But within weeks, my nights spent tossing and turning in a pool of sweat came to an end due to thermal adaptation—something I was quite familiar with having been raised in a country with winters so cold that ice cream cake could be left in your backyard all season.

I pressed my legs against my chest, rested my chin on my knees, and looked around. We were hiding inside a shallow rock shelter, hidden from view by crusted plants hanging at the entryway like a torn-up curtain you'd find covering a window in an old haunted house. There wasn't much space, but with only five of us remaining—Nyla and her two devoted followers having stayed behind and the injured woman having refused our help—we managed to fit.

Aside from Hammer and Fisher, the other two women were complete strangers to me. Being that we were practically touching arms and recycling each other's breaths, it was only reasonable that I got to know them.

"I'm Brone," I said, my teeth clattering. "I'm a Hunter, and I can get us food."

Everyone remained silent. I wasn't sure if this was because they already knew who I was and they didn't like me or because they were intimidated.

I eyed Fisher, who uncrossed her arms and placed both hands on her hips. "I'm Fisher, as I'm sure you know. It's pretty simple—don't attack me and I won't attack you."

I watched as several eyes averted her stare, and I couldn't help but smile.

"Fisher's the best fighter I know," I added quickly. "If she's on your side, she'll protect you."

Fisher scoffed and turned away, but she knew I was right.

Hammer cleared her throat, breaking the tension. "I'm good with my hands," she said.

I glared at her, remembering her doughy body holding me down on the jungle floor. She sat there, arms folded over her large bare chest, her hands hidden underneath her armpits.

"I can build weapons... tools. You name it," she said.

She glanced at me, but only for a second. Although I despised her ugly, swollen face, she was valuable to us. I'd have to get over what had happened.

I looked up at the woman who was standing guard at the shelter's entryway.

"What about you? What can you offer?" I asked.

I wasn't used to being the one leading a discussion, but these women followed strength, and being that I had killed our attacker and maimed Nyla, I was currently their symbol of strength.

"I'm Franklin," the woman said, alternating her gaze between us and the jungle.

She looked confident, her chin raised high and her small lips always tight on her face. Her short, shoulder-length hair, which appeared to be brown due to the rain, was most likely strawberry blonde. She had a stunning sugar skull tattoo on her left shoulder, its hair flowing down her arm and around her elbow, forming a half sleeve, and tribal markings on her other arm.

"I was assigned Battlewoman. I won't be of much use, though"—she eyed my quiver sticking out over my shoulder—"I don't have a weapon."

"I'll hook you up, girl," Hammer said.

Ugh, she was so repulsive.

Franklin nodded as a way of acknowledgment, and our eyes all shifted to the last woman. She was older than the rest of us—sixty-something, maybe—with shaggy gray and white hair, flabby arms that looked like pancakes against her sides, and a face so stern I couldn't read her whatsoever.

"I'm Everest," she said, her r's rolling off the tip of her tongue, "you know, cause of—" and pointed up at her hair.

Hammer let out a deep laugh, but Fisher slapped her on the chest.

"This place echoes, you twit!" Fisher said. "Are you tryin' to get us killed?"

Hammer looked away like a child caught picking her nose.

"I'm a..." Everest started, "vell, used to be, a

Farmer."

There was no smile on her face, nor any form of kindness whatsoever. In fact, her lips were turned upside down. Was she reserved, or just cold?

"I'm good at preserving and preparing food," she added, gesturing a partially closed fist in the air. "One of ze best cooks in Alchevst," she went on.

Hammer scoffed. "Never heard of the place. Must be some tiny little—"

"Is Ukraine," Everest said, "you foolish—"

"Perfect," Fisher cut in. "Brone will kill, you'll cook."

"Well," Franklin said, popping her head into the discussion, "looks like we might just stand a chance after all."

Hammer was about to laugh again, but she caught a glimpse of Fisher's glare and looked back down at the leafy floor.

"We need to eat soon," I said. Although I'd passed the stage of hunger and stomach pains, I knew my body was hungry. I hadn't eaten in two days, and basic movements were becoming difficult due to light-headedness and muscle weakness.

The only upside to the storm was the rain. I stepped out of the rock shelter and tilted my head back, swallowing mouthfuls of fresh rainwater.

"If we can make it to the Grounds," Fisher said, "we can make a fire inside the waterfall."

"And how do you expect to find any food?" Franklin said. She pushed aside the curtain-like barrier to further prove her point. There was nothing but decay out there.

"Vat's ze matter vit' fish?" Everest asked.

"The hell's that supposed to mean?" Fisher moved toward her.

Everest's unimpressed eyes rolled up at Fisher. "Fish. Vater. Food," she said, gesturing her hand toward her mouth.

Fisher retraced her steps, chest puffed out. "Ah, kay," she said. "Thought that's what you meant." She stood there for a moment, one arm crossed over her chest and the other hand up by her face, pulling on her bottom lip.

"Is fish even safe to eat?" Fisher asked, peering outside. "I mean, any fresh water around here is probably filled with ash by now."

"Fisher's right." I then remembered a news article I'd read at work following a devastating wildfire that had spread across several regions and lasted for days. "The water could be contaminated due to all the ash and cinder. And if the water's contaminated, the fish could be, too."

Everest shrugged her shoulders. "Zat's probably true."

"So what," Franklin chimed in, "we supposed to go back toward shore? Go fishing? With what? Sticks?"

"I can build—" Hammer started.

"We just traveled for hours," Franklin continued. "We'll probably collapse before we even get to the ocean. And what about drinking water? I haven't had anything in over a day. And you know what they say—"three days without shelter, three days without water."

"We get it, Frank," Fisher said.

Franklin glared at her. "It's Franklin."

Fisher rolled her eyes. "Whatever."

"She's right," I said, my eyes meeting Fisher's. "We need to find food and water."

"That's why we keep moving," Fisher said. "If we can get to the Working Grounds, Murk may have left resources in—"

"Are you insane?" Franklin said. She'd completely abandoned lookout duty and was now facing us, arms swaying in all directions as she spoke. "How do we know the Northers aren't waiting there for us, huh?" Her eyes were large and round, her tight-muscled posture full of confidence. Even I wouldn't have spoken against Fisher like that. She had courage, to say the least. "And how do we know the wildfire didn't spread across the entire fucking island? It's not like a magical barrier prevented the fire from spreading backward!"

"Well, actually," I cut in, "the fire spreads depending on the wind, so technically—"

"We don't have anywhere to go!" Franklin went on. "We don't know what's beyond the Village and the Grounds! What if the entire other half of the island is Norther territory? What if there's a bunch of Ogres the farther we get into the jungle?"

"All right!" Fisher finally snapped, but she immediately lowered her voice when it echoed across the inside of the shelter. "All right, okay? I get it. It's a huge risk. But what do you want us to do? If we go back toward shore, we're putting ourselves out in the open. Not only that, but we'll never make it in this weather. It's not like we can fish with huge waves crashing on us anyways. Our best option is to keep moving and hope for the best."

Franklin scoffed. "Hope for the best? Look, I get it, Fisher. You're a good leader, and you know this island better than any of us, but we need to be smart about—"

"Shut up!" Fisher hissed.

Franklin stopped talking, cocked an eyebrow, and continued. "Seriously? I'm trying to communicate, and you think you can—"

In one swift movement, Fisher spun around Franklin and pulled her in against her body, one arm snug over her chest and the other covering her mouth so tight that her fingers turned white.

Everyone went silent, realizing that Fisher wasn't just being Fisher.

Someone was walking outside the shelter.

CHAPTER 9

Franklin's bulging eyes shot from side to side above Fisher's hand.

There was rustling amid the sound of pouring rain, followed by faint voices bickering back and forth.

Fisher looked at me, and I immediately prepared my bow, aiming it straight at the entryway. We waited, listening to what sounded like a heavy body being dragged through the mud. Fisher slowly released her grip on Franklin and grabbed her knife.

Right when I saw movement mere inches away from Fisher, I pulled back hard on my bow's elastic, preparing to kill whoever dared set foot into our hideout.

But then I heard a voice, and I immediately felt at home.

"Brone? Is that you?"

I lowered my bow as she walked into our enclosure.

"Ellie?" I said, wanting nothing more than to

throw my arms around her.

I couldn't believe it was her. Not only was Ellie the first friend I'd made on Kormace Island, she was the only person I'd ever trusted. I thought she was dead. I thought...

She ran into the rock shelter and threw both arms around my neck and squeezed me tight.

"I thought you were dead," she whispered.

I couldn't describe my emotions, but I wanted her close to me. I squeezed back, feeling her soft chest press up against mine, and inhaled her scent—a woody, earthy smell combined with a subtle hint of coconut. She always did love moisturizing with coconut oil.

I hadn't realized how much I'd missed her.

"I thought you were dead, too," I said, my throat swelling.

"Would someone help us?"

Ellie let go and rushed back to the entrance where one woman stood covered in blood, and another lay by her feet in the mud. The woman in the mud winced as rain soaked her face and belly, and only then did I notice her two fists clenched around the shaft of an arrow. It was sticking out of her, right below her stomach.

"Bring her in." Ellie stretched out her arms, gesturing everyone in the shelter to make space.

Aside from her bubbly personality and unwavering loyalty, the one thing I admired most about Ellie was that she was always there to help others, even if it meant putting her own life at risk. There was something so pure about her—a kindness unlike any I'd ever encountered before. I didn't understand how this part of her still existed on Kormace Island.

Even I—a girl who used to cry at dog rescue videos on YouTube—had begun to feel numb toward the pain of others. I was losing myself. I was losing my sensitivity.

"What happened?" Fisher asked.

Everyone circled the injured woman and bickered back and forth.

"Mia got hit," Ellie said, "in the Village."

I recognized her face—soft and childlike—but I hadn't known her name.

"Ellie," Mia said choppily, "Ellie saved... She got me out."

Ellie brushed Mia's wet hair out of her face and gently massaged her forehead with her thumb.

"It's okay," she said, her voice so soothing that my knees buckled. I was exhausted.

"Just fucking pull it out already! It's killing her!" said the woman who'd followed them in. She reached down toward the protruding arrow, but Fisher's hand clasped the woman's wrist so hard the clap-like sound echoed around us.

"Don't," Fisher said. "You'll kill her." She knelt beside the woman, examining the wound and the arrow's remaining shaft and fletching.

"This is gonna hurt," Fisher said, before slowly twirling the shaft of the arrow to one side.

Mia groaned, her eyes sealed shut and her mouth stretched so wide I could see all her back teeth tightly pressed together.

"What the hell are you doing?" asked the nameless woman standing by her side.

I stepped in. "Back off."

I didn't know what Fisher was doing, but she had more experience than any of us dealing with wounds—especially those inflicted by arrows.

Fisher stood up, wiped blood from her hands and onto her pants, then said, "Well, it's not lodged in bone, so that's good. But there's no telling what it's damaged."

"So take it out!" the woman yelled.

"I can," Fisher said, calmer than I'd ever seen her, "but it'll hurt. And even if I do, there's no guarantee your friend'll make it. It looks pretty deep."

The woman took a step back as if she'd only just realized that the possibility of her friend dying wasn't merely a dream. She threw a hand over her mouth, her eyes filling with tears.

"Do what you have to," Ellie said, glancing up at Fisher. She continued to stroke Mia's head.

Fisher grabbed her shiv and came back to Mia's side, then pressed a firm hand on her belly. "You sure you want me to take it out?"

Mia nodded, her face pale and glistening with cold sweat.

"Somebody give her something to bite on," Fisher ordered.

Everest stepped forward. For the first time, her face bore more than a blank expression. Whether it was disgust or heartbreak, I couldn't tell. She handed Fisher a piece of brown material—

350

something I'd noticed fastened to her wrist.

"You'll want to bite into this," Fisher said, placing the material inside Mia's mouth. "I'll be digging a bit inside to try to pull out the arrow with its head. If the shaft separates from the head, you'll probably die." Mia blinked quickly, although I wasn't sure she was even listening. Fisher glanced up at her friend. "You should probably wait outside."

The woman shook her head, knelt by Mia's side, and grabbed her hand.

Fisher glanced up at the circle of women surrounding her, took a deep breath, and pointed her knife toward the wound and began cutting into it.

Mia threw her head back and growled, teeth clenched tight into the brown cloth. Once an incision large enough had been made, Fisher slowly slid a finger along the arrow's shaft and into the woman's belly, causing black blood to gush out.

Mia screamed, saliva splashing around the cloth and at the corners of her mouth. She squeezed her friend's hand so hard that it turned white and blue. But the sound came to an abrupt halt nearly as quickly as it had begun. Her head fell back to the ground, and her grip immediately loosened.

"Mia," her friend said, a terrified urgency in her voice. She shook her friend's lifeless hand, then quickly looked up at Fisher who was still digging her finger inside the wound.

"She's alive," Ellie said calmly. "She just passed

out."

The woman pressed Mia's hand against her teary cheek. "Hang in there, girl."

Fisher repositioned herself, forcing even more of her hand inside the woman's wound. "Got it."

She pulled back slowly, one hand gripping the arrow's shaft, and the other slowly sliding out of the hole. There was so much blood that I couldn't differentiate Fisher's hand from the arrow. The tip of her index finger was pressed into the arrowhead's point.

"Fucking bastards," Fisher growled.

She wiped the arrowhead into the earth by her feet to clean it, then raised it back at eye level. "Broadhead arrow made of shell. Sharpest thing I've ever touched. I'm surprised it didn't go any deeper than that."

Ellie rushed into Fisher's position and held both hands over the wound. "Someone get me something to stop the bleeding."

Mia's friend slid off her shirt and handed it to Ellie, who bunched it up into a ball and pressed it firmly over the wound.

Fisher looked at Mia's friend and waved the bloody arrow in the air. "You need to take care of that wound. Pulling out the arrow is only half the battle. Keep it clean, whatever you do. The other problem is... I'm not a doctor. I didn't feel any damage to any major organs, but I can't be sure. She's lost a lot of blood, too. Make sure she doesn't lose any more. And if you can," Fisher went on, "find some garlic cloves to help with the healing.

Garlic is antibacterial. Just don't leave it on the skin too long, it'll burn her."

I wondered how many wounds Fisher had seen in her life on this island, and how many people she'd lost to infection. Things would have been so much easier with Tegan around. She had a potion for everything.

Then I thought of Navi. How would we survive without our Medic? Sure, Fisher had managed to pull out the arrow, but this didn't guarantee anything. Without proper care, Mia was exposed to so many risks.

There was an eerie silence inside the rock shelter as we waited for Mia to come to. But she didn't. She lay there with her eyes closed and her dry lips parted slightly. I stared at her blanched face and thought perhaps she'd already succumbed to her injury.

CHAPTER 10

"We need to move," Fisher ordered.

But no one did.

Everest stood up in a stretch and said, "And vat? Gonna leave ze girl here? Let some hungry leopard drag her away?"

Her accent was so pronounced it was hard to understand her.

Fisher quickly glanced at Mia's still body. "We don't have a choice. Dragging her around with us is only gonna slow us down."

Mia's friend held her motionless body, tears sliding down her rosy cheeks.

Fisher was right, but at the same time, I knew that had Mia been one of us—one of the Hunters—Fisher would never have suggested we abandon her simply to get ahead.

"We need food," Fisher went on. "Water. More weapons. We can't stay here."

The sound of rain flooding the jungle finally stopped and was replaced by a gentle trickling. Light shone through a curtain of vines, forming short yellow strips inside the rock shelter. For a moment, it even felt warm.

"Fisher's right," Ellie said. She peered outside, then back at us. "We're probably in the eye of the storm right now. If we don't move, who knows how long it'll take for the storm to pass, which means we won't be able to hunt."

"You heard the woman, let's go!" Fisher said.

"No!" shouted Mia's friend. She threw her arms around Mia and began sobbing. "She's not dead. I can hear her heart. She's not dead!"

I didn't want to disobey Fisher, but at the same time, she wasn't my leader—at least not in an official hierarchal sense. I couldn't let someone die.

"What's your name?" I asked Mia's friend.

She glanced up at me with big red eyes. "Impa."

I smiled. Seriously? Another reference to The Legend of Zelda?

"Like an imp?" Franklin scoffed.

My eyes rolled up to Franklin. "You. Grab her feet."

Franklin's nose crinkled as though I'd asked her to pick up a fresh pile of shit.

"Now!" I said.

I hadn't meant to sound so authoritative, but if I wasn't the one to step up, no one would. I reached down to grab Mia by the arms when Hammer stepped in. "I got this. We need you up front, Hunter."

I was both shocked and reluctant. Was this some sort of trick?

"I'm sorry about what I did to you," Hammer

said softly. I stared at her, noting the sincerity in her one eye. The other was now nothing more than a slit across a red and blue mass of skin.

I wanted to say, 'I'm sorry, too,' but the words didn't come out. Instead, I nodded and stepped aside, allowing her to pick up Mia.

"If you can't keep up, we're not waiting." Fisher glanced at me, before stepping out into the jungle. I followed her closely, my feet sinking a few inches into the mud with every step.

Fisher turned to me when I caught up. "I hope you know what you're doing. This could get us all killed."

"It won't." I peered back at the others, who were all stepping out of the rock shelter, their eyes fixed up at the sunny sky. Hammer and Franklin were the last to come out with Mia in their arms. To my surprise, Impa, Everest, and Ellie stayed close to the duo, prepared to step in if Mia's dead weight became too much to bear.

"What would you have done if that was Rocket? Trim?" I asked.

Fisher worked her jaw.

"Or Flander? Biggie?"

She let out a laugh—something I wasn't expecting.

"Girl, if that was Biggie, we'd all be helpin', and we'd all be sinking knee-deep into this mess." She flicked her toes from side to side, brown goo splashing everywhere.

I smirked. Although a funny image, she'd just admitted that she'd stop at no length to help a friend.

"You have heart," she said.

I rolled my eyes. I didn't have heart—at least, not much of it. I was only doing what I knew was right.

"How much farther until we reach the Grounds?" I asked.

Fisher looked up at the sky and the surrounding trees. "If I'm right, we're closer than I thought."

"Do you really think it's safe to go back?" I asked.

"We don't have much choice," Fisher said. "It's the only home we know. I'm hoping there are resources in Murk's quarters. I'm also counting on the Northers' impatience. It wouldn't be like them to sit around and wait for survivors to come back. They're probably long gone by now."

I hoped she was right. The last thing we needed was to march straight into a trap.

We followed Fisher's lead through the hollow forest, eyes shooting in every direction as we moved forward. Surprisingly, the women had managed to keep up by sharing the lifting duty.

"Do you hear that?" Franklin said, running up ahead of us. She turned back around, a yellow grin stretching her face. "Home, sweet home."

I could hear the Working Grounds' waterfall—a powerful roar in the distance.

"Grab anything you can before we get any closer," Fisher ordered, sliding the Norther's mask she'd stolen over her face. "Anything you can use to fight."

The women rummaged through rotten debris as they searched for sticks on the forest floor. I prepared my bow, and together, we moved in slowly.

I remembered this path—although now, it was completely open and colorless, whereas when I'd first been brought to the Working Grounds, we'd tramped through layers upon layers of bushes and plants to make it out into the main area.

The moment we set foot on the Grounds, it was like looking at an unsaturated image. Everything was completely gray, including the water. It was nothing like it had been before the attack—full of bright greens surrounding the bay of turquoise water.

Even the sand was gloomy. But something else caught my eye... something far more disturbing than colorless sand and dark water.

Across the bay's shore were several ash-coated bodies lying still. Franklin stepped forward, prepared to inspect the graveyard, but Fisher threw a hand across her chest.

"Wait."

Fisher crouched and slithered forward in the mud, scoping out what remained of our home.

"We move around the edge and go straight into the waterfall," she ordered, gesturing a loop in the air.

"But what if—" Franklin tried.

"There's nothing you can do for them," Fisher said. "They're dead. And if by some miracle one of them isn't... they will be by nightfall. We can't walk out into the open like that."

We followed Fisher's lead along the forest trees which had once formed a circular enclosure around the Grounds. Although not completely hidden from sight, now that the trees were nothing more than leafless trunks, it was far safer than exposing ourselves in open space.

I stared at the bodies as we made our way to the waterfall. Although covered in ash, they didn't appear to be burned. I wondered if they'd been injured in the Village and had attempted to seek shelter at the Grounds.

As I observed the scenery, I noticed something else—all stations had been left intact. Had the fire not spread to the Grounds? And then it dawned on me: the waterfall's mist must have protected its surrounding area from the wildfire's flames.

The Needlwomen's station was still set up at the forest's edge, across the bed of water. Maybe there were arrows or weapons lying on the ground. And then I saw it.

Food.

"Fisher," I said quickly. "There."

Fisher's eyes lit up. At the edge of the waterfall was the Farmer's station, which, aside from being drenched, was still in once piece. The garden had flooded, which was to be expected, but the meat's storage unit—a wooden rack with uneven shelves and an angled roof to protect its contents from the rain—was just fine.

There were slabs of meat across its top shelf,

and beside the rack, a boar's bloody carcass.

"Do you think the meat's still good?" Fisher asked.

"Ve only put cured or smoked meat on ze top shelf," Everest said. "I'll go grab vat's still safe to eat."

She scurried toward the Farmer's station while remaining as close as possible to the forest's edge. Fisher led us inside the waterfall. It was as dark and moist as I remembered it.

I followed Fisher's broad, fur-outlined figure and the sound of her footsteps, which were delicate and calculated.

"Do you think she'll make it?" I whispered.

Fisher's head turned toward me. "What?"

"Mia," I said. "Without Tegan—"

But suddenly, Fisher was tackled onto the stone ground, a loud crash resonating throughout the entire cave.

CHAPTER 11

"Goddamn Northern piece of s—"

I heard a punch, and then another, and another.

"Stop it!"

"I'ma kill you! You hear me?"

Another hit.

"I'm not a N—"

And another.

I ran toward the sound of the fight and grabbed whoever was on top, but a hard fist knocked me right in the mouth, pushing my tooth through my bottom lip.

"Don't move!"

The sound of rapid footsteps echoed around us, and dim orange lights spread across the rock ceiling above. There were three of them standing there—one holding a torch in each hand, the others on either side of her pointing hunting spears at us from above their shoulders.

Fisher was lying flat on her back with someone straddled on top of her.

"Coin?" Fisher asked, tearing off her mask.

"Fish?" the woman said. She had dark brown skin and a shaved head with only a narrow strip of hair reaching down to the base of her skull. She was built like a bulldog—short and stocky.

Franklin ran up to the scene of the fight and grabbed the woman—Coin—by the back of the hair, then raised a fist. Coin's lip curled up as she anticipated the blow, and I noticed something gold glimmer from inside her mouth—a gold tooth. Coin, I realized.

"Stop!" Fisher shouted, her words repeated around us in a diminuendo.

Franklin released her grip, and the rest of our crew caught up, including Everest, who stood clueless with two big pieces of meat in either hand. "Vat's going on?"

Coin climbed off Fisher and grabbed her by the arm to help her up. "Yo, I'm sorry, man. I thought you was one of them Northers."

Fisher wiped her bloody nose. "No sweat."

"You guys are Murk's women?" I asked.

Coin nodded. "We barely escaped... I'm sure y'all noticed da bodies out there. We weren't all so lucky."

"I'm sorry," Fisher said.

Coin shook her head. "Ain't nobody to blame but them Northers."

"Did you see anyone from my crew? Any Hunters?" Fisher asked.

"Naw, sorry, man," Coin said. "It all happened so fast."

364

A deep moan rumbled behind us, and Coin's eyes followed the sound. "Someone hurt?"

"Arrow," Ellie said, popping up beside me. "She's awake, but the blood is starting up again. We need to lay her down and put pressure on the wound."

"Let's go," Coin said, throwing her head toward Murk's quarters.

I licked the rusty taste of blood from my bottom lip, feeling the split with my tongue. But the warmth of someone's hand grabbing mine immediately pulled my mind away from the pain.

"You okay?" Ellie asked.

"I..." I stuttered. "Yeah. I'm good."

She held on a few more seconds before letting go and falling back with Mia, who was now groaning and squirming. I swallowed hard and shook the weakness out of my legs.

How did Ellie always manage to make me feel so weak?

When we reached Murk's quarters, relief and sadness enveloped me. Where was Murk, anyways? Was she dead? Was she hiding? There was a strange emptiness as we walked in—a void that had once been filled by Murk's presence.

Hammer and Impa rushed Mia to the back of the room, where a pile of leaves formed a bed. There were torches fastened all around the room, offering a cozy, camp-like atmosphere.

The woman who'd been carrying the two torches slipped them into empty sconces on the wall, before turning back toward us. "Have a seat."

There were blankets of fur positioned sporadically across the floor, and several leaf-constructed beds were lined up against the back wall.

My attention was suddenly drawn to that wall, where Murk's chalk drawing was still intact. She'd been staring at it the last time I saw her—a drawing of a gazelle with surrounding birds which supposedly depicted the meaning of freedom on Kormace Island. I remembered thinking that she was probably high, and I couldn't help but smile.

I dropped down into one of the fur blankets, appreciating the soft texture against my aching skin. I'd never been so tired in my life. The entire room was filled with a warmth I hadn't known in days. I listened to the sound of the torches burning—a sound similar to the crisping of paper in a campfire—and I began to drift away.

* * *

"Not too long, sweetheart," my mother said, pulling my marshmallow stick out of my hands. "You see that? That's all you need. A nice golden color."

I slid off my wool-knitted mittens and with my tiny fingers, pulled the melted marshmallow off the stick's pointed tip.

My friends at school always thought it strange that every year, on Christmas day, my mother would make it a point to light a fire in our backyard and roast marshmallows, no matter how cold the weather was.

She'd always dress me up in layers, even if I

ended up looking like a marshmallow myself.

As I sat chewing on the sweet gooey treat, I smiled up at my mother and thought to myself: this is exactly where I want to be on Christmas day.

* * *

"Hey, sleepy."

Ellie was lying sideways beside me with her head in her palm and a smile on her face. And although I wanted to return the smile, I couldn't.

I missed my mom, my friends, my life.

They were all gone.

"Hey," Ellie said, noting the pain in my eyes. She reached a hand around the back of my neck and pulled me in against her chest, gently rubbing her fingers through the back of my hair.

Although I didn't want to cry, I couldn't help myself. Everything came pouring out. It hurt so much. I sobbed on and on, my wet face pressed against Ellie's neck. I reached an arm around her and dug my fingers into her skin.

I'd never experienced so much pain before.

"My mom..." I said. "The Hunters... Rocket. Trim... Biggie. Everyone."

She stroked my hair and held me tight until the tears finally stopped. I sniffled the snot back up into my nose and pulled back, my eyes fixated on hers.

"How do you do it?" I asked.

She smirked at me. "Do what?"

"Stay so positive all the time."

She looked up toward the ceiling and shrugged. "I've been here a long time. I went through it too, you know—the grief. You feel like everyone you love in the real world has died because you know you'll never see them again. And then, people you learn to love on the island do die... But you can't hold onto it. It doesn't fix anything."

I swallowed hard. I didn't want to start bawling again.

"There's a secret, though," she said.

My eyes lit up.

"Hope."

"Hope?" I repeated.

"Exactly," she said. "Hope. Faith... I refuse to believe that I'll be stuck in Kormace for the rest of my life. Think about it—if word gets out about the government's corruption, reporters will be all over that, and eventually, they'll come back for us."

I pondered this for a moment. It had never crossed my mind. My idea of hope had always been to build a raft and *hope* for the best.

Maybe Ellie had a point.

Maybe, despite all the horrors this island had to offer, there was still hope.

I stared into her soft brown eyes, suddenly feeling reborn. She must have sensed my change in mood, because her thick lips formed a crooked smile, and she slowly pressed them against mine.

I stopped breathing.

I didn't understand what was going on, but I didn't pull away. I didn't want to.

I lay there, enjoying the feeling of her soft plush lips as butterflies filled my stomach.

"Wooooooo!" someone shouted and everyone

cheered, creating an echo across the cavern walls.

Ellie pulled away and laughed. "Sorry. I've wanted to do that since I first met you."

I smiled. If I put too much thought into it, I'd freak myself out. I'd never identified as a lesbian, or bisexual, for that matter. And the last thing I wanted to do was introspect or ponder my sexuality.

Whether stuck on Kormace Island forever or not, only one thing mattered most above all else— if something made me feel good, I'd welcome it with open arms. There was enough negativity on this island to last a lifetime.

The savory smell of smoked meat then filled my nostrils. A shadow darkened the space around me, and I looked up to find Fisher bent over with a piece of brown-edged, red meat dangling inches from my forehead.

I tore it out of her hands and swallowed it so fast, I barely tasted it.

"Whoa, whoa, now," Fisher said. "There's plenty more where that came from."

"For now," Everest said. "Zat's ze last of ze smoked meat ve have. Rest, ve vill have to cook up. But it von't last us very long. Ve vill need to hunt—"

"Yo, White Mountain," Fisher said through hard chews, "would you shut up and let us enjoy this moment? Most of us haven't eaten in days."

Everest threw both hands into the air and walked away. She reminded me of a grumpy grandmother who always felt underappreciated by her grandchildren.

Fisher plopped herself down beside me and handed me another piece of meat.

"Guess what?" she said.

I stared at her. What the hell did she have to be so happy about? Had she found Murk's stash of funny leaves?

"Was chattin' with Thompson over there." She pointed her chin out at one of Coin's friends—a young Native woman with a long French braid over one shoulder. "She saw Trim and Rocket... said they got out after the fire started. Headed south like us. We must've just missed 'em."

I sat up.

Fisher was grinning from ear to ear. "If those two are alive, you can bet your ass the others probably are, too."

I glanced at Thompson, who was sitting with both legs pressed up to her chest, one arm dangling over her knee. She held a cigarette or a joint.

Maybe they *had* found Murk's stash.

"Is she sure it was them?" I asked.

Fisher slapped me on the shoulder, her smile stretching so wide I noticed missing teeth in the back of her mouth. "Yes, she's sure. Everyone knows who the Hunters are. And with that untrimmed head of hers, it isn't like anyone would confuse Trim for someone else."

I pictured Trim's bushy eyebrows and dark frizzy hair—a helmet almost—and smirked.

"We got ourselves some Battlewomen here,

Brone. A Farmer." She then shot Thompson another look. "Even a Needlewoman. All we need is to find ourselves a new home. Some place the Northers would never think to look. I figure we gain our strength, gather as many resources as we can, then move out by dawn and find the others."

I looked at Ellie, who was smiling at me with profound tenderness, and back at Fisher, who was nodding so fast her curly baby hairs danced by her face.

Hope, I thought.

Maybe we did stand a chance, after all.

Visit **shadeowens.com** for more works by Shade Owens.

Printed in Great Britain
by Amazon

16429556R00221